A Lot Like
CHRISTMAS

A Lot Like
CHRISTMAS

JENNIFER
USA TODAY BESTSELLING AUTHOR
SNOW

Entangled Publishing, LLC
10940 S Parker Road
Suite 327
Parker, CO 80134
Visit our website at www.entangledpublishing.com.

Amara is an imprint of Entangled Publishing, LLC.

Edited by Liz Pelletier and Lydia Sharp
Cover design by Bree Archer
Cover art by PH888/shutterstock and MikeLaptev/GettyImages,
pljvv1/Depositphotos, ricardoreitmeyer/GettyImages,
and borchee/GettyImages,
Interior design by Toni Kerr

Print ISBN 978-1-64937-090-7
ebook ISBN 978-1-64937-102-7

Manufactured in the United States of America

First Edition October 2021

AMARA

ALSO BY JENNIFER SNOW

BLUE MOON BAY SERIES

A Lot Like Love
A Lot Like Christmas

WILD RIVER SERIES

An Alaskan Christmas
Under an Alaskan Sky
A Sweet Alaskan Fall
Stars Over Alaska
Alaska Reunion

COLORADO ICE SERIES

Maybe This Time
Maybe This Love
Maybe This Christmas

*To all the wrong paths that
finally led to the right one.*

A Lot Like Christmas is sweet small-town romance with a happy ending. However, the story includes elements that might not be suitable for all readers. Depression, anxiety, and symptoms of PTSD appear in the novel, and a child's illness and death are relayed through a character's backstory. Readers who may be sensitive to these elements, please take note.

CHAPTER ONE

"Be honest, you at least spit in the frosting, right?"

Jessica Connolly placed the bride-and-groom topper on the white-and-silver, tastefully Christmas-themed, three-layer cake and stood back to admire her work. "The only joy in all of this is that they will never know." She winked at her best friend Whitney as she carefully boxed up the forty-hour labor of love.

Later that day, her beautiful creation would be enjoyed at ex-boyfriend number three's wedding. Three weddings in the same year for three guys she'd had relationships with. Unbelievable.

"No one would blame you if you did." Sitting at the counter of Jessica's bakery, Delicious Delicacies, her not-so-recently engaged friend flipped through the book of wedding cake designs that she'd looked at a dozen times already. Her beautifully manicured, candy cane-themed nails flicked the pages so fast it was a wonder she could actually see the choices. Whitney shook her head. "I can't believe these guys, asking you to do this."

"To be fair, I'm the only *real* bakery in town. And besides, John, Cameron, and Dallas are great guys. They just weren't the right guys for me," Jessica said, repeating her mantra. She could put on a brave face, but this was getting exhausting.

Three brides in the last year. None of them her.

And worse, there wasn't anyone in her small hometown of Blue Moon Bay that she wanted to date that she hadn't already. At almost thirty, she'd been hoping to design her own wedding cake soon.

"The funny thing is," Whitney said, "they all found 'the one' after they ended things with you."

"Thanks for pointing that out, Whit."

Her friend's laugh was apologetic. "Sorry. I'm just saying, you're like a good luck charm for these guys. Wasn't there a movie like that?"

"Believe me, if this was a movie, I'd have your legs and Sarah's butt."

Whitney paused her page-flipping, her expression contemplative as she tilted her head to the side.

Did they have a winner? Excitedly, Jessica leaned over the counter to see which design had caught her friend's attention. Her heart stopped. It was the three-tier cascade wedding cake, white with lavender accents and sugar work doves adorning the top. Jessica's favorite. The cake she'd always wanted for her own wedding...if it ever happened.

Please don't select that one.

If her best friend wanted it, there was no way Jessica could deny her from having it. She held her breath, waiting...

It's only a cake. No big deal. She could design a new one for herself. Nothing would be as pretty as this one, but...

A second later, Whitney resumed flipping.

Oh thank God.

Letting out a breath of relief, Jessica tagged the box with the couple's names and then struggled to carry it to the freezer without dropping the fifty-two-pound cake. "Can you grab the door?"

Whitney hurried to open the walk-in freezer and shivered as a blast of cold air escaped. "I think you should charge them more, at least," she said, pointing to the price tag on the box. "The ingredients alone cost more than this."

Jessica removed the price tag and avoided her friend's gaze as she said, "Actually, the cake is my wedding present to them." She set the box inside on a shelf and closed the door.

"Wait. You're going to this wedding?"

"I was invited." Watching her ex proclaim his everlasting love to someone else may be challenging, but she was secretly hoping there might be a single guy at the wedding that could help ease the sting a little. John's fiancée, Emily, was from out of town and she had six siblings. She was gorgeous, and good looks had to run in the family, right?

Whitney's disapproval was written all over her face. "Can I talk you out of it?"

"Nope." The truth was, Jessica was infatuated with weddings. She'd even been known to crash a few, but she always brought cookies or something—she wasn't a total creep. She just couldn't walk past a beautiful beach ceremony or a wedding reception in the park without stopping to say congratulations to the bride and groom. She'd been that way since she was four years old, wearing lace doilies on her head as a veil while she forced the kid next door to "marry" her.

"Are you going?" she asked Whitney.

She checked her watch, avoiding Jessica's frown. "I have to work. Which I should get to now. Trent will be there, though." She gave Jessica a quick hug. "Enjoy!" she called behind her as she made her exit—which seemed suspiciously more like an escape—from the bakery.

She watched her best friend climb into her banana-yellow Miata convertible, crank the music, put on her oversize sunglasses, and drive off. Jessica sighed, unable to shake the nagging feeling that Whitney wasn't completely sold on this whole marriage thing that Jessica would do just about anything to have.

Hours later, from her seat as far in front as the Reserved signs allowed, Jessica scanned the ceremony setup at the bay's country club, the best venue in town for large weddings. Ceiling-to-floor windows provided a spectacular view of the ocean and the boats along the marina. Thirty-foot open-beam ceilings with a light wood decor throughout gave the space a warm and intimate feel, despite the posh exclusivity of the members-only club.

Exactly a hundred chairs covered in white satin sat facing a large archway decorated with white flowers and silver snowflakes. The wedding colors of white, silver, and crystal blue weren't the traditional red-and-green holiday choices but instead gave an air of a chilly winter wonderland, and the large crackling fireplace along the side of the room completed the cozy vibe.

December weddings had to be the most romantic. If and when Jessica ever got married, December would be her month.

Her ex-boyfriend John stood under the archway, speaking to the marriage officiant. Dressed in his black tails with a pale-blue tie and cummerbund, his dark hair gelled to one side and his face freshly shaven, he looked amazing, but not even the slightest flicker of lingering emotion for him dared to surface. It had been eighteen months since they'd dated. Jessica was completely over him.

Had she been trying to force a connection in the first place? If it had been real love, the way she'd thought it was, wouldn't this be harder on her? Wouldn't the previous weddings have had some heart-wrenching impact on her, too?

John glanced her way with a small, casual smile, and she returned it before shifting her attention to the other guests arriving. Groomsmen ushered family members to the reserved seats near the front, and Jessica could already feel the customary wedding tears gathering in her eyes as she saw the couple's grandparents and aunts and uncles arrive for their big day.

The most important day of their lives. Nothing was as powerful as connecting to another person in a way that said *let's grow old together*.

As she scanned the room, she noticed a tall, gorgeous-looking man surveying the seating selection.

Almost all the chairs were taken and the ceremony was about to start. She lifted her purse from the "saved" seat next to her as he made his way down the center aisle. Her heart raced when he paused at the end of her row, glanced her way, and…then took a seat next to some gorgeous woman on the bride's family side of the room. Jessica sighed and set her purse back down. She'd been right to assume Emily's family members would share her hotness, but unfortunately, they all had dates.

Soft piano chords started to play, then, and she turned her attention to the back of the room. The wedding procession was about to start.

"Can I sit here?" a male voice asked.

Jessica flashed her very best flirty smile as she turned to see…Trent. Her cousin.

"The seat's all yours," she said, lifting her purse. So much for a hot guy offering her a tissue to wipe her eyes during the ceremony. Not that Trent wasn't good-looking or a gentleman, but he was family.

Everyone stood as the wedding procession started, and Jessica ran a hand over her flared dark emerald-green crinoline skirt as she turned to watch the wedding party step toward the altar. She loved this part. Everyone looked so excited and happy, and the groom was so adorably nervous, his hands clenched tight in front of him, a look of apprehension on his face as he waited for his bride.

It didn't even bother her that this groom was someone she'd once entertained the thought of forever with herself. John beamed when his bride appeared with her dad at the end of the silver-carpeted runway.

Jessica was happy for them.

Mostly.

Jealous of the bride's gown—a mermaid-style, strapless, lace design that Jessica could never pull off—but otherwise happy.

Definitely, mostly happy.

At the altar, an emotional father lifted the veil over his daughter's head and kissed her cheek, and then Emily joined John.

Tears had already gathered in Jessica's eyes when the officiant started the ceremony. "Dearly Beloved, we are gathered here today…"

"This is the fourth wedding Whitney's skipped out on in three months," Trent whispered next to her.

Jessica nodded, her gaze locked on the wedding couple.

"I know it's not the idea of commitment freaking her out, though," he went on, "because Whitney doesn't make decisions lightly. Once she commits, she commits."

An older lady sitting in front of them turned and shot him a look.

"Shhh…" Jessica said.

At the altar, John was reading his personalized vows, and her chest tightened. How Emily wasn't a big, sobbing mess, she didn't know. She hadn't realized John could be so poetic. Guess the right woman brought out the best qualities in a man.

"Tell me the truth, is it me?" Trent whispered, moving closer. "Is she getting cold feet because she doesn't want to marry me?"

Jessica sighed as she tore her eyes away from the ceremony. "Trent, I love you like a cousin—"

"We *are* cousins."

"Exactly. But you need to shut up. This is my favorite part," Jessica hissed.

"Sorry," he mumbled, sitting back and turning his attention to the wedding that was actually happening.

But now Jessica was distracted. *Was* Whitney getting cold feet? Something was definitely up with her, but was it that? When the two had first gotten engaged, Whitney had been all about a short engagement, but then a couple of months later, her time frame changed. The two of them never kept things from each other, but Jess was sitting on her own secret. Maybe Whitney had one as well.

"You'd tell me, though, right? If you knew something?" Trent whispered.

Would she? She was loyal to her friends, but she was also close to Trent and her family. She wouldn't want to see any of the people she cared about end up hurt. "I'd tell you," she said, and the couple kissed at the altar.

Trent handed her a tissue, and she dabbed the tears away from her eyes, then stood and clapped as the couple were announced husband and wife. They made their way back down the aisle together while guests tossed silver and white confetti after them.

As people dispersed, Trent asked, "Where are you sitting?"

Jessica checked the seating card she was given.

"Table nineteen. You?"

"Three."

"How did you get VIP seating?" she asked, following the procession to the receiving line.

"I played football with John for years. You're welcome to take Whitney's seat by me," he said.

She shook her head. "Your table is no doubt all couples. I'll take my chances at the singles' reject table far in the back."

"Want me to sit with you?"

"Nope. You're too cute and I don't want the single guys here thinking I'm taken." Although most of them seemed to be. Maybe there was someone she'd missed in her perusing...or someone worth a second look.

Trent laughed. "Okay. Good luck, tiger."

She pretended to growl and pounce as he headed toward the bride and groom to offer his congratulations. Instead of joining the long line of well-wishers, Jessica headed into the reception area inside the country club. She'd have plenty of time to talk to the happy couple later. She wanted to choose a great seat at table nineteen with the best view to watch the speeches and the couple's first dance.

Inside, tables of eight were positioned around the head table in the center of the room. White tablecloths reached the floor and bouquets of white roses in silver vases kept with the look of crisp, clean elegance. Tea lights would illuminate the room beautifully once the sun set. Tiny light blue and silver heart-shaped confetti littered the tabletop and a small box of chocolates sat at each place setting. In the middle, next to the table wine, were white disposable cameras for anyone to take candid shots of the evening.

Jessica loved that idea. The best wedding photos were often the non-formal, spontaneous moments captured between the bride and groom. She was the one who'd suggested it to Emily the day the bride had selected her wedding cake design. Or rather, the third and final time she'd selected a design.

A pianist played soft, romantic notes in the corner, but a DJ was already setting up near the dance floor. She'd worn flats, prepared to dance the night away. Hoping she'd have a tall, dark, and handsome partner to twirl her around the room.

She'd settle for short, cute, and interesting.

"You're at this table, too?"

Flirty smile in place, she looked up at average height, blond, and sexy. And alone. "Yes. I'm Jess," she said, extending a hand.

"Niall."

She loved that name. Strong and masculine. "Nice to meet you. Are you a friend of the bride or groom?"

"Bride. I'm actually her hair stylist."

"Really? Wow. I used to date the groom…and I made the cake." Geez, why had she mentioned the first thing? "I made the cake. Full stop."

Niall laughed. "So this is the hired help table?"

His smile revealed the straightest, whitest, most perfect teeth Jessica had ever seen and dimples that seemed endless. So far this guy was checking a lot of the right boxes.

"Should we get into the wine early?" he asked, pulling her chair out for her.

Manners. A gentleman.

She wouldn't start naming babies yet…but a little girl with his blue eyes and her dark hair would be adorable.

"I'd love a glass of white," she said. She preferred red, but she wasn't letting fate ruin this for her with a stain on her light tan blouse.

Niall opened it and poured a glass for both of them. "To table nineteen."

She accepted the toast and took a sip. "So…are you here with anyone?" She glanced around, but no one else was approaching their table. She'd be okay if they ended up being the only two sitting there.

"Nope. Flying solo," he said, running a hand through his hair.

She bit her lip. That didn't mean he didn't have a glamourous supermodel girlfriend somewhere. After all, Trent was here alone and he wasn't on the market. Not that that would stop a lot of women from flirting with him. Good thing Trent was head over heels in love with Whitney and her friend had nothing to worry about.

"George, my partner, had a Christmas modeling shoot in Paris this weekend," Niall said.

Or supermodel boyfriend.

"Paris, wow. Guess Blue Moon Bay can't really compete with that." She sipped her wine and gazed longingly at Whitney's empty seat at table three as the other members of theirs joined them. Two seventy-year-old men that golfed with John's dad, three of Emily's female university alumni friends, and her old babysitter. No sexy singles.

It seemed they'd all evaporated from the bay in recent years.

Soon she, too, would have to decide if staying in the small town, clinging to the safe and familiar and comfortable, was the way to get the future she'd always wanted.

"So, wait, *you're* the Jessica that John dated before he met Emily?" Niall asked, turning to her with renewed interest.

Still not the kind of interest Jessica had been hoping for, but she nodded politely.

"Emily told me all about you."

"She did?" Had the subject of all of John's exes come up with her hairdresser or just her? She was the only one in attendance, but that was primarily because of the cake.

He lowered his voice as he shimmied his chair closer. "You're the good luck charm, right?"

"I'm sorry, what?"

"That's the rumor circling around. A man dates you, then he finds his true match."

Holy shit. So it wasn't just Whitney who'd noticed that uncanny connection. She cleared her throat. "I...don't think that's a real thing. Coincidence," she mumbled.

"A three-time coincidence? Not likely. The New Brides Club has deemed you their lucky charm."

Jessica's gaze fell on the New Brides Club, her ex-boyfriends' wives all sitting together at table four. Their new husbands at their sides. Her ex-boyfriends. Emily would now join that group, too. And who would be next?

"They actually call me that?" she asked.

Niall laughed. "It's in an endearing way, believe me. They're all super grateful."

Grateful. That her heart had gotten broken so they could find true love? That men she thought she had a connection with dumped her for them?

Who the hell even believed this weird shit was really happening anyway?

They looked her way and caught her staring, and their smiles were indeed full of gratitude.

They believed it.

"There's no way Emily started this rumor, though, she's one of the nicest people I've ever met," she said. One of the other women, she could believe, but not Emily.

Niall glanced around him as though making sure no one else could hear. "Okay, I could totally lose my hairstylist-therapy reputation for this, but…Emily made a play for John while you two were still dating, hoping it was true. That your magic would work for her." He glanced toward the couple. "Obviously, it did."

Jessica's cheeks flushed with an uncommon rush of rage. Emily actually saw her as the reason for her happily ever after? She was gossiping about her behind her back? And now she had people soliciting her services?

No freaking way!

"How far-reaching is this rumor?" she asked.

"My sister heard about it in L.A." He shrugged. "So

at least that far."

She'd had enough. Enough of these weddings that weren't hers. Enough of these embarrassing singles tables. Enough of her time and talents being used to make the meals at her exes' weddings that much more delicious.

Jessica set her glass down and pushed her chair back as she stood. "Great meeting you, Niall. It's been…enlightening." Without overthinking it or letting common sense seep in, she strode across the room toward the head table, ignoring the pleasant greetings or compliments on the cake as she passed. She barely heard them, laser-focused on a mission.

She stopped in front of Emily and John, where her beautiful creation sat on a cake display rack for all to admire. Their silver knife engraved with their names and the date sat next to it. They both glanced at her in surprise.

"I wish you both a lifetime of happiness," she said. Turning to Emily, she added, "You're welcome." Then, taking a deep breath, she picked up the fifty-two-pound masterpiece she'd spent days working on and carried it straight out of the country club.

Only the audible gasps of surprise and disbelief from the crowd and the flash of the tables' disposable cameras followed her out.

CHAPTER TWO

As the wheels of the plane hit the runway, Mitch Jameson's eyes snapped open. Sweat covered his entire body and his breathing came in short bursts. His hands clutched the armrests on either side of him, and registering his surroundings took a moment.

Damn, another nightmare.

Propping himself higher in his seat, he looked around to see if any of his fellow first-class passengers had noticed, but no one was looking at him. Everyone was preoccupied with gathering their things as the plane taxied toward the gate. The long-haul flight from Cambodia to California had everyone desperate to get their feet on solid ground.

Outside his window, the sun was starting to rise. Bright red and purple streams of light were cast across the early morning sky.

Mitch blinked the exhaustion from his eyes and reached for his carry-on under the seat in front of him. He switched off airplane mode on his cell as the plane pulled up to the gate, his knee bouncing while he waited for the cell service to connect him to the airport's wifi.

Three new email messages. His heart raced.

But they were all spam.

He let out a long *whoosh* of air. Was he relieved or disappointed that he hadn't received his new placement assignment yet?

After the last six months at camp in Cambodia he wasn't sure he'd ever be ready for the next one, yet he knew he'd be back on a plane and headed to another part of the world to help provide medical attention to children as soon as the holidays were over.

He wouldn't even be taking this break now if it hadn't been "recommended."

He stood as the plane doors opened and smiled politely at the flight attendant, then collected his larger duffel bag from the overhead bin. Short, thin, with pretty, big brown eyes, she'd flirted with him several times during the flight. Her extra attention hadn't gone unnoticed or unappreciated, but decompressing after a mission didn't provide much headspace for casual conversation with a lovely woman.

She stopped next to him and gently touched his shoulder. "Nothing in that medical bag of yours that can help?"

Great, so his night terrors hadn't gone completely unnoticed. His old sleep-talking habits better not have returned or he'd have to book another airline in the future.

He shook his head, avoiding her sympathetic look. "Unfortunately not."

Over the years he'd learned there was nothing that could block the images of man at his utmost worst from a person's mind. The memories of the haunting things he saw overseas just started to fade to gray over time. Then they blurred, one into the other, until they had become one long montage of pain and suffering.

But they never completely went away.

"You home for the holidays?" she asked, the slightest hint of flirtation back in her voice.

"Yeah. I guess so," he said as the line moved and people de-boarded. The timing of this break just happened to be the seasonal time of year. He'd never purposely take the holidays off. He hadn't celebrated them in years. December 25th was just another day.

"Well, happy holidays," she said, sliding a card into his jacket pocket as he exited the plane. He'd be lying if he said she was the first flight attendant to hit on him, or that he'd never taken anyone up on their offer to *hang out* while he was laid over somewhere. But right now he knew he wouldn't be the best company.

"Merry Christmas," he said with a final wave.

In the airport, he grabbed a double shot of espresso and managed to convince the young woman at the car rental desk that he was okay to drive, despite his blood-shot eyes and dark circles. Then, somehow, he made the two-hour drive along the coast to his hometown of Blue Moon Bay without crashing into the ocean. The bright sun rising above the water and the waves lapping gently onto the sand below the windy stretch of highway were breathtakingly beautiful. He rolled the windows down and cranked the radio, relying on the cool breeze and loud music to keep him awake.

But pulling into the parking lot of Dove's Nest B&B,

he thought maybe he *was* asleep at the wheel. The old inn looked amazing. Completely transformed. The last time he'd seen it, it had been closed and nearly condemned. He'd known from his sister, Lia, that Dove had passed away earlier that year and she'd left the place to her granddaughter, Sarah. She'd renovated it in time for the family reunion Mitch had missed months before, but he hadn't expected such a dramatic change.

It was slightly unsettling. He'd wanted something less pretentious. Something understated, slightly beaten-up and neglected. The new siding, roof, windows, and decks off the bedrooms made the B&B almost unrecognizable, and the hundreds of white Christmas lights along the trim of the exterior and the decorated evergreen on the front yard were warm and inviting. His gut twisted.

Did he deserve warm and inviting?

Any other time of year, he'd camp out on the beach with a tent and sleeping bag, but the temperature drop on the coast that month along with the unpredictable winter storms would have local beach security forcing him to pack up and move indoors.

Mitch reluctantly climbed out of the car and walked on heavy, lead-like legs to the large double front doors. The thick evergreen holiday wreath was decorated with seashells and surfboards, and it served as a reminder that Blue Moon Bay Christmases were a lot different from the ones he'd celebrated overseas the last four years. Here, life was quiet, simple…easy. No worries or cares.

The contrast between his hometown and the war-ravaged, poverty-stricken countries he'd spent the last few years in almost made him nauseous.

What right did he have to get the luxury of escaping when so many others couldn't?

He opened the door and entered the large, impressive foyer of the inn. Despite the upgrades and renovations, he was happy to see not much of the esthetic had been changed inside the main common areas. The double spiral staircases had been refurbished, but they were still the focal point of the foyer. One leading to the guestrooms on the second and third floors, the other to the living quarters of the house. As kids, they'd sneak in and slide down the rails whenever Dove was working in the yards outside.

From where he stood he could see the big ballroom and a dining area to his right. A fresh coat of paint and new lighting fixtures really brightened up the space. The library and front sitting room to the left had been almost untouched except for some cosmetic improvements and new furniture.

Right in the middle of the foyer stood a twenty-foot artificial tree, with boxes of decorations next to it on the floor. Looked like Sarah was planning to continue Dove's holiday tradition of inviting the community to decorate the tree together.

As a kid, his family had participated every year. Each family brought a special ornament to add to the collection, and Dove served cookies and hot chocolate. The tree always looked like two-year-olds had decorated it— no theme, hundreds of homemade items mixed with elegant glass bulbs, garland, and strands of cranberries and popcorn—but it had reflected the various family traditions in Blue Moon Bay.

His gaze was still locked on the tree when the sound of retching in the bathroom down the hall caught his attention. Doctor instincts immediately kicked in as he moved toward the door. He tapped once. "Hey, you okay in there?"

More retching, then, "Sorry! Be right out."

He stood back and, a moment later, heard the toilet flush and the faucet running. Then the door opened and a young woman who looked about mid-twenties exited. She smiled politely at him. "Hello…sorry to keep you waiting."

She quickly led the way toward the check-in desk, so he kept pace with her at her side.

"No problem," he said. "You okay?"

She nodded, but pressed a hand to her stomach. "Totally fine. Just a random burst of nausea." She picked up several holiday-scented candles from the desk and blew them out, her face momentarily disappearing behind a thin cloud of smoke. "I guess the combined scent of pine and cinnamon spice was a little too much."

Mitch sniffed the air. "Maybe not the best combination. Try one at a time?"

"Or just let the actual scents do the work," she said with a small laugh. "Anyway… Welcome to Dove's Nest. Do you have a reservation?" she asked.

He scanned her face for any sign of recognition. He hadn't been home in six years, so he didn't expect her to know him.

"Yes, Mitch Jameson," he said, laying his bags down on the floor. His arms ached from carrying the weight of them so long.

A wide, genuine smile lit up her face. "You're Lia's brother!"

He nodded. "Sarah?" Seemed like a safe guess.

"Yes. Nice to see you again. How was your flight?"

"Long."

She sent him a sympathetic look. "You look exhausted. Let's get you checked in and I'll show you to your room. You're here until…December twenty-fifth?" She frowned as her gaze returned to his, a puzzled look in her dark brown eyes. "You're leaving on Christmas Day?"

No doubt she found that odd, but he hoped to get his new assignment by the twenty-third, when the next postings were scheduled to be announced. He was already feeling the itch to go again. Staying in Blue Moon Bay for twenty-two days would already be difficult. He hadn't spent that much time in his small hometown since he'd left for college and med school.

Living in L.A., with a successful private practice, he'd liked the fast pace and noise that drowned out the silence he'd been trying to escape for years. Then traveling the world with Doctors Without Borders had given him the lifestyle he wanted. Seeing the world— the *real* world, not just touristy, pretty places.

Staying in one place for too long, a peaceful, pictur-esque place at that, made his privilege guilt become unmanageable.

Following Sarah up the staircase, it took all his

remaining energy to propel his legs forward. "So many upgrades and no elevator?"

She laughed. "Don't let your sister hear you say that."

His fitness fanatic sister, right. The one who would be home next week herself for the holidays. Her law firm in New York always shut down for a month in December, and she and her husband, Malcolm, were heading to Blue Moon Bay for an "early" Christmas with their parents before continuing on to spend "actual" Christmas with Mitch's parents at their winery in Napa.

His sister couldn't get here fast enough. With ten years between them, they weren't super close. By the time she was a fun age to do things with, he'd graduated and moved out of the small town, but her energetic spirit and fiery personality was quite possibly the only thing that could pull him from this slump. He always admired her determination and success and wished they could be closer despite the distance he put between them with his career. Unfortunately, he always felt like she was annoyed with him, being the firstborn and not so secretly their parents' favorite child.

"Here we are. The Seaview Room," Sarah said, stopping in front of it. She handed him the room key, a digital swipe card that was definitely an upgrade from the traditional turn-key lock that used to be there. "It's one of the bigger suites."

He opened the door and scanned the accommodations that would be his home for the next three weeks. Seafoam-green decor with a king-sized bed in the center of the room. Surfboard decorations on the wall and an old black-and-white photo of a local surf star from the fifties.

Fresh paint but still the same old feel.

"This is great, thank you," he told Sarah.

She nodded. "Enjoy your stay. If you need anything, don't hesitate to ask."

"Hey, Sarah," he said as she headed down the stairs.

She turned back to face him.

"Is the inn going to be busy this month?" He wasn't sure which answer he wanted. Being surrounded by lots of people and noise might help drown out his own depressing, anxiety-filled thoughts, but he wasn't sure repressing his feelings instead of taking time to process them and deal with them was the best solution.

"We decided to reserve December for locals, host some fun events, and offer the guest rooms to people coming home to spend the holidays with their families. Lia and Malcolm will be here as well, and there are two other families arriving next week. Other than that, it should be fairly quiet," she said.

"Great...thank you," he said, closing and locking the door behind her. He set his bags down on the floor, unpacked his toiletries, and undressed down to his underwear. In the bathroom, he brushed his teeth quickly and splashed warm water on his face.

He plugged in his cell phone but turned off the volume and then approached the big double balcony doors leading out onto the deck.

Black-out blinds. Thank God. He hit the button on the wall and within seconds he was enveloped in complete darkness.

Mitch crawled in between the soft, down-filled sheets, so exhausted that he thought he might sleep his entire holiday away.

• • •

He'd slept for sixteen hours. He would have slept longer if his cell phone hadn't woken him. It had somehow vibrated its way to the edge of the nightstand and crashed onto the floor. Obviously, he'd missed some calls.

His body felt stiff as he rolled over in bed and fumbled to find his phone in the dark. When he did, the display screen nearly blinded him and he squinted to read without his glasses.

His mother. Right. She knew he'd arrived the day before and no doubt had expected to see him right away. She never quite understood his need to process, to have time to unwind a little before seeing his family after his missions overseas.

It was for their benefit, too.

They did not want to see post-mission Mitch. Especially not this time. He still wasn't feeling his best, but he felt okay enough to answer the phone, at least.

"Hey, Mom," he said as upbeat as possible, lying on his back and staring up at the ceiling, his eyes still adjusting to the dark.

"Darling! You're home!"

The high-pitched excitement hurt his brain and he

winced, pulling the phone away from his ear a little. Maybe he should have let the call go to voicemail, but he'd have to answer eventually or she'd show up at the inn. The unmistakable sound of Kenny and Dolly's *Once Upon a Christmas* played behind her. Her favorite holiday CD. She always started listening to holiday music in October, with zero guilt about skipping the holidays of Halloween and Thanksgiving. She said the world could always use more joy.

Mitch didn't disagree, but unfortunately country music's famous duo couldn't offer nearly enough joy needed to erase the world's problems. But it made his Christmas-loving mom happy.

"Yeah," he said, "got in yesterday, just sleeping off the jetlag."

"Don't you love the new inn?"

Sure. He loved the black-out blinds and the fact that the owner hadn't woken him for breakfast or house-keeping. "It's different, but yeah, it's great."

"It was so nice of Sarah to open it up to locals coming home for the holidays this year."

"Yes, it was." She was procrastinating with the small talk. Mitch could hear the looming question on her mind. When would she see him?

"So, darling…"

Here it comes.

"I know you like your time to…decompress, so no pressure…" His father had to be standing next to her, otherwise there would indeed be pressure and maybe even guilt added to her request. "But we would love to see you for dinner tomorrow."

He'd agreed to spend the holiday season in his hometown. What had he expected? That his family and old friends wouldn't want to see him? Truthfully, he wanted to see them all, too. But in small doses. Too much socializing and celebration only irritated him. He couldn't expect everyone to see the world through his grim, realistic perspective, but it was difficult singing "Jingle Bells" and drinking eggnog from a cup shaped like a moose's head when there were children who had no idea there was something in the world to be excited about at all.

At least she was giving him another day and not expecting him there bright and early the next morning. "Of course. Six?" he said, suppressing a yawn and blinking the remaining fog of tiredness from his eyes.

"Perfect! Oh, and I ordered dessert from Delicious Delicacies on Main Street. Could you pick it up on your way over?"

Dessert. That meant one thing. It wasn't going to be a private family dinner. His mother had obviously invited others, but he'd agreed and there was no backing out now. "Sure, Mom," he said. "See you tomorrow."

"Love you, darlin'."

"Love you, too." He disconnected the call and released a sigh before tossing the bedsheets back and climbing out of bed. As much as he wanted to hide out in the room all season, he had to start shaking off the dark cloud that continued to loom over him. He couldn't go back overseas allowing this last mission to haunt him and affect his judgement.

If only things hadn't gone so wrong…

At the window, he opened the blinds and shielded his eyes from the bright sun. These balconies off of the bedrooms were a new addition from Sarah. He didn't hate them.

He stepped out onto the deck, a chilled December breeze blowing through his hair, and leaned against the cool metal railing, peering out over the ocean in the distance with sunlight sparkling on the waves. An ocean away, there was death and destruction and hopelessness, and he was there in Blue Moon Bay, where the only hardship was trying to catch the perfect wave.

Could he survive the season of joy and giving, self-ishly enjoy it, even, when his heart told him he should be out helping others?

CHAPTER THREE

DECEMBER 3ᴿᴰ...22 DAYS UNTIL CHRISTMAS...

She'd stolen the wedding cake.

Technically, it had been hers. But the pissed off bride and groom weren't likely to see it that way.

Spooning a forkful of it into her mouth, Jessica scanned her whiteboard on her kitchen wall Monday morning. Six orders needed to be filled that day. Well, maybe five. She was fairly certain the gift opening cupcakes John and Emily had ordered for their event that day was one of the flashing messages on her phone, canceling the order.

What the hell had she been thinking? She could have cost herself every wedding business in town after this rumor circulated. Only the delicious, not-too-sweet, not-too-chocolatey cake on her tongue made her feel even the slightest bit better about her actions. They were hardly professional, but she'd snapped. No one could possibly understand how hard it was, constantly surrounded by brides-to-be and not having an engagement ring on her hand herself.

And then to hear that she was being used, not only for her cakes, but as some weird mythical token of good luck? Now she'd be looking at every potential suitor with a cautious eye. How could she trust anyone's interest in her now?

She shook her head. Either way, her actions had been wrong.

She sighed and tucked the phone into her apron. It was in the past and she had current pressing matters at the moment. Rolling up the sleeves of her oversize plaid shirt, she started on the busy day ahead.

A bar mitzvah cake, several holiday cookie orders, a time-suck cheesecake—plain, not even an exciting flavor—and a stream of walk-in customers later, her phone ringing off the hook with new, last-minute holiday orders, she was exhausted.

Jessica refilled her frosting bag, then retrieved the yet-to-be decorated birthday cakes on the order list. Michael, Ross, and Elliott. All boys around the same age.

Sorry, kids, everyone is getting the same blue frosting this year.

The front door opened again and she shut her eyes tight, hoping whoever it was had walked into the wrong store. If that chime over her door jingled once more today, Jessica was going to lose her shit. Had everyone in Blue Moon Bay fallen off their latest health fad diet in the last eight hours?

It had to be the rain.

Rainy days were common this time of year on this part of the coast, and when the skies decided to open, it resulted in dark, overcast downpours that lasted for hours. It was pretty to watch from inside the bakery, but unfortunately, it spurred a need for a sugar fix in the locals and tourists alike. Something to do with a change in barometric pressure…

"Hello?"

The unrecognizable male voice had Jessica counting to ten.

Where the hell were they all coming from? Hadn't she served everyone within a five-mile radius by now? She'd expected her business to be slow because of the wedding stunt.

"Anyone here?"

"No, I just leave my bakery unattended…hope the Keebler elves sneak in to do all the baking at night," she muttered, pushing through the screen door that led to the front of the bakery. "How may I help—" She stopped and her jaw dropped. "Mitch Jameson?"

He hadn't changed at all in the years since she'd last seen him. If anything, he'd gotten hotter.

Or maybe, as a teenager, she just hadn't noticed Lia's older brother in that way.

She sure as hell was noticing him in that way now.

Tall, thin in an *I have muscles under this shirt but I'm not a gym junkie* way, and handsome in the traditional dark hair, dark eyes stereotype, he was definitely the best-looking disturbance so far that day. Or any day in recent memory.

"I'm sorry…you're…" He glanced at the stack of business cards on the counter. "Jessica?"

She didn't take offense to him not recognizing her— she'd been a chubby kid, a teenage friend of his sister's the last time he'd seen her, and he'd already been completing his medical degree. They may have said ten words to each other the entire time she'd hung out with Lia. "Yes," she said. "Hi... It's just Jess."

His dimpled smile and dark-rimmed glasses seemed to contradict each other. Like when Adam Levine tried to downplay his hotness by wearing glasses, the "hot geek" look was definitely working for this guy. She rubbed at her chest beneath beneath her shirt. It was really hot in here.

"Hey, do you think I could borrow a small towel...or napkin?" He removed his glasses and ran a hand over his face, and rain dripped from his dark hair. Shorter around the back and sides, longer in the front. It looked soft and thick, the kind of hair that her hands could run through forever. "A paper bag, even?"

"Oh, yes." She had to quit gawking. It wasn't as though she'd never seen an attractive guy before. She reached for a clean dishtowel in the drawer and handed it to him. "Here you go."

"Thank you," he said, wiping his face and exposed neck in his open-collared blue dress shirt.

He wasn't dressed for the weather...or for Blue Moon Bay at all, really. In dark, charcoal dress pants and shiny leather shoes, he stuck out among the board-short-wearing crowd of the coast. Even in the rain, the humidity would have made what he was wearing look uncomfortable on anyone else, but Mitch looked cool and relaxed, as though the rolled-up sleeves were the only casualness he needed.

"I was sent to pick up an order for my mom," he said, looking around.

Her eyes widened. "The Jameson Nightmare Christmas order? That doesn't need to be ready for another week and a half." The family always placed a massive Christmas order for their holiday entertaining. Usually, Jessica had until the twentieth, but that year they were celebrating early with Lia, reducing her deadline.

"You have a name for it?"

Oops, had she said it out loud? "Yes?" She winced. "Sorry, no offense, it's just a really big order and... It's just that I haven't actually started it yet this year." She might regret admitting that, but he had a trustworthy face. And if he was there to pick it up early, he was going to be leaving empty-handed, so she may as well be honest.

"Well, you're off the hook for now," he said. "Today, there was just some cookies and cupcakes..."

She released a sigh of relief. "Right. *That* order is almost ready. Just waiting on the oatmeal raisin cookies."

"I'm surprised you continue to take on the...what did you call it? Nightmare Christmas order every year," he said with amusement. "With all the dietary restrictions I'm sure you're trying to accommodate, you may as well just tell us to serve gluten-free rice cakes and fuck off."

"Right?" He really got it, and she liked him immediately. "So, Lia says you're working with Doctors Without Borders now." Good-looking *and* charitable, an incredibly tempting combination.

He nodded, but his expression darkened slightly. "Just back from Cambodia—wonderful country, amazing people. The scenery was breathtaking."

He was a little breathtaking. "Yeah."

"You've been?" Interest showed on his features, and the temptation to lie was strong. Compared to his life, hers would sound so boring. *She* might be boring. Just a small-town baker who had never been farther out into the world than L.A.

"No, I've never been," she said, just as the timer on her oven went off. Another cake that would need icing within the hour. "Excuse me for just a sec."

"Take your time." He climbed up onto one of the counter stools. "Can I grab one of these muffins?"

"Help yourself to anything you want," she said, then feeling herself blush, she added, "In the display case, I mean."

Or otherwise.

Pushing through the kitchen door, she released a deep breath. Damn, what the hell was happening to her? She donned her oven mitts and opened the top oven, then retrieved the chocolate cake and set it on the cooling rack, before resetting the oven's temperature and sliding in a tray of oatmeal chocolate chip cookies. After that day's traffic, her display case was practically empty. Luckily the muffins in the bottom oven were almost done.

Removing the mitts, she hurried into the bathroom and checked her reflection in the mirror.

Holy hell!

A large red smear of icing sugar covered part of her left cheek. She grabbed a cloth, wet it, and quickly scrubbed at the stain, but the stubborn dye simply faded to a pale pink.

Her hair was falling loose from her bun and she'd long ago licked her new mango-flavored tinted gloss from her lips, but hearing the bell chime again, there was little she could do about it. Even if there was time to reapply her makeup and fix her hair, she couldn't waltz back out there looking better without him knowing she'd gone through the effort.

Besides, it was Mitch Jameson. The guy was a world-traveling doctor, who was ten years her senior. Impressing him would be futile energy she didn't have.

With no other choice, she went back into the front to start packaging his family's order and send him on his way before he could distract her further…and found her shop neighbor, Mrs. Barnett, standing there.

This day could end anytime now.

She forced a polite smile. "Hi, Mrs. Barnett. How are you?"

Pissed, if the woman's body language could be trusted.

Jessica thought fast. The smoke detector hadn't gone off in weeks and she hadn't made any more of the spiced apple muffins that Mrs. Barnett said competed with the scent of her therapeutic oils she burned in her apothecary shop next door.

Something new must be annoying Mrs. Barnett.

All four feet eleven inches of her. So much fiery passion was bundled inside such a tiny person. She was nearly always on a rampage about something and Jessica tried hard to steer clear of her path. Odd that a woman who made her living from selling the idea of a calm and balanced existence was always so wound up.

Had she ever tried her own products?

"Can you explain this to me?" the older woman said, placing a letter on the counter.

Jessica picked it up and, seeing the logo for Not Just Desserts on the letterhead, her heart raced.

Uh-oh.

Her offer from Not Just Desserts, a big dessert chain in California to buy Delicious Delicacies, to buy her bakery was weighing heavy on her. They'd approached her earlier that year and she had three months left to decide if she wanted to sell her business. She was keeping it to herself for now, and not being able to discuss it with her best friends was torture, but she didn't want to freak anyone out just yet. Especially now that she'd promised Sarah she'd be here supporting her new venture of running the newly renovated B&B Sarah had inherited from her grandmother.

The thought of moving away made her nauseous, but the idea that she could die alone surrounded by half-eaten baked goods was becoming a reality with each ex getting married.

Unfortunately, she didn't know what to do. Eventually, she'd have to talk to her friends about it. She never made any big decisions without asking for their opinions and advice. She, Sarah, and Whitney had been best friends since grade school.

Though *they* were both recently engaged, and Jessica would be lying if she said she didn't fear being left behind as her two friends got married and started families. Being "awesome Aunt Jess with the yummy treats" only appealed to her so much.

"I'm not selling my shop or the space it's in," Mrs. Barnett said, taking the letter back before Jessica could read beyond the first line.

She'd read enough to understand Mrs. Barnett's irritation. "You don't have to."

Mrs. Barnett shook the paper. "According to this, I might. Says here, you're selling this space to them and they need my shop and Frankie's Fabrics to sell, too, so they can expand to put in a full seating area."

They'd really assumed a lot. Jessica hadn't given them an answer yet. She still had months until the deadline to respond. And besides, her bakery had nothing to do with the other two businesses in this building. If they wanted space for customers to sit and eat, they could expand outward with a deck or build a rooftop terrace.

Mrs. Barnett turned, as though noticing Mitch there for the first time. Her neighbor's expression changed and suddenly she was eyeing Mitch as though the fact he was thirty years her junior didn't matter one little bit. And his movie-star smile back at the woman wasn't doing him any favors. Had he forgotten Mrs. Barnett's reputation for being a man-eater in her earlier widowed days?

"I'm sorry, Mrs. Barnett," Jessica said. "Unfortunately, now's not a great time." A quick look at the clock revealed that two customers were due in thirty-six minutes to pick up holiday cakes. Thank God, one was a basic chocolate icing, but the other one was a red, green, and white poinsettias design. Even on her best day, that would take longer than thirty-six…make that thirty-*five* minutes.

"You're telling me. I have an essential oils bachelorette party starting in an hour, but these bastards keep sending these letters. They even sent someone to my shop yesterday. I was out. They left a business card under the door." She removed her glasses and slid them to the top of her head, fluffing her red curls around her shoulders.

The company was sending reps now? Jessica's stress bubble exploded over her head, drowning her as though she'd stepped outside into the downpour. They were really starting to put the pressure on. They'd called that morning, too, and she'd pretended to be an employee and said she wasn't in. Maybe her ancient landline needed to be at least upgraded to include caller ID.

"Look, I'm really sorry. I haven't given them an answer yet. And it's really up to you if you sell your space."

"You need to tell them no, and I have a few other choice words you can add…"

"Hey, you own Barnett's Bottles next door, right?" Mitch interrupted.

Mrs. Barnett's anger dissipated. "Yes. Gabrielle Barnett, widowed…and you are Mitch Jameson, the local hero doctor everyone talks about all the time."

Oh jeez.

Mitch laughed. "I don't know about that. However, *you*…your reputation precedes you. I hear you make the best coconut-infused massage oils on the west coast."

Mrs. Barnett giggled—*actually giggled*—the letter from Not Just Desserts completely forgotten. Jessica wanted to reach across the counter and kiss Mitch.

"I don't want to brag, but I do get a lot of customers who say it's the best they've tried. I mix different natural ingredients to create a line that meets any of your massage needs. My MintoCoco really soothes aching muscles." She eyed his forearms resting on the counter. "If you'd like a demonstration of it, I could set up the massage chair…"

Oh my God! Jessica wasn't sure which was worse, angry Gabrielle or flirty Gabby.

"Actually, that sounds amazing, but it's not for me," Mitch said smoothly. "My mom's sciatica is back, so I thought it would make a nice gift for her. Could you package up several bottles for me, with anything else you can recommend, and I'll stop by to pay once I leave here?"

Mrs. Barnett nodded, touching his shoulder. "Such a wonderful son, looking after his mom. I'll give you my special discount."

She looked ready to give him more than a discount, and Jessica shuddered. "Thank you for that," she said after Mrs. Barnett left the bakery.

"No problem, but do you mind me asking what she was so fired up about?"

Jessica sighed, checking the clock on the wall. She'd much rather spill her problems to the hottest man to walk into her bakery in years, but she still had cakes that needed to be decorated, boxed, and out the door within the hour.

"Sorry…raincheck? I'm swamped." She paused. "Actually…" Reaching under the counter, she grabbed a plastic cake stencil and a bag of icing she'd been using to pipe elf faces on some shortbread cookies that morning. "I'll tell you the story, but you need to help me catch up."

His eyes widened. "Oh…um…" He checked his watch. "I've got dinner…"

"The rest of your order's not ready yet. Write 'Happy Birthday,'" she said, nodding toward the stencil.

An amused smile spread across his face as he climbed off of the stool and rolled his dress shirt sleeves higher. "That's it? That's the challenge?" Mitch rotated his shoulders and bent over the stencil.

Jessica stared at his face as he worked, his look of concentration zapping every last ounce of hers. Having him in her kitchen might slow things instead of speeding them up.

"Do I pass?" he asked.

Jessica studied the slightly off-center script lettering. It was readable and time was ticking. "It will have to do," she said, lifting the section of the counter to give him access to the employee area.

"I'm hired?"

"You've volunteered. Donating your time to a cause. That's your thing, right?" She handed him an apron and waited for him to refuse the Christmas-themed, ruffled fabric.

Instead, he took it and slid it over his head, which only made him the most insanely attractive man on earth. "You think you have me figured out, huh?"

"Don't I?" This felt like flirting. Was this flirting? Should she be flirting? Did she have time to flirt?

"No act of selflessness is completely altruistic," he said.

"You have ulterior motives for helping me?"

"Two."

Definitely flirting. "The explanation about Mrs. Barnett is one…so what's the other?"

"Maybe by helping you, you'll have time to go to dinner with me…say tomorrow night?"

Her heart raced. Dinner? With the sexy, kind-hearted, charismatic doctor?

Hell, yes!

Her agreement was on the tip of her tongue when Niall's voice popped into her brain. *The good luck charm*… Damn it! There was no truth to it and yet… Maybe she should lay off dating for a while. She'd be setting herself up for heartbreak. The last thing she wanted was another guy finding the love of his life, aka *not her*, after she went out with him.

Wait, was that his motive?

Her eyes narrowed. "You heard the rumor, didn't you?" Made sense. He was getting older, probably looking to settle down…date her a few times and *BAM!* Connect with the love of his life.

He looked genuinely confused. "What rumor?"

She sighed. "About me being the magic link to you and your soul mate."

"I'm not following."

Her cheeks flushed. Obviously, he hadn't heard. Damn, why had she said anything? "Never mind."

"No, I definitely need to hear this," he said, looking amused. "You're not getting out of it now."

"It's just a silly rumor that if you date me, once we end things, you'll find your true love. It's happened several times," she mumbled, avoiding his gaze.

He laughed. "I tell you what, you have dinner with me and I promise you that I will not fall in love with the next person I meet. In fact, I promise not to fall in love with anyone."

She wasn't sure how she felt about *that* exactly... Didn't "anyone" include her?

"I'll take your silence as a yes," he said, giving her a second to compose herself as he diverted his attention to scan the kitchen. "Now, where do we start?"

• • •

Opening the door to his family home half an hour later, Mitch's sense of foreboding hadn't completely subsided, but maybe being home for a few weeks wouldn't be as torturous as he'd thought. Since leaving the bakery, his mood was considerably better and it wasn't completely from having done a good deed.

In fact, his awkward lack of basic skills in the kitchen

had probably put Jess even further off her schedule, but he couldn't bring himself to regret hanging around while she worked. He vaguely remembered her from when she'd spend time at their family pool with his sister after school and on summer break. She was always the smiling, nice one out of all of Lia's friends.

And she'd grown up to be quite a beauty. He hoped the ten-year age gap between them wouldn't freak her out, because he already knew one dinner with her wouldn't be enough. She was interesting and intriguing and hilarious. Her story about the Good Luck Charm curse had made him laugh harder than he had in over a year, and laughing with her had felt good.

Almost exactly the cure he'd been needing.

The sight of the holiday decor throughout the house as he entered immediately brought him back to his childhood. The garland wrapped around the staircase railing and his mother's collection of different-colored trees—different heights and thickness—in the center of the foyer were all familiar. The big white snowflakes hanging from the ceiling were now yellowing from so many years of use, and the number of snow globes positioned on every flat surface in the house had to be reaching close to two hundred by now. She'd collected them since she was a child.

His mother believed in traditions. She decorated the same way every year. She cooked the same foods. And their Christmas morning routine had always been the same. Awake before sunrise, stockings first, then hot chocolate and cookies for breakfast, and last, gift opening under the tree.

Voices and laughter drifted to him from the dining room, making him the slightest bit uneasy. He missed his family when he was away, but he knew they'd drill him with questions about his missions. They were interested. That was a good thing. He knew his parents were proud. But he wasn't in the mood to talk about the last tour overseas.

Man, he wished he was still at the bakery, where the conversation had been flirty and light.

Carrying the boxes of desserts, he entered the dining room, where it appeared his entire extended family were gathered. As usual, his mother had gone completely overboard. A big WELCOME HOME banner hung on the wall, and photos he'd sent from various missions had been blown up and displayed on racks all over the dining room. The shrine-like feel made his stomach twist, his high from meeting Jess unfortunately not enough to counteract the weight of the pressure bringing him back to earth.

Obviously, there'd be no deflecting the conversation away from his last mission.

His gaze fell on an image of him playing soccer with a group of kids in Cambodia, the smile on his face the last one before the incident. It took little to feel as though he were back there, living the nightmarish moments.

"My baby!" The joy in his mother's voice made him feel like an asshole for not visiting more, but this over-the-top setup was precisely the reason why.

He set the desserts down just in time to receive her hug, and kissed her cheek when she refused to let go. "Hey, Mom. Went a little overboard, don't you think?" Trying to keep his tone light and trying not to offend was difficult. He knew she meant well, but she could never quite understand that he'd chosen his field of work to help others, to serve…not to be treated with this kind of reverence. He didn't like the spotlight she insisted on putting him under all the time.

"No such thing as overboard," she said, squeezing him even tighter.

He laughed awkwardly as he scanned the room, and his other family members smiled and waved in greeting. His father came to his rescue.

"Okay, okay, let the poor man breathe, Ally," he said, gently pulling his wife away and then extending a hand to Mitch. "Great to see you, son."

Mitch shook it. "You, too, Dad." He greeted the rest of the family and made small talk as they took their seats around the table. His mother opted for the one next to him instead of her usual chair. It was the same each visit, as though she were afraid to let him out of her sight, for fear that she may never see him again.

He'd never tell her how close that had come to being true.

To avoid the topic altogether, he turned to his Uncle Doug. "Hey, how's the tree business this year?" His uncle was an independent truck driver, and this time of year he was kept busy hauling Evergreens and Blue Spruce from the tree farms farther north.

The older man *tsk*ed. "Even slower than last year. Folks opting for those pre-lit, no-mess, plastic, rotating, singing trees more and more…" He sounded disgusted.

Beside him, his mother whispered, "I bought one of those this year."

And so went dinner. Mitch successfully diverted the conversation to every other family member to avoid the discussions he didn't want to have. Luckily, his older relatives could talk about the everyday mundane pace of the small town for hours, thinking they were catching him up on all that he was missing.

He'd never admit he didn't feel like he was missing a thing. Same old stories. Same old life. Wonderful if it suited them all, but he'd never be happy living in the simplicity and predictability of small-town life every day.

"Can we chat in the study?" his father asked him, as his mother cleared the dinner plates.

Mitch popped the last piece of strawberry-filled va-nilla cupcake into his mouth and made a mental note to compliment Jess on their dinner date the next evening. She was as amazing a baker as she was intriguingly in-teresting.

"Sure thing, Pop," he said, standing and reaching for his coffee cup.

His father shook his head. "Leave it. I got the good stuff in the liquor cabinet," he said quietly.

"Thank God," Mitch said with a grin, sneaking out of the dining room and following his father to the study. The two of them barely had a chance to chat whenever Mitch visited, with his mother always hovering. He loved his mom, but these one-on-ones with his dad helped him handle his time at home a little better.

Sitting on the slightly worn leather chair near the fireplace, Mitch accepted a glass of scotch from his dad and folded one leg over his knee.

His father sat across from him, studying him for a long moment before saying, "The last mission didn't go so well, huh?"

Mitch stared at his glass and shook his head. "Some are worse than others. It's the nature of the business we're in." As a family doctor for over forty years, Clyde Jameson had seen it all in his own career. Mitch remembered days when his father would come home beaming after delivering twins or crushed with disappointment when one of his senior patients passed away. It was his father's compassion and dedication to helping others that Mitch had always admired most, and he was grateful that he'd inherited those traits.

His father nodded. "You doing okay?"

Was he? Two days ago, he'd been a complete mess. Burned out, exhausted, eager to get back but unsure whether or not he could handle a new assignment with his current mindset. Today he was rested, more relaxed, still on edge but better. A big part in thanks to meeting Jess that afternoon. "Getting there," he said honestly.

There was no point in trying to hide how he was feeling from his father. His mother would worry too much, and Mitch didn't like adding to her anxiety, but his father understood the stress that came with this career, even if he chose to treat clientele in a small town instead of poverty-stricken countries.

"Well, I'm here, son. Anything you need."

Mitch nodded. He could always count on his father. "Thanks, Dad. I appreciate that."

His father took a breath and leaned forward in his chair. "On that note, I have a proposition for you."

Uh-oh.

"Your mother and I have built a wonderful life here in Blue Moon Bay. We have everything we could imagine we wanted when we started out with a small one-bedroom apartment and struggling to repay my medical school loans," he said with a smile. "But I think it's time to retire."

Mitch blinked. "What?" He'd assumed his father would die holding a thermometer to a toddler's mouth.

"I'll be sixty-five next year and we want to do more traveling and, you know, just be together more." Clyde stood and refilled his own glass, and Mitch recognized it as a way of avoiding his son's perceptive gaze.

Mitch had also inherited his father's ability to read people and situations.

How much of this decision had to do with his father being ready to hang up the stethoscope, and how much had to do with his mother wanting him to? She'd been asking Clyde to retire for several years now, claiming soon they'd be too old to enjoy retirement.

"You sure that's what you want?" It certainly wasn't what Mitch wanted for his father.

He'd heard of very successful, very intelligent people having a hard time with retirement. As though they lost their purpose. His dad could very well be someone like that. He'd spent his entire life caring for others and thriving in a fast-paced, high stress environment—even at the small family clinic level—this change would be hard on him.

But his father nodded. "It is."

"What will you do? Other than travel with Mom?" His father had no hobbies or interests beyond medicine. Without it, even the traveling wouldn't fill the void. His father had never taken more than two weeks off a year. Ever.

"That's it, I guess."

"Is this because of Mom? Is she putting the pressure on?"

His father twirled the ice in his glass and stared at the amber liquid. "She's been convincing me that it's the right choice," he said slowly. "I have to hang up the stethoscope at some point, and I'm not getting any younger. Don't want to be one of those old folks who save forever to finally enjoy life and then croak within days of being free to do so. And I have to be fair to your mom, too. She's stood by me and my decisions all these years."

Clyde always put his wife and family above all else, so there was no point in trying to talk him out of what had to be a difficult decision. "Well…congratulations, I guess. I'm sure the community will miss you and the practice."

His father cleared his throat. "It would be an easier transition on everyone if you'd consider taking it over."

Mitch's stomach pitched and he frowned. "Take over your office?"

Clyde nodded, setting his glass aside. "It's the logical thing to do. I've had offers on it, but no one I'd rather leave it to than you."

Only one other time had his father approached him with a similar offer of working together at the practice, and Mitch had gently but firmly explained his own goals and visions for his future, and that had been the end of the discussion. His father had respected his choice. To say this was coming out of left field would be an understatement. "I sold my practice in L.A. because I wanted to travel, remember?"

"Yes, but that was seven years ago. I thought maybe it might be something you'd consider now? You've traveled all over the world, done some real good. Have you given any thought to settling down a little, staying in one place for a while? Maybe find someone to share your life with, start a family?"

Mitch's eyes widened. "When have I ever expressed an interest in all of that?" He was almost forty, but he was far from wanting to settle down in any capacity. He'd never really considered marriage, enjoying the freedom of casual, no-strings attached relationships and he loved kids, but he wasn't sure he wanted any of his own.

"I just thought you might if an opportunity like this presented itself," his father said, failing to hide his disappointment.

Mitch shook his head, slightly annoyed that this

opportunity had presented itself. Now, it was on him letting his father down, letting the community down by not wanting to continue the legacy he'd built here in Blue Moon Bay. Mitch had never felt familial obligation before and it irritated him that he was feeling it now.

"I'm not ready for anything like that yet, Dad. I'm still doing good work overseas even if things don't always turn out the way we hope." He knew that.

In his heart, despite the recent tragedies and disappointments, he wasn't ready to walk away yet. Maybe after this last disastrous trip, he had to go back and prove to himself once again that there was a point and purpose to the direction his life had taken. A successful trip to restore his faith in his career and himself. Staying in Blue Moon Bay had never even been a consideration.

"I understand," his father said without an ounce of resentment or pressure, which only made Mitch's rejection feel even worse. "Just know the offer is there if you change your mind."

Unfortunately, just knowing he had that option made Mitch want to skip out on the holidays in his hometown and get his ass back to reality—before any more unexpected surprises threatened to derail his own plans for his life.

CHAPTER FOUR

"I suppose this isn't the most unique idea for a dinner date around here," Mitch said, gesturing toward the other picnicking couples as he spread a checkered blanket under a tree on a grassy area near the beach.

Jessica laughed and set down her wicker basket. "It's perfect." She'd actually been nervous about the idea of a dinner date with him. Blue Moon Bay loved new gossip, and with few dining options to choose from, they'd no doubt be spotted by someone they knew if they'd gone to a restaurant. Not that she was reluctant to be seen with Mitch, but it just felt nice keeping this attraction to herself for a while.

Besides, Mitch was only here for the holidays, so he'd probably only invited her out to keep himself busy while he was in town. She wouldn't get ahead of herself, thinking her intense attraction to him was mutual.

"No matter how many oceans I see, this view is always the most special," he said, removing his shoes and sitting on the blanket. He stretched his long legs out and crossed his bare feet at the ankles.

He had nice feet. Figures he couldn't have the decency to have one obvious flaw, like ugly toes, that she could use to remind herself that they'd only spent a few hours together in her bakery the day before—she barely knew him. Yet, something about being with him felt eerily right. Natural.

"I love it, too," she said. "I couldn't imagine not having this right in my backyard."

His sister, Lia, living in New York and pre-in-love Sarah could rave about city life all they wanted, but nothing could compare to beachside living for Jessica. Fast pace, hustle and bustle wasn't her style. Her bakery was busy, but she controlled that schedule and when she needed a breather, she took one. Working for someone else, part of a bigger company wouldn't offer that flexibility.

"You've lived here your whole life, right?" Mitch turned to look at her and the wind blew his dark hair across his forehead.

Jessica shoved her hands under her legs to resist the temptation to push it back. "Yes. My parents traveled a lot as antique appraisers, but they never took me with them, so other than a few trips into L.A. to visit Sarah, I've never been anywhere else." Which made him that much more appealing to her. Just being near him, knowing the places he'd been, the adventures he must have experienced, brought out a sense of wanderlust in her that she didn't feel often.

"That's incredible," he said. "I couldn't imagine staying in one place that long. Before Lia was born, I'd been all over the world with my mom. Dad was always reluctant to take too much time away from the clinic, but Mom wanted me to experience different cultures from an early age, so we'd often go alone. I remember the school holding a conference with my parents after I'd missed too many weeks of class in grade two and my mom telling Mrs. Remy that I was getting a much better education by seeing the world than just reading about it in a book."

"Really? How did that go over?" Ally Jameson had a reputation as being a bit of a firecracker in town. Very spirited and friendly, even if her holiday baking order was a source of nightmares.

"The teacher really couldn't argue with Mom's reasoning, so she based part of my grade on written reports about my travels," Mitch said.

"Didn't that just feel like extra work?" Jessica had never enjoyed school, doing the bare minimum to squeeze by. Culinary college and pastry school had been her first experience enjoying learning.

Mitch smiled as he shook his head. "I actually liked writing them and I still have them. They're great to look back on and remember the adventures from my younger point of view, especially when I revisit those places now as an adult. And it's a habit I've kept up."

"You journal your trips?" Could the man get any more impressive?

"Yeah. That's corny, right?" He was adorable when he blushed.

Jessica shook her head. "Not at all. Of course, using the word 'corny' is slightly 'corny.'"

"I'm showing my age a little, huh?"

"Maybe a little."

"Does my age bother you?" He appeared legitimately concerned that it might.

Jessica laughed. "You're thirty-nine, not fifty."

"So...that's a no?"

"That's a no."

"Good," he said with a smile.

And it was impossible to tear her gaze away. How had she never noticed those deep-set dimples before? She'd spent hundreds of days at Lia's place growing up, but Mitch had always been just the older brother that Lia would shoo away whenever he tried to hang out wherever they were. Of course, the age difference back then felt huge.

"Should we eat?" she asked.

"I'm starving." He opened the takeout bag from the beach-hut a few blocks away. They'd picked up sandwiches and fruit, and she'd packed dessert and wine in the basket.

"I can't remember if you have any siblings," he said, unwrapping a sandwich and then taking a bite.

Jessica opened the wine and poured it into two plastic wineglasses. "I don't. I'm an only child. I think my parents felt like they needed to have at least one child, but they barely had time in their busy schedule to spend much time raising me." She shrugged. "Don't get me wrong, I'm not traumatized over it or anything. It was the family dynamic I grew up used to and I spent a lot of time with my aunt and uncle. They had four children, so I guess I got the best of both worlds."

Time with her parents may not have been the

traditional upbringing with their frequent absences, but she'd come to appreciate the relationship for what it was. They were close in a different way.

"I feel the same way," Mitch said. "I was an only child for over ten years, so I got to experience having all of my parents' attention, and then Lia came along and I was fortunate to have a sister."

Fortunate. Lia didn't see their relationship that way at all. She thought her brother was annoying and irritating and she'd never been close to Mitch. Did Mitch even realize how his sister viewed their relationship? She'd planned a family reunion earlier that year specifically when he couldn't make it.

So far, Jessica couldn't find fault with the man at all, so maybe Lia's irritation was directed more at her parents and their apparent preference for Mitch.

"When's your next trip?" she asked, then took a bite of a strawberry.

"In three weeks." His gaze was on the sandwich he was unwrapping and she couldn't read how he felt about that. "I'm hoping for Cambodia again. We accomplished a lot while we were there, but there's more work to be done."

Three weeks. Just until Christmas. She'd been hoping he was staying at least until the New Year. "Will you be in Blue Moon Bay until you leave again?" Did she sound hopeful? Playing it cool wasn't something she'd finessed over the years.

"I haven't really made any plans yet. I'll spend time with my family, but I also might drive north to Big Bear for a few days. See the snow. Do some skiing." He laughed. "The travel bug never eases up for long."

She nodded. "That sounds nice. I've never actually seen snow."

"Really? Never?"

"Never," she said.

"Well, maybe you'll expand your horizons a little and come along." He paused, studying her a moment. "I just meant that I'd love to have company…only if you're interested. No pressure."

She was definitely interested. The problem was she was afraid of getting *too* interested. Falling hard and fast was not an issue for her. It was knowing when the other person was as fully committed that she struggled with. And this guy had promised that he wouldn't fall in love this holiday season…

"Sorry, that was too forward," he said quickly in her silence.

"No! I'd actually love to go." She could close the bakery for a few days, or hire someone to just run the front end for a weekend.

After all, she was contemplating giving up her bakery completely. Maybe a few days away from it might help in her decision-making. Help her see what not going into her own business at five a.m. every morning felt like. See if it could be an option for her future.

"Why don't we play it by ear?" he said.

"Good idea."

"So, we got distracted yesterday with your Good Luck Charm story and you never did tell me much about this offer from Not Just Desserts. How much longer do you have to decide?"

She stared out at the evening sun setting over the ocean, the crashing waves lapping over the sand. "Another few months." Though they were increasingly putting more pressure on.

"Are you leaning more one way or the other?"

"No idea. At first, I thought no way…but lately, I'm not sure."

"You love it here, though, right?"

Yes, but she had no one to love here.

Not that she could tell him that. She refused to sound alone and desperate, hounded by the sound of a ticking biological clock and wedding bells.

She hadn't had a first date in a while, but even she knew that would drive a man off. Fast. "I do," she said honestly. "I guess I'm hoping I'll know what to do when the time comes."

"You will," he said.

"How do you know?"

"The way I see it, there's no wrong answer. Whatever you decide to do will turn out for the best."

He sounded so sure and confident, but this was one decision she'd second-guessed over and over. She didn't think that would end even after making the decision. Either way, she'd wonder what if she'd gone the other way.

All she could do was live in the moment. This moment with him, right now. Her troubles had no place on this date with this gorgeous, interesting man.

. . .

Kiss her or not?

That was the million-dollar question that had plagued him the entire drive to her place after they left their beach dinner date. They'd held hands whenever they weren't eating and she'd allowed him to wrap an arm around her as they watched the sun set over the ocean.

But was a kiss too much, too soon?

Would she think he was only interested in a physical, casual fling? They both knew he wasn't staying in town beyond the holidays and that he obviously wasn't looking for a relationship.

But he knew two things—he wanted to see her again, and he desperately wanted to kiss her.

He shot a quick glance toward her in the passenger seat of his rental. She'd licked her dark mauve colored lipstick from her lips during dinner and she hadn't reapplied it. Did that mean she'd be open to a good night kiss? He'd read in a *Cosmo* magazine left behind on a flight once that the lack of reapplying lipstick was a sign…

Jeez, now he was getting his relationship advice from a magazine he had no business reading.

She looked at him, and he quickly turned his attention back to the road. "I'm just the next left," she said, as he came to a stop sign. The speed limit in the neighborhood was thirty, but he couldn't be going faster than ten. He was reluctant to see the night end, but inviting her back to the inn for a drink had seemed too sleazy…but would she invite him into her place?

It had been far too long since he'd been on a real first date, and it was quickly becoming evident that he had no idea what the dating etiquette was these days in the era of apps and hookups. She'd been quiet on the drive back to her place, so it was hard to read her.

He turned onto her street and cleared his throat. "So, on a scale of one to ten, how would you rate tonight's date?"

She grinned as she turned in the seat to face him. "Like if I was leaving a Yelp review?"

"Yes. Yelp review me." He could take it. Hopefully, she wouldn't dock him for his use of the word "corny" or his unimaginative date suggestion.

She looked as though she were thinking for a long moment. "Um…I'd say it was a solid eight."

"Eight." He nodded slowly. Not bad. Not a ten. "What could have I done for a better score?"

Jessica's cheeks flushed slightly as she stared at their joined hands between the seats. "I docked you two points because you are a limited-time offer."

He swallowed hard. So, she was looking for something a little more serious in a guy. Normally that response would have him doing the logical, responsible thing—breaking it off before the woman got too invested or got her feelings hurt. So far, he'd been honest and clear in his intentions. Saying good night and thanking her for a fun evening was the way to play this.

But he really wanted to see her again. More than he'd wanted a second date with a woman in a long time. He didn't want to see her get hurt, of course, but maybe they could take things casually and see what happened.

All he knew was he'd been dreading this time in his hometown. Dreading the downtime, the holidays with his family, being in one place for too long...but Jessica was already helping him cope.

"Sorry if that put any pressure on," she said.

He squeezed her hand. "Maybe I like the pressure."

She smiled shyly as she pointed to a small bungalow on the right. "That one's mine."

He pulled into her driveway and cut the engine. "Is it too old-fashioned of me to walk you to your door?"

She shook her head. "It just might earn you another half point."

"Eight and a half. I'll take it," he said, opening the door and climbing out. He quickly made his way to the passenger side and opened her door for her. Then, taking her hand in his again, he walked her up the walkway and to the door.

He scanned the front yard and nodded toward the Santa on a Surfboard inflatable she had displayed. "Cute." Other than the white and blue lights lining her roof, it was the only visible holiday decoration. It was a relief that she wasn't as Christmas-focused as his mom.

"It was a gift from Sarah," she said. "She found it in a surf shop in L.A. last Christmas and had to have it, but she didn't have anywhere to put it when she lived in an apartment building, so she gifted it to me."

"Dove's Nest owner, Sarah?"

"That's the one," Jessica said, reaching her front door and fumbling with her keys.

Key fumbling was also supposed to be a sign of a kiss being welcome. Procrastinating meant prolonging the good night. But unfortunately, he couldn't place his fate of another date in the hands of a secondhand *Cosmo* magazine. He cleared his throat. "I had a great time... both yesterday and tonight."

"Me too." Her dark brown eyes reflecting the glow of the holiday lights were warm and inviting, and as much as he knew he should walk away before things had a chance to get complicated, he wasn't sure he'd survive the holidays in his hometown without spending time with her again. A lot.

And it was totally arrogant and presumptuous of him to think she'd fall for him in a few weeks anyway.

"I have two questions," he said. He had to go for it. If she rejected him, it was better than not even trying.

"Okay..."

"Can I kiss you, and can I take you out again?" Blurting them both out wasn't exactly smooth, but he was rusty with this whole dating thing.

Jessica smiled as she hesitated, contemplating.

He held his breath.

"No to the kiss." She paused. "But yes to the second date."

Thank God. Out of the two options, at least she'd said yes to one. The most important one. He brought her hand to his lips and placed a gentle kiss on her palm. "I can definitely live with that. 'Night Jess," he said.

"Good night, Mitch."

He waited until she'd unlocked the door and gone inside, but then high-fived himself on the way back to the car.

CHAPTER FIVE

"You said no to the kiss? Good for you!" Sarah sounded impressed on the other end of the call as Jessica walked down the street toward the bakery the next morning—a little later than usual. She cradled her cell between her shoulder and ear, carrying several boxes of holiday lights and decorations for her shop window.

"Yeah, only my playing hard to get left me wanting all evening, too." As soon as she'd gone inside, she'd had to resist every urge to open the door and run after his car. The date with Mitch had been perfect. She refused to consider that she may have put him off by the rejection of the kiss. There was always next time.

At least there would be a next time and she wouldn't get hung up on just how many next times. One date at a time.

"Well, he looked happier last night entering the B&B than he was the day he checked in, or yesterday when he was heading out, so he obviously had a good time," Sarah said. "And wow, Mitch Jameson. Mitch and Jess... has a nice ring to it."

Jessica laughed. This was why she loved Sarah. She could dream-plan a future with a man she'd dated once and Sarah was along for the ride. At least, this new blissfully in love version of her best friend. Before reuniting with Wes, Sarah would have been a tad more cautious or cynical in her advice, but after getting an unexpected chance at happily ever after with her longtime secret love, Sarah was definitely a different woman these days.

"When are you seeing him again?" Sarah asked.

"Not sure. We didn't make any real plans, but he took my number." He'd sent a "thanks again for a great night" text about an hour after dropping her off. But she did that even after nights out with her aunt, so she wasn't sure she could read too much into it, and he hadn't texted yet that day...

"Well, keep me posted," Sarah said.

Seeing a man dressed in an expensive-looking suit and shiny brown dress shoes, leaning up against the exterior brick wall, Jessica sighed. "Hey, Sarah, I have to go. Call you later." She let her phone slide from her shoulder into the top of the box as she approached the bakery.

That was a Not Just Desserts rep. She could spot them a mile away. Unfortunately, his timing sucked. So much for the euphoric high she'd been riding that morning. The temptation to turn and walk back in the other direction was strong, but he'd spotted her.

Too late.

"Good morning," she said, stopping next to him and juggling a box on one hip. She unlocked the bakery door.

"Is it still morning?" He checked his Rolex.

She clenched her jaw. "It's not noon yet. Mr. Dorsey, I presume?"

He nodded. "Getting a bit of a late start, though, aren't you?" He pointed to the HOURS OF OPERATION sign in her window.

"I didn't realize I was punching a time clock." He didn't own her bakery yet and he'd never own *her*. She pushed against the door, and surprisingly he held it open as she entered, then set the box down in front of the window. She flicked the lights on and flipped the open/closed sign so the OPEN side was facing out.

"Just an observation," he said, scanning the bakery.

"I had a later than usual night." Wait a minute, why was she explaining herself to this guy? He should be explaining why he was lurking outside her business. Of course, he probably thought it was the last resort, seeing as she'd been avoiding his calls and emails over the last two weeks.

She hated that of all mornings, he'd chosen this one to stop by. She was a professional business owner and being late to work was something she rarely did. But that morning she'd still been riding high from her date with Mitch the night before and hugging the bed for an extra hour had seemed blissful.

"Coffee?" she asked. She hoped not too many people had seen him outside. If she decided to sell, *she* wanted to be the one to tell her customers. They were her community and friends. Already there was a rumor circulating, though. Lia had even caught wind of it earlier that year when they'd first approached Jessica, but she didn't want anyone thinking that the sale was a done deal, just yet. It wasn't.

"Decaf, please," he said, surveying the delivery shelf. "These all for today?"

She nodded, her teeth clenching.

Please step away from the shelf.

"Eighteen deliveries for one day? Is that standard?"

"This time of year, yes. Some days are slower, but I have most of the business accounts around here and most generally place an order once a week for catered staff meetings and office parties throughout the month of December, so the work is steady."

He glanced into the kitchen. "What about custom cakes for birthdays and weddings? How well are they doing this time of year?"

She filled the coffeepot and changed the filter before answering. "Mr. Dorsey, I've spent a lot of time building this business to what it is. People order from Delicious Delicacies because they are confident in the consistency of my products. If you are successful in buying this bakery, you can't assume the business will automatically transfer."

He smiled, but it didn't look sincere. "We're not worried about it."

Of course not.

She reached for her favorite mug and a paper to-go cup for him and willed the coffee to hurry up. She had more cakes to decorate before noon, a holiday window display to create for the Night of Lights that weekend, and the rain had let up momentarily, but once it started again, she'd be busy with walk-ins. And she did not want anyone coming in and seeing him or overhearing their conversation. She needed to get him out of there.

May as well cut straight to the chase. "So, why are you really here? I still have a few more months before I have to give you my final decision."

"We are reaching the end of the terms of our offer. Typically, these kinds of acquisitions don't take this long."

"I still haven't made a decision, so if you need to retract the offer…" That would be easiest of all. Have the opportunity taken away so that it was no longer her choice.

That would be better, right?

Mr. Dorsey shook his head as he climbed up on a stool and opened his briefcase on the countertop. "We are actually willing to make it more appealing for you and your neighbors. Maybe help the decision come along a little faster."

She turned away, needing a moment, and with an unsteady hand, she poured the coffee and handed him a cup. "Cream? Sugar?" she mumbled.

"Black is fine."

No doubt like his cold heart.

"Look, Miss Connolly, we're not trying to bully you into making a decision. I get it. I understand your attachment to this place." He looked around the shop as though he found the small-town local business charming and quaint.

She doubted he could possibly understand it. She sipped the hot coffee and burned her lip.

"The first business I acquired was my parents' little

mom and pop bookstore in San Diego."

Yep, heartless.

"I grew up in that store, I worked there during the summer—it was special to my parents and to me," he said, wrapping his hands around the cup and leaning forward, "but selling it made sense. Local independent bookstores aren't making profits these days and my parents would have put all of their savings into keeping the doors open, and for what?"

For what? Was he serious? Was it really just about a healthy bottom line? "How about for the community? The people who still love those indie bookstores?" She loved Book Pages, Blue Moon Bay's bookstore down the street. It would be like losing a friend if that place ever closed.

Though, when was the last time she'd visited and actually supported the store?

Mr. Dorsey shook his head. "In the end, they hadn't busted their butts for years just to retire poor. It was for the best. But my point is, I get it. I know what it's like to let go of something that you've worked hard to build, and this bakery is nothing like that bookstore—it's actually thriving, which is why we want to increase our buyout offer." He reached into his soft, leather briefcase and slid the new offer toward her.

She didn't want to look, but she was curious... Her gaze landed on the dollar amount they were offering and she blinked.

A million dollars?

"You'd never have to work again if you didn't want to,

and if you invested right, of course," he said.

A million dollars was double their original offer and it could set her up for life…whatever direction she decided to take.

Her head was nodding almost as though on autopilot, and she quickly reversed its direction. So quickly, she got a neck cramp. "I'm twenty-nine. I'm not interested in retiring." Though not having to worry about a slow season would alleviate any stress she experienced throughout the year, but this decision couldn't be strictly based on money.

Mr. Dorsey shrugged. "Then go work somewhere, with the peace of mind that money is no longer an issue."

"Money is not a huge motivator for me." She'd never really had to worry about it. Her parents had loaned her the money to open the bakery years before and she'd since paid them back, and she lived a modest life. She had no debt or any huge expenses.

But she sighed, her thoughts immediately going to Whitney, who was struggling financially. She'd admitted in recent months that her mother's medical bills were a concern. If Jessica took this offer, she could help her friend out with her debt. Take some of the burden away. Then maybe Whitney would be comfortable moving forward with wedding plans and having a family with Trent.

Then again, selling the bakery for the money might allow her to help Whitney, but she'd be letting Sarah down. She'd agreed to be the main supplier of baked goods for the inn, and Sarah's decision to keep it had

been partially based on Jessica's promise. Not entirely…
and she'd understand, but…

There seemed to be no winning in this decision.
"How long do I have to think about it?"

"Until the original offer expires," he said. "However,
we'd like to move forward with our plans as early as the
new year, so an early decision would be appreciated."

Meaning more money, no doubt.

"And Frankie's Fabrics—you're offering her the
same?" Her aunt was getting close to retirement age.
Frankie may not have jumped at the first offer, but this
one would be tough to turn down, especially if she too
saw the potential benefit of helping Whitney and Trent.

He nodded. "Really give this some thought, Miss
Connolly. I'd hate to see you regret your decision. May
I?" he asked, nodding toward the wrapped day-old
muffins in the basket on the counter.

"Help yourself," she said. As if she could ever deny
anyone a muffin.

He unwrapped a white and dark chocolate chip
espresso muffin, and Jessica watched as he took a bite.
"Mmmm, this is good."

"Thanks," she mumbled.

He checked his watch and stood. "I better go. The
rest of the shops are opening up and people in small
towns get nervous when they see a guy in a suit around."

Nauseous was more like it.

"I'm taking this with me, though," he said, picking up
his coffee. "It really is the best coffee-and-muffin combo
on the coast. You'll have to tell me your secret," he said

with a wink.

Not a chance. Not Just Desserts may get her bakery one way or the other, but all her recipes went with her. They thought just because they were a big chain, they could win. Well, she had more faith in her community and her talents. And if only that were enough, she'd tell him where to shove his million-dollar offer.

She waited until he was gone before heading into the kitchen. While she still had her business, she had work to do.

. . .

Could he casually stop by the bakery and claim he was just there for the baked goods, or would Jessica see right through it?

Mitch strolled along Main Street late that morning, after another long sleep. The jetlag was taking a while to wear off, but the night before was the first real peaceful sleep he'd had in months. And for the first time, he hadn't woken with a heavy sense of dread weighing on his chest. He'd woken with a smile, thinking about the evening before and the gorgeous brunette who'd coyly refused his kiss.

Seeing the bakery's awning a block away, his palms sweat and he wiped them on his dress pants. Would it appear stalkerish to just show up at her work?

He'd love nothing more than to surprise her and catch her in her element — messy hair and frosting smeared on her face like the first time he'd seen her.

Damn, she'd been cute. The sight of her had instantly lifted his sour mood.

But she'd said she had a busy day. Christmas was a chaotic time of year for her. He'd offer to help, but he was probably more of a hindrance in the kitchen than anything else. Sighing, he turned at the corner and headed back the opposite direction. He needed to be chill, play it cool…

Was it too soon to text? Maybe he'd waited too long. Pulling out his phone, he hesitated then tapped out a text.

Mitch: *Can I see you tonight?*

He stared at it…no. Too eager. Back-to-back dates might be overkill. He didn't want to come on too strong. And she probably had other things to do. She did live here and she did have a life. He deleted "tonight" and typed "tomorrow night." He could last thirty-six hours, right? He barely knew her.

Screw it. He deleted "tomorrow night" and rewrote "tonight" and hit send before he could overthink it. Or, overthink it even more. He walked several more blocks, trying to enjoy the various holiday displays in the storefront windows, but his unchiming phone was a major distraction.

Damn, he had to relax and find something else to occupy his time. She was at work…she was most likely busy. She may not have even given him a second thought since the night before.

He crossed the street and made his way to his father's office three streets over. A bell sounded as he entered the nearly empty reception area. His father's receptionist looked up from her computer, and her face lit up when she saw him. "Modeling agency's four doors down," Mrs. Platner said teasingly.

She always said he'd missed his true calling of becoming a professional model. She claimed he was a ringer for Adam Levine. She even had side-by-side photos of Mitch and the mega superstar in a photo frame on her desk and asked people if they could tell them apart. He was flattered, but the thought of posing shirtless for a jeans ad made him nauseous. Far too self-conscious and shy for that kind of attention.

"Hey, Mrs. P, how are you?" he asked, approaching the desk.

She stood and wrapped him in a big hug. "I'm great, honey. How are *you*?" She moved back and eyed him.

"I'm good." He was. Mostly. He was getting there at least, thanks to his evening with Jess.

Mrs. Platner seemed pleased with her assessment. "You look healthy and rested."

"I've gotten the best night's sleep over at the old inn," he said, leaning against the counter.

She nodded. "That place looks amazing. We have a staycation booked for our fiftieth wedding anniversary in February."

"Fifty years. Wow." Mrs. Platner and her husband had met when they were teens and had been together ever since. True, real, long lasting commitment like that was so rare these days.

"About time you started thinking about putting a ring

on it," she said, eyebrow raised. "Those good looks won't last forever."

"Ouch." He feigned offense.

"You here to see your dad?"

He hadn't really been heading there for anything in particular, but it was almost lunch, so maybe they could grab something together. He still felt uneasy about the last conversation they'd had and they might not get a chance to really clear the air at the family home. "If he's not busy."

She shook her head. "He's been taking fewer patients lately," she said, lowering her voice. "Transferring a lot of new clients to Dr. Royerson on Elm Street."

So he was really moving forward with the retirement plans. Mitch swallowed hard. "How are you doing with the…transition?" She'd worked for his father for thirty-two years. This change impacted her as well.

She waved a hand. "Don't you worry about me. I was ready to call it quits five years ago," she said, but something in her voice made him suspect it was a lie. Mitch knew her husband was diabetic and suffered from high blood pressure. He had been retired for fifteen years and it was just her income supporting them now. She could still use the job and the steady paycheck it provided. Finding another one at her age would be stressful and difficult in the small town.

If he took over the practice, though, she wouldn't have to.

He shook his head. His father would make sure she was taken care of. Or maybe whoever bought the practice could keep her on. After all, she knew the patients better than any new receptionist could.

His cell phone chimed as she paged his father and Mitch reached into his pocket for his phone. Seeing the text from Jessica, his face formed into a smile.

Jess: *You can if you're okay tagging along on my exciting life…*

Mitch: *What do you mean?*

Jess: *I have bowling league tonight. Still interested?*

Mitch hesitated. Was he? He'd never been interested in small-town life before, finding the slow pace boring. But if he wanted to spend time with her, he'd have to learn to adjust. He definitely wanted to spend time with her.

Mitch: *Pick you up at six?*

He watched the tiny dots appear and waited for her reply.

Jess: *Wish it was sooner.*

CHAPTER SIX

Unlike their picnic date, this one would be a lot more public. Bowling league was a big deal in Blue Moon Bay. With few weekday options for entertainment, the multiplex was a local hotspot for all ages. Could they keep their attraction on the down-low to avoid gossip spreading through town?

People seeing them together having a good time wasn't her concern. It was the other less-than-flattering rumor of her Good Luck Charm curse that bothered her. Everyone might be watching to see if the hot, single doctor would meet his own match after spending time with her this holiday season. There were more than a few single women in town who might be waiting in the wings.

The thought made her stomach twist.

But the sight of Mitch standing next to the passenger side door in her driveway hours later turned that uneasiness into butterflies. He was gorgeous, dressed in jeans, a black crewneck sweater, and a green thermal vest. His hair was gelled to one side and the five o'clock stubble along his jawline was her ultimate weakness.

"Hi," he greeted with a wave as she approached.

A simple word and yet she could hear the note of

anticipation in his voice, as though he'd been looking forward to that evening as much as she'd been.

"Hi," she said with a smile. He opened the passenger door and she climbed in. Once she was settled on the seat, he closed the door and walked around the front of it to the driver's side.

She took a deep breath to steady her thundering heart rate.

This was going to be fine.

Even if Mitch did find the love of his life after dating her this holiday season, it would no doubt be someone overseas and she wouldn't have a front row seat to the relationship.

And if he came back to get married, she'd refuse to make the wedding cake.

"You okay?" he asked, studying her as he climbed in behind the wheel.

She shook off the unsettling image of him waiting at the altar next spring with a bride that wasn't her. "Perfect."

"And you're sure about this? About me tagging along to your activities?"

"Are *you* sure about this? You're probably going to be bored to death." She let out a nervous laugh.

"I guess we'll find out," he said with a wink that sent her pulse racing. He took in her bowling polo shirt and read aloud: "Bay's Singles?"

Her cheeks flushed slightly. "It's a singles' league." She couldn't claim to have been passionate about the sport when she'd first joined. It had been in the hopes of meeting someone, but now she actually enjoyed the weekly meet-up, despite not having found Mr. Right among the pins.

"Aw. Any ex-boyfriends I should be worried about?" He put the car in reverse and backed out of her drive.

"All blissfully married," she said.

He glanced at her, his gaze far too perceptive. Had he heard the note of longing in her voice?

She needed to change the subject. "What did you do all day?"

"Went for a run on the beach this morning, played golf with my dad in the afternoon, took a nap…" He paused. "And thought about you almost the whole time."

Heat flushed through her. She'd been thinking about him all day, too. There may be a cake out there missing an ingredient to prove it.

"Almost the whole time?" she asked, a teasing note in her voice.

"Well, I think there might have been at least a few minutes throughout the day that I tried not counting down the seconds until tonight," he said, reaching for her hand.

He interlaced their fingers and happiness over-whelmed her. Whatever happened once the holidays were over was out of her control. Right now, she'd try to relax and enjoy their time together.

He rotated his shoulders and grimaced slightly.

"You okay?" she asked.

"First time golfing in a while. Didn't realize how tight my muscles were." He glanced at her. "You wouldn't know a good masseuse by any chance, would you?"

She grinned. "I do, in fact."

"Oh yeah?" he asked huskily, bringing her hand to his lips and kissing it.

It was hard to concentrate when he did things like that, but still, she said, "Yes, Mrs. Barnett. I'm fairly sure her offer was a standing one."

He gently bit her knuckle. "Tease."

A lump lodged in her throat at the sexy gesture, and she fought the urge to take the wheel and force them to the side of the road so she could get that kiss she'd foolishly turned down the night before. Instead, she cleared her throat and focused on the least sensual topic she could think of. "So, when does Lia arrive?"

"A few days."

"Do you think she'll freak out about us spending time together?" How could Lia possibly be angry about this when the two of them were so obviously happy and having a good time together? She may find her brother irritating, but she'd want him to be happy, right?

"Nah. Why would she?"

His words weren't as reassuring as she'd like. Maybe he thought there was nothing for Lia to freak out over, and that caused an unsettled feeling in her stomach.

Far too soon, he pulled into the bowling alley lot and peered at the two-story building that also housed a new and improved arcade, the axe-throwing rooms, an escape room, and a small bar. "I actually think I was here on opening day for the old arcade."

"Oh, come on!" He wasn't that old.

"No shit. There was a Pac-Man competition and I entered."

"Did you win?"

"I don't think so…" He unbuckled his seat belt and stopped her as she reached for the door handle. "You're sure you're cool with me being here? I don't want to cramp your style all week." He paused. "The thing is, I really like hanging out with you. I thought I was going to get bored being home for three weeks."

"Won't you still, though?" Dragging him to all of her commitments would be fun, but it would definitely paint him the perfect portrait of what life was still like in Blue Moon Bay. A life he'd decided wasn't for him. Bowling and axe-throwing were two of the highlights around town during the week, along with the holiday events. Other than the cinema and the beach and boardwalk, there wasn't a lot of excitement.

The fair came to town twice a year, but Mitch wasn't exactly a twelve-year-old adrenaline-seeker, so that feature probably wouldn't make him want to stick around.

"It's not that I find Blue Moon Bay boring," he said slowly. "Just slower paced, but I don't get to do this whole relaxing thing very often. This will be good for me. And as I said, I just want to spend time with you." He kissed her hand again and his eyes fell to her lips.

What the hell was he waiting for? She hadn't even put lipstick on tonight. Her lips were free and clear and his for the taking. She leaned slightly forward. Maybe he just needed a nudge. After all, she had turned him down the night before.

His gaze burned into hers and his grip on her hand tightened as he pulled her closer.

She closed her eyes, her heart pounding in her ears. *This is it. Mitch Jameson is about to kiss me...*

Tap. Tap.

Jessica jumped and Mitch released her hand and pulled back. Turning, she saw Trent at the window. "Hey! Ready to raise some—" He stopped at her murderous stare.

She widened her eyes and cocked her head toward Mitch, hoping Trent understood what she wasn't saying out loud.

He looked past her into the car and, seeing Mitch, gave a little wave. "Oops, sorry—I'll see you inside." Trent quickly walked off.

"Who's that?" Mitch said.

Jessica grinned, detecting the slightest note of jealousy in Mitch's voice as she turned back to face him. Trent was six foot five and two hundred and fifty pounds of solid muscle, tattoos covering 70 percent of his body—he was intimidating to most men, to say the least. "That's my cousin, Trent," she said. "He owns the bar on Main Street and the one inside the multiplex."

Mitch touched her cheek. "Thank God. He's huge. I would *not* have wanted to compete with that dude," he said.

"In bowling?"

"No, for your attention."

Was it possible to smile too much? Was too much

happiness a thing? Mitch was like an addiction—the more of him she got, the more she craved. And she didn't want to come down from this high anytime soon. "There'd be no contest," she said.

• • •

Her cousin and self-designated bullshit detector, Trent, eyed him as he waited for the round of drinks at the bar. Mitch shifted from one leg to the other and readjusted his glasses, feeling the giant man's unyielding gaze on the side of his face as he leaned against the bar. Tattoo sleeves covered both the guy's arms, and the tight T-shirt he wore clung to chest and shoulder muscles that would make The Rock jealous.

Jessica had made the introductions when they'd entered, but he sensed there was more info Trent was bent on finding out.

He tapped his fingers nervously against the bar to the tune of some Justin Bieber holiday song playing on the overhead and surveyed the decorated space. The bar/bowling alley could compete with his mom for the most holiday spirit. Strands of light garland were draped along every surface, and oversize red, green, and gold baubles hung from the ceiling. Reindeer centerpieces sat on every table, and a big rotating Christmas tree was set up in the corner near an old jukebox. Even the bartender and waitstaff were sporting elf costumes. It had been so long since he'd celebrated the season, he'd forgotten how much his hometown really got into the festivities.

Unfortunately, Trent didn't look so holly jolly as he continued to silently assess whether or not Mitch was worthy of his cousin's time.

"Mitch, right?" he finally asked while filling a pint glass.

"Yes. I'm Lia's older brother." He seemed to feel he needed that info to validate his hanging around, even though Lia wasn't in town yet.

"How old are you?"

"Thirty-nine. I'll be forty in February."

"Jessica is twenty-nine."

"I'm aware." She'd said the age difference didn't bother her. It certainly didn't bother him. Would her friends find it odd that she was dating an older guy? They hadn't really discussed previous relationships or whether or not he was her usual type. It didn't really matter.

"And you're single?" Trent pressed.

He sighed. "I wouldn't be dating Jess if I wasn't." Was he overstepping with the word "dating"? Relationships were a lot more complicated these days. What term would she have used? Seeing one another? Hanging out?

Trent shrugged. "Not like it hasn't happened before that some jerk thought he could get away with using her as a sidepiece without her knowing."

Damn. First the good luck charm thing, now this. Obviously her track record with men wasn't the greatest. His gut twisted slightly and he wasn't sure if it was because he hated the thought that she'd been previously hurt or that there was the potential with him that she could get hurt again.

"Do you have any kids?" Trent's interrogation continued.

"Not that I know of," he said, then realizing Trent wasn't the right audience for the bad joke, he said quickly, "I definitely don't."

"You're a doctor?" Trent asked.

"Yes."

"What kind?"

"Pediatrics."

Trent nodded, his shoulders relaxing slightly. Mitch's working with kids had garnered him some bonus points, obviously. "You live in the city?"

"Actually, I'm kinda homeless at the moment," he said.

Trent's thick dark eyebrows met in the middle.

"I mean, I travel the world with Doctors Without Borders, so I don't keep a place in the city anymore." He had for the first year, but then it had seemed pointless for the few weeks a year he actually used it. Closing his practice and selling his condo had been the most liberating experience. No ties. No real material possessions. No obligations or commitments. Life this way suited his nomadic spirit.

"Doctors Without Borders?" Trent continued to study him as though not fully trusting that it wasn't just some line he used to attract women.

He nodded. "Yes. I just came back from Cambodia a few days ago."

"So, you're leaving again?" Trent asked as he placed their drinks on the bar in front of him.

Mitch nodded as he opened his wallet, retrieved enough cash for the round, and placed it on the bar. He picked up the drinks, but Trent stopped him before he could walk away. "Well in that case, just do me one favor."

His palms sweat slightly and he felt his grip slip on the glasses. "What's that?"

"Don't go breaking any hearts this Christmas," he said.

"You got it," he said over the lump forming in the back of his throat.

Mitch's gaze met Jessica's as he approached a little slower. She literally seemed to glow under the neon holiday lights. Her dark hair reflected the red and green, and her bright, beautiful smile shined brighter than all the lights in the room ever could. She was gorgeous and smart and funny and sexy as hell. He'd desperately wanted to kiss her moments ago in the car. He'd desperately wanted to kiss her every minute that they'd spent together so far, but he'd held back out of fear of crossing that line.

He suspected once he did, there'd be no turning back. *Don't go breaking any hearts this Christmas…*

He wasn't sure he could fulfill that promise to Trent and the heart he was concerned about was not only Jess's.

He handed her a drink as he sat next to her on the plastic bench seating.

Jessica sighed. "Let me guess. You got the big brother speech from Trent."

He cleared his throat. "Nah. He just asked me about a dozen questions, that's all." He was actually surprised the guy hadn't asked to see his driver's license and a copy of his credit report.

"Sorry, Trent's a little overprotective."

"Totally understandable," he said with a smile. He was starting to feel protective over Jess, too. He didn't want to see her get hurt, either, and that certainly wasn't his intent.

She introduced him to the rest of the team. Several couples around his age and an older man that Mitch recognized from the hardware store in town. They all welcomed him warmly, but there was definitely curiosity among the group. No doubt they were surprised to see him there with Jess.

"Nice to meet all of you," he said. He took a swig of his beer and his gaze landed on the pins at the end of the alley as they scattered. "Are those Christmas trees?"

Jessica laughed and nodded. She reached for a bowling ball and showed him the white, spiral-y pattern that made it look like a snowball. "Holiday-themed bowling. Every December, the alley changes out the regular pins and balls for Christmas trees and snowballs. The league donates a dollar to the local food bank for every strike made during the month."

"Bowling for charity, I like it," he said, feeling even better that he'd tagged along. Blue Moon Bay was a close-knit community, so it didn't surprise him that residents supported one another during what could be a challenging time of year for some.

Maybe he'd fill some of his free time by throwing some balls himself.

"Thought you would," she said. Their gazes met and held for a long beat.

From the corner of his eye, he saw her teammates staring, taking in the interaction. Best to keep things as cool and casual as possible in front of their audience. He cleared his throat and nodded toward the group of gawkers. "I think they're waiting for you."

She blushed. "Right. I'm up first."

"Good luck," he said, sliding over into her vacated spot on the bench to get a better view. When she bent to pick up the ball, his mouth went dry. Her ass in skin-tight jeans was the sexiest ass he'd ever seen. He was actually jealous of the light, faded, stretchy denim. Over the last two days, it had been nearly impossible not to check her out whenever she wasn't looking. The curvy hips and thin waist, full chest and round, soft-looking skin were so incredibly tempting. She was 100 percent his type. She checked all of the boxes physically with the long dark hair, soft features, and vibrant, expressive eyes, and her cheery personality was almost too good to be true.

He watched as she swung the ball back then released it down the center of the lane. It connected just slightly left of the middle Christmas tree and sent all the pins scattering. Her hips wiggled and she raised her arms in a victory dance as their team took the lead, and his body instantly reacted to the intoxicating sight. There was no way he was going to be able to say good night to her this evening without kissing her.

Luckily, she'd seemed to have drawn the same conclusion.

* * *

As soon as he put the car in park in her driveway two hours later, she was moving toward him. "I'm sorry, I'm not waiting on you any longer," she said before her mouth crushed his.

Surprise had him hesitating only for a fraction of a second before his arms went around her waist and he pulled her closer. Her arms circled his neck and she pressed her chest higher into his, closing the gap between their bodies. The smell of her soft, gingerbread-scented body lotion tantalized his senses and made his mouth water. He wasn't normally a fan of gingerbread, but right now, given the chance, he'd lick her entire body.

Her lips were warm, soft, and full, everything he'd thought they'd be. Inviting, intoxicating kisses full of desire had his body awakening in ways it hadn't in quite some time. His grip on her tightened and he deepened the kiss, slipping his tongue between her lips. She moaned softly against his mouth. He was a goner.

Her hands tangled in the back of his hair as she draped one leg over his, bringing her body even closer. She held him in place, kissing him harder, and her confidence and assertiveness in that moment blew him away. Such a contrast to the sweet, cute woman he'd met in the bakery only two days before.

Her contradictory qualities captivated him. How many more sides were there to Jess? He wanted to know them all.

His hands slid up the side of her slowly, until he felt the edge of her underwire under her shirt. He paused, torturously close to her breasts. He wouldn't go any further. This was a first kiss…

But then she reached for his hand and placed it over her breast, and he pretty much fell in love despite his claims that he wouldn't. He massaged the beautiful mound gently until they were both panting with desire.

She reluctantly pulled away and her eyes opened and met his. "Too fast," she said, catching her breath.

He lowered his hand back to her waist, forcing his own body to simmer down. The evidence of her effect on him was impossible to conceal. He cleared his throat and nodded. "Definitely too fast."

She frowned. "Yeah?"

He laughed and touched her flushed cheek. "I don't know. You're in control here, Jess." He'd take her that very moment right there in the car if it was up to him. But their pace would always be her call.

"Wonderful, now I want you even more," she said with a strangled-sounding laugh full of desperate desire he could totally relate to.

"There's no rush." Despite her words, he knew she wasn't fully ready to take things further. Which he was completely okay with. Her pace. Her rules.

She sighed as she slowly slid her leg off of his and moved back into the passenger seat. He held onto her hand and kissed it, savoring the feel of her warm flesh against his lips. He glanced up at her, and her expression full of emotion and obvious attraction was one that should have terrified him, but it didn't.

"I'll walk you to your door?"

She nodded. "Probably for the best."

He wasn't so sure about that, but he was prepared to wait as long as necessary. This holiday season just got a whole lot more interesting, and he was fully onboard for whatever happened next.

CHAPTER SEVEN

Jessica hummed a holiday tune as she opened her oven the next morning and took out a fresh batch of cinnamon rolls. The tantalizing scent reached her nose and she smiled appraisingly at the pastries as she placed them on the cooling rack.

Everything was turning out to perfection this morning.

Wiping her hands on her apron, she returned to the front counter, where Whitney continued her search through the cake design binder. Her friend hadn't mentioned whether or not Trent had told her about seeing Jessica with Mitch at the bowling alley the night before, and normally she'd want to gush to Whitney about the new man she was seeing, but something about her friend's vibe that day gave her pause. Whitney had a lot going on in her own life, and in truth, Jess wasn't really sure her practical, no-nonsense friend would be on board with this holiday fling that could end with Jess brokenhearted. So she decided to hold off on that conversation.

"See anything you like?" she asked instead.

"They are all gorgeous," Whitney said. "How does anyone choose?"

Jessica beamed. Her collection of cake designs was something she was proud of. Three hundred and fifty-two different styles, all sizes, all flavors. All lovingly, painstakingly baked and decorated. She loved her job, and it didn't even bother her that all her hard work vanished off the ends of forks within minutes.

Cakes made people happy.

"Have you narrowed down colors for the wedding yet?" she asked. "That could help."

"Almost," Whitney said, but she was hardly convincing.

Whitney had yet to make a final decision about anything for her wedding, and that was odd. Head of marketing for the Blue Moon Bay Tourism office, her friend was a driven, type-A personality when it came to everything else. She was always organized and her attention to detail was mind-blowing, so her lack of wedding preparation had Jessica wondering if her friend might be unsure about the lifelong commitment.

Putting off decisions meant putting off a wedding.

"Well," Jessica said, "I start my diet tomorrow so I can fit into my bridesmaid dress. Any hint on what style of dress I'll be wearing?" She was desperate to get anything at all out of Whitney, but she was kidding about the diet. At five foot four, a hundred and seventy pounds, she liked her body. She'd always been a little overweight according to some B.S. BMI chart and she'd struggled with it as a teenager, wanting to be tall and thin like her best friends, Sarah and Whitney, but now, she embraced her curves.

Who trusted their baked goods to a skinny person?

"I'm thinking I'll let you decide on your own dress style, whatever suits your body shape best and whatever makes you comfortable," Whitney said.

It wasn't as though Whitney had any fear of being shown up at her own wedding. Tall, thin, blond, and gorgeous, her friend looked like she should be the biggest bitch in the Bay, but nothing could be further from true. Whitney was kind and caring, and her devotion to her mother with failing health was endearing. She could be a success anywhere in the world, yet she put her family first and stayed in the small coastal town.

"How's your mom?" Jessica asked, switching subjects. Whitney had recently moved the older woman into Rejuvenation Assisted Living when Lydia's Alzheimer's made her afraid of Whitney and she didn't recognize her own home.

"She has her good and bad days. Yesterday was great. We had almost an hour before we lost her again."

An hour. She knew Whitney cherished every moment they were lucky enough to have when her mother was lucid, but it was heartbreaking. "It can't be easy."

"It isn't." Whitney shook her head. "She asked about the wedding. She's afraid if we wait much longer, she'll be too far gone to remember anything." She closed the binder and the vein in the middle of her forehead appeared—the only tell that her friend was stressed.

"Then what are you waiting for?" Jessica asked gently. "No pressure, friend, you know that's not my intent, but you and Trent have been together for five years. You love him, right?"

Whitney nodded. "He's everything. He's been there for me through so much. I don't know what I'd do without him."

Jessica felt a tinge of guilt at the love in her friend's voice. She wanted that. A real connection, a real relationship. Her short time with Mitch had only solidified the fact that she was 100 percent ready to fall in love and settle down. She'd enjoyed her life alone…but having him with her the past two evenings had reemphasized how much more fun life could be with someone to share it with.

"Look, you thrive on deadlines, right?" she asked Whitney. "So why not give yourself a deadline to make the decision on a date, at least? Baby steps. That's how you achieve your goals. You taught me that."

And Jessica would soon have to take her own advice. Weeks to make a life-changing decision wasn't a lot of time, but she couldn't put off making a decision regarding the sale of her bakery forever.

She needed to decide what mattered most to her…

Whitney stood. "You're right. That's what I'll do, but right now, I have to get back to work." She leaned across the counter and hugged her. "Thank you."

"Anytime," she said, and then Whitney left.

Sighing, she checked her order whiteboard on the kitchen wall. There was barely any whitespace left. This time of year was her busiest. Orders for holiday cookies, cakes, and pies were all coming in, and her workdays were getting longer with each day closer to Christmas. It was the same way every year. Jessica had learned after the first hectic Christmas season to buy and wrap all her presents, decorate her own tree, and do all her own personal baking in November.

Her anxiety over actually delivering on all the orders was starting to mount, but she was determined to pull it off again that year, even if it meant hiring some holiday help. She had a reputation in Blue Moon Bay as the sugar princess. As a joke, she'd even had a "Sugar Princess" Halloween costume custom made for her, and she prided herself on the fact that she hadn't let the health-craze of this decade dictate her business. People deserved a treat now and then, and her bakery was the place to find it. Offering healthy lifestyle options might bring in a few more customers, but she didn't want to risk making those that preferred the taste of real sugar feel guilty for choosing delicious.

She grabbed a cranberry muffin from the display case, broke it apart, and popped a piece into her mouth, then got to work on the first order—frosted sugar cookies shaped like elves.

"Jessica!"

The shrill sound of Mrs. Barnett's voice made her jump, choking on the piece of muffin. She coughed and pounded on her chest until the big lump made its way down.

"Jessica, you here?"

Unfortunately.

She pushed through the swinging door and wiped her hands on her apron, forcing her best smile. "Good morning."

"I received another one," Mrs. Barnett said, waving a letter from Not Just Desserts.

"What does it—"

"Jessica Lynn Connolly, tell me you haven't sunk us all," her aunt Frankie interrupted, entering the bakery with an identical letter in her hand.

"Dramatic much, Aunt Frankie?" Jessica said with a heavy sigh.

Her aunt winked at her and shot a side-long glance toward Mrs. Barnett, letting Jessica know she was overreacting for the other woman's sake.

Mrs. Barnett huffed her approval, missing the gesture and feeling justified in the solidarity.

"You're not really selling the bakery, though, are you?" Frankie asked, her tone less dramatic, but slightly concerned as she studied her.

Looking at her aunt was like looking in a mirror. They were often mistaken for sisters. The fifty-seven-year-old didn't look a day over forty and had more energy than anyone Jessica's age. With just one employee, she'd operated the fabric store on Main Street for thirty years.

"No. I'm not. At least, I haven't made my mind up yet." Jessica pointed to the letters. "Those are completely premature. I can't believe they sent those to both of you without my answer." Someone was getting an earful today.

Other than her.

"But you're thinking about it?" Mrs. Barnett said, folding her arms across her chest.

"I'm not *not* thinking about it." No sense lying to them. It would be far worse if she then did decide to sell. "But whether I do or not doesn't matter. You don't have to."

"Actually, we might," her aunt said, climbing onto a stool at the counter.

"Why?"

"It's called progress," Mrs. Barnett said. "If Not Just Desserts can convince the town's committee and Mayor Rodale that it's better for the economy to have a large, eat-in-bakery and café instead of two semi-lucrative businesses, they can push us out." She toyed with the rings she wore on each finger and Jess could see the mood-revealing, color-changing stone around her neck was a deep, dark blue. She'd once explained the different colors to Jessica and she couldn't remember if dark blue meant annoyed or murderous.

She shook her head, forcing her voice to sound confident. "The town would never decide that. Barnett's Bottles and Frankie's Fabrics have been here for like…a million years."

"Watch yourself, girlie," her aunt said.

"You know what I mean. No one's going to push you out. And besides, I haven't told them I'm selling." Yet. One minute she thought there was no way she could. Then the next, especially after finishing a wedding cake that wasn't her own, she thought it might be the right decision.

But selling the bakery was just one step.

Then what? Where would she move? What would

she do? She could get a job anywhere working as a pastry chef and she might be just as happy. But how would she decide where to go?

So far, fate hadn't helped her find Mr. Right, and flipping a coin or pointing to a random spot on the map didn't seem like it would be any surer of a bet than staying right where she was and letting *him* find *her.*

A memory of Mitch's kiss made her cheeks flush.

Had he already found her?

"Well, I'm not going anywhere." Mrs. Barnett ripped her letter in half and stormed out of the bakery, her patchouli-scented perfume lingering in her wake.

Jessica sighed. "Sorry, Aunt Frankie. I had no idea they were going to pressure you." They'd mentioned expanding, but Jessica hadn't let it bother her, not having made up her own mind yet.

This made the decision much harder. Other livelihoods could be affected by it. Not to mention Not Just Desserts would charge her friend a fortune to provide baked goods to Dove's Nest. She'd be an awful friend if she bailed on Sarah now.

Her gut tightened into a knot.

Frankie leaned forward. "Listen, Jess…I understand. You're twenty-nine years old, you have a successful business, and your family is here, but you want more. I don't fault you for that. You have to decide what's right for *you.*"

Her aunt could always read her, and Jessica had confided her deep fear of dying alone to the woman on more than one occasion. "Thanks, Aunt Frankie. But is

Mrs. Barnett right? Could they squeeze you both out as well?"

Frankie shrugged. "Who knows? But you can't let that determine what you need to do."

"Thank you for being so supportive." Her aunt had always been there for her. Jessica had confided secrets to Frankie before she'd told anyone else, even her own mother.

"Hey, was that my beautiful daughter-in-law-to-be I saw in here a few minutes ago?" she asked.

Jessica nodded. "She stopped by on her break."

"Does that mean we have a cake design?" Frankie looked like she was holding her breath.

She hated to burst her aunt's bubble. "Not yet."

"Is she okay? We haven't seen much of her lately. They usually come by every second Sunday for brunch, but the last few times, it's just been Trent."

Whitney was definitely acting out of character. Jessica was a loyal friend and she wanted to give Whitney whatever support she needed, but it was impossible when no one knew what was going on with her these days. She'd always been career-focused, but the last six months, it seemed like the only thing, besides looking after her mother, that she cared about at all. Even their monthly girls' night out had stopped, and Whitney hadn't attended their Wednesday morning yoga session in almost a year.

Jessica was prepared to lose some of her friend's time to married life and children in the near future...but losing her to something unknown made her anxious more than anything else. Before Sarah had moved back from L.A., Jessica had felt like they were slowly losing her, and she had a similar gut instinct about Whitney now.

But soon enough, *she* might be the one leaving.

"I know work has been busy for her," Jessica said. "I'll talk to her."

Her aunt Frankie looked relieved. "You two are so close. I'm sure if anything was wrong, she'd tell you."

Jessica wasn't so sure anymore, but she nodded reassuringly.

"Just let her know, I'm here for her. I know it must be hard thinking about wedding plans when her mom can't be there to help. It breaks my heart and I know I'm second best, but I'd like to be involved in the plans. Three other boys off and married bridezillas, each one worse than the other, and I got no say in anything. And who knows if Kara will decide to get married." She shook her head.

Jessica touched her aunt's hand. "I promise you, if I ever get married, you're head of the planning committee." There was no one else she'd want helping her. She was closer to her aunt than anyone. She'd always longed to be part of her aunt's family, envious of the connections between her cousins that despite being there all the time, she didn't feel she had.

Aunt Frankie laughed. "Sweetheart, there's nothing left to plan. You've had every detail of yours figured out since you were five years old and Shawn Thompson asked you to marry him at recess."

Jessica smiled. It was true about the wedding plans—she had a binder filled with dress sample fabrics from her aunt's shop, and she'd designed a one-of-a-kind cake for her own special day—but she'd forgotten about Shawn Thompson and the kindergarten proposal. If only she had as many guys into her at twenty-nine as she had at age five. "What happened to him anyway?"

Aunt Frankie grimaced. "Last I heard? Jail for armed robbery."

"Guess I dodged a bullet there."

Hearing her own store's bell chime next door, Frankie stood. "Well let me know if Whitney needs anything, and just give me a heads up when you decide what you plan to do about this"—she held up the letter—"okay, darlin'?"

"I promise I will."

As her aunt left the bakery, Jessica retrieved her own offer letter from Not Just Desserts from the drawer under the register and shook her head. Something about the underhanded way they'd approached the two neighboring businesses without waiting for her answer first made her stomach turn.

Did she really get to decide the fate of her business, or would they find a way to force her out if her answer was no?

• • •

Jessica locked her front door and then hurried down the stone path to her driveway, where Mitch was waiting, at five fifty-five later that evening. Once again, he stood by the passenger side door, ready to open it for her, and her chest swelled upon seeing him. Not just because he looked amazing in a pair of faded jeans and gray hoodie under a worn leather jacket, but because he was always doing these nice, sweet gestures—opening doors, picking up the tab despite her protests, and being considerate of her time.

She'd been a little surprised when he'd texted her that day asking what the plan was for that evening, but he'd obviously meant it when he said he was tagging along to her extra-curriculars. And so far, he seemed to be enjoying himself. Though one week of this was a lot different than a lifetime. She refused to get her hopes up that Blue Moon Bay could ever be enough for him. He was a nomad by nature and enjoyed that kind of life.

"Okay, this is the sexiest shirt ever," he said, hugging her quickly, then pulling back to eye her black, form-fitted, long sleeve, V-neck T-shirt with the words "I'm a Blue Ball Buster" on the front.

She laughed, then blushed slightly. "It's an axe-throwing term. The bullseye has two blue balls…"

He grinned, watching her with amusement in his dark eyes as she explained.

"You knew that!" She hit him playfully and climbed into the car.

"Yes, I did know that, but watching you blush as you explained it was too hard to resist," he said before shutting her door and walking around to the other side.

Jessica watched him, unable to believe things were

going so well. He was smart and interesting and he seemed to be enjoying their time together as much as she was. Often in past relationships, there was a power struggle with one person more committed to the relationship than the other, but with Mitch, it felt like they were on the same level.

"So, axe throwing is in the same building as the bowling alley?" he asked as he climbed in.

"Usually, but tonight we're doing something a little different. Turn right on Main Street and I'll direct you from there."

"I'm intrigued." He put the car in reverse and backed out of her driveway, heading toward Main Street. He turned the volume a little higher on the Christmas music playing on the radio then reached for her hand, drawing it over onto his lap and interlacing their fingers while he drove.

She smiled. Since the first time they'd gone out, he'd been doing that. Holding her hand in the car. It felt so freaking good, it was hard to let go once they'd reached their destination. They were keeping things casual in front of everyone, but the residents in Blue Moon Bay would have to be dead not to notice the sparks flying between the two of them.

His little text messages throughout the day were nice, too. Hearing her phone chime every now and then made her feel like a teenager with a crush. He was thinking about her when they weren't together, and she was enjoying this new-relationship rush.

"Turn here," she said, pointing to the side road as they

approached their destination.

"Christmas Tree Forest?" He slowed as he drove along the dirt road to the gravel parking lot already full of cars. That evening's event sign hung above the farm entrance. "Another charity event?"

She grinned. "Yep," she said, unbuckling her seat belt as he put the car in park.

Mitch's look of approval had her heart soaring. She'd suspected the town's charity spin on all the local activities would appeal to his humanitarian side.

"How does this work?" he asked.

They climbed out and headed toward the group of people wearing similar shirts to hers near the entrance to the Christmas tree farm.

"We're putting our axe-throwing skills to the test and to good use," she said. "Each team paid an entry fee to compete in the farm's competition. We rallied support from sponsors and raised over two thousand dollars to buy trees for families in need this holiday season."

Mitch paused several feet from the others and pulled her closer. Her heart pounded in her chest as his expression held her hostage, a look of deep respect and admiration reflecting in his eyes. "You, Jessica Connolly, are truly incredible."

She swallowed hard and forced her response to be casual, despite the intensity of the chemistry radiating between them. "Wait until you see me throw an axe."

• • •

Damn, she wasn't kidding.

Standing among the tall, thick evergreens on the tree farm, illuminated by brightly colored holiday lights, Mitch watched as Jessica stood twelve feet from the target in the farm field. The scent of hot cocoa and chestnuts roasting on a nearby open fire made his stomach rumble, but he refused to hit up the snack booth and miss her shot.

A look of concentration on her face, she took aim, then let the axe fly through the air. The hatchet completed its full rotation and then stuck just shy of the bullseye.

Her skill was impressive, but it was the look of happiness radiating on her face that held him captivated. She was so beautiful and so caring. Charity bowling, charity axe-throwing… She was doing a lot of good that holiday season for the community and the residents of Blue Moon Bay, and he couldn't deny the tug in his chest.

Did he do enough for his hometown?

He'd always known he wanted to follow in his father's footsteps and go to med school. His own practice in L.A. had hosted a lot of free clinics and offered medical care to everyone in need, whether they had insurance or not. Then he'd left to try to make the world a better place, to make a difference, traveling overseas with Doctors Without Borders. He knew he was achieving his goal of helping the world, and he couldn't deny the sense of pride and accomplishment he felt. But what about on a smaller scale? Had he ever truly made a difference to the people he'd grown up with, his neighbors and friends? The community that raised him in Blue Moon Bay?

He could easily donate money to the local charities, but suddenly it hardly felt like enough. Jessica and the rest of the teams out there that evening had put in the time and effort to raise funds through their competition. They showed up. The night before, the members of the local bowling leagues were upping their game to raise money for the food bank. He hadn't realized how much his own community needed the support. Growing up in the touristy, coastal town with all the advantages he could ever have wanted, he hadn't seen the fact that not everyone in Blue Moon Bay was as fortunate as he was...

He swallowed hard as Jessica walked toward him. Her flushed cheeks and hair blowing in the evening breeze caused his pulse to race. In two days he'd actually started to crave that beautiful smile of hers whenever he wasn't with her.

"Great shot," he said.

"I would have hit the bullseye, but the wind took it," she said with a teasing grin, as she watched her teammate step up to the mark.

He cleared his throat. "Hey, um...I was wondering if there were any other charity events like this one that maybe I could get involved in..."

She looked slightly surprised that he was wanting to go from spectator to participant. She wasn't the only one, but it just felt right. He was home that holiday season. He should try to be more involved.

"This was the last one I'd signed up for..." She paused. "But I did hear Mr. Cranston say they could use some volunteers to help cut down the trees for delivery."

He nodded quickly. That he could do. "Perfect. Can I borrow your axe?"

She beamed at him, and it was definitely true that no act was truly altruistic. Mitch would cut down the entire lot if it meant that she'd continue to smile at him that way.

CHAPTER EIGHT

Jessica pulled her delivery van into the driveway of Dove's Nest B&B early the next morning. She lowered the visor and checked her reflection in the mirror. Hair curled, makeup on, a new pair of jeans that she'd normally never waste on work, she couldn't deny that she'd dressed up a little that day just in case she ran into Mitch during her delivery of the inn's baked goods. It was early, but maybe he was awake. She stared through the windshield at the guest rooms on the third floor and a memory of his smoking hot kiss the night before that had steamed up the car windows made her pulse race.

Maybe she should deliver breakfast to his room. Right, and then the rest of the deliveries would not make it to their destination that morning. She climbed out of the van, went around to the back, and opened the doors.

Wes, Sarah's fiancé and co-owner of the inn, exited through the kitchen door on the side of the old Victorian house. Dressed in paint-splattered jeans and an old sweater, he was obviously headed out to a construction job that day. "Hey, Jess."

"Good morning." It was a good morning. She was still enjoying that euphoric feeling of a great make-out session with promise of more to come. And she refused to get too far ahead of herself and start thinking about what would happen after the holidays. Stressing about tomorrow didn't change the future, it just stole today's peace, right?

Stay in the moment, enjoy the moment—that was her new motto.

"You're early," Wes said, eyeing her with suspicion.

No doubt it was the lack of yoga pants and ponytail, her usual delivery look, that had him perplexed. "Yeah, the holidays are busy for me, so I thought I'd start the deliveries early."

Her gaze drifted to the balconies. Which one was Mitch staying in? Damn, all the blinds were drawn. Not even a chance of catching a peek of him.

"Where's your helper this morning?" she asked. Wes's ten-year-old daughter, Marissa, loved living at the inn. The family had officially moved in with Sarah the month before, and the little girl practically ran the place when she wasn't at school. Marissa helped at the front desk, in the dining room, and she always helped unload the baked goods. Jessica suspected it was to get first dibs on the sweets.

Wes reached inside the van for a tray of fresh bread and dinner rolls. "She and Sarah were up and gone this morning at four a.m. Some new iPhone they both wanted released today, so they drove out to L.A. to line up outside the store." He shook his head. "A phone. You'd think it was a basketball signed by Michael Jordan or something."

Jessica laughed. "Different priorities, I guess."

His daughter was a techie like Sarah. The two of them had formed an amazing bond that summer over their mutual love of coding and web design.

Jessica nodded toward the pad of paper he was writing on. "The online inventory system down?"

"Nope. This is the old school method."

"Still haven't learned how to use it, huh?" Marissa was usually the one working the iPad during deliveries.

"Nope," he said honestly. He carried the trays into the kitchen and Jessica followed with her invoice. She scanned the main dining area, but there was only one woman sitting in there, enjoying a tea. "Is it busy here for the season?"

"Not yet. But Mitch just left about ten minutes ago to go pick up Lia and Malcolm from LAX. They should all be back here soon. And then we have a family from Maine arriving...Mrs. Darkington's family..."

Jessica was barely listening as Wes continued to detail the arriving guests. Lia and Malcolm were going to be here soon. Sweat pooled under her arms, and it had nothing to do with the heat in the kitchen. *That* might hinder things if Lia had an issue with them seeing one another. How was Lia's presence going to affect her budding relationship with Mitch? She hoped he'd still have time to hang out. She'd kinda gotten used to seeing him every evening, but obviously now that his sister was in town, he may not be as available. What if he told Lia, and she did freak out about the two of them dating? Her mouth felt like sandpaper.

"Hey, you okay?" Wes asked, a look of concern on his face as they headed back to the van. "You look a little pale."

"Yeah. Totally fine," she said. As long as Lia didn't turn out to be the Grinch who stole her sexy Christmas.

• • •

Whatever couples therapy his sister and her husband had going on was definitely working. Maybe a little too well. Earlier that year, there had been trouble in paradise, according to his mom, and the two had been headed for divorce. But their falling out seemed to be long forgotten as they'd made out like teenagers in the back seat of Mitch's rental the whole way from LAX to Dove's Nest.

Now they were taking a hell of a long time getting "settled" in their room, while he paced the foyer and fended text messages from his mother asking why they were late. He suspected his sister was in less of a rush to get to their family home than he was, and he wasn't all that eager himself. He'd rather be spending the day with Jessica.

The smell of fresh-baked bread coming from the dining room reminded him of her. Would he ever smell delicious baked goods again and not think of her? He suspected every spiced latte and cinnamon roll he had in the future would remind him of how she'd smelled and tasted during their make-out session the night before.

Man, he was getting soft for her. He had to be careful.

Hearing a guest room door open at the top of the stairs, he turned to see Lia and Mitch coming out of their room.

Finally.

He tapped his watch as they descended the stairs. "We're late."

His sister blushed, fastening several of the buttons on her emerald green blouse. "Sorry…we, uh, had a little trouble unpacking."

Mitch rolled his eyes and Malcolm just shrugged with a satisfied Cheshire cat grin. Gross. He did not want to think about his sister and her husband's intimate life.

"Okay, let's go." He opened the door and allowed them to step outside first. The forecasted rain had started, so they all ran toward the car and climbed in. "There's an umbrella in the trunk," he said.

"That's helpful now," Lia mumbled from the back seat.

Once again, Mitch was alone in the front. It wouldn't surprise him if his sister gave him a chauffeur hat for Christmas. Lia was always this way, slightly cold and distant toward him. She obviously harbored a not-so-secret resentment toward him for the way their mother made her preference of children obvious, but that wasn't Mitch's fault. He couldn't help it if he was the firstborn and had had ten years to bond with their mother before Lia came along.

He'd like to be closer to her, but she made it impossible. Whenever he called from overseas, she was always just rushing into court or headed to a consultation with a client or at the gym or yoga. Her lack of effort to make time for him hadn't gone unnoticed, but he still kept trying whenever he could.

"So, Mitch…where are you headed next?" Malcolm asked.

"Cambodia again. We still have work to do over there." He glanced at his brother-in-law through the rearview mirror. He'd only met him once before, at their wedding, and he wanted to like the man, but he gave off a *better than everyone* vibe with his expensive clothing and jewelry, and his arrogance rubbed Mitch the wrong way. But he seemed to be making his sister happy again these days, so it wasn't his place to judge the guy.

"Don't you miss the money, though?" Malcolm said. "From your own practice?"

The guy was definitely money motivated. He was a very successful defense attorney in New York and his hourly rate wasn't for the faint of heart. His parents owned a third-generation winery in Napa and their multimillion-dollar home was truly impressive. So Mitch could understand the question, but money had never been his motivation for getting into medicine. He'd wanted to help people like his father did. Not that he was always successful…

He shook his head. "Not really. This is more fulfilling, I guess."

"Mitch is very altruistic," Lia said.

He couldn't tell if she meant it as a compliment or not.

"But you can do good and still make a good living.

There's no shame in that," Malcolm said.

There wasn't, and Mitch knew that as an attorney, Malcolm had helped defend a lot of innocent people in his career. "You're right. I guess the other part of it is being antsy if I'm in one place for too long."

"He has commitment issues," Lia said in a loud whisper.

Okay, that one definitely wasn't a compliment. "That's not true."

"When was your last relationship?"

He shrugged. He could tell her about Jessica, but that would probably only confirm her thoughts about it. He was really only there for a few weeks and he wasn't sure what would happen after he left. He'd like to stay in touch, obviously, but he wouldn't give Jessica any false notions about where the connection between them could lead. His immediate future didn't include Blue Moon Bay…or a life partner.

"You can't even commit to one place long enough, let alone one person," Lia said. Then her expression softened slightly as though recognizing the edge in her tone. "And that's okay. That's just who you are."

Why did it sound so bad when she said it like that? He loved his life. He was living a life of charity and commitment—albeit to a cause, not a person or place, but he felt fulfilled. Wasn't that enough?

He pulled into the driveway of their family home, and Lia peered through the pouring rain, taking in the holiday decorations that were more than a little over the top. "She wasn't kidding when she said she'd added a few new things this year, huh?"

Apparently not. There were even more inflatables and figurines on the lawn than when he was there a few days ago, and the Santa and eight reindeer on the roof was definitely a recent addition to the decor. "Wait until you see the inside," he said.

"It couldn't possibly be worse," Malcolm said, looking at the house like it was the tackiest thing he'd ever seen. No doubt his Napa mansion was tastefully decorated by a hired interior designer.

"Just wait," Mitch mumbled, cutting the engine. "Anyway, her last text said coffee and tea was poured, so…"

"We better get inside," Lia said, sounding like she was about to walk the green mile.

Malcolm retrieved the umbrella first and then held it above their heads as they hurried up the slippery, cobblestone walk to the front door. Chivalry definitely wasn't in the man's wheelhouse before their reconciliation, so Mitch was happy to see it.

Under the protection of the awning, Lia stepped away, smoothed her hair, and squared her thin shoulders like she was about to walk into a high-profile court case. His sister normally oozed confidence. He never saw her nervous. Ever. Until she had to come face-to-face with their mother.

So strange how the joyful woman full of more holiday spirit than the big jolly man himself could evoke so much fear into his baby sis.

He opened the door. "After you."

Here we go.

"Jesus, you weren't kidding," Malcolm said, ducking to avoid a stretch of holiday garland draped across the doorway.

"There you are," their mother greeted them. Dressed in a pair of jeans, a festive green-and-red striped sweater, and reindeer antlers on her head, she almost blended in with the decorations.

"Hi, Mom," Lia said, removing her jacket and hanging it in the closet.

"Can I get you to remove your shoes, darlings? We just had the carpets cleaned yesterday."

They all removed their shoes and set them in the closet before following Lia into the dining room, where Dad was reading the paper. "Hi, Dad," Lia said.

Malcolm's eyes were still wide as he scanned the collection of snow globes on the side table. "It's like a holiday museum in here...or an episode of *Hoarders*," he mumbled.

Mitch hid a grin. "Don't worry. It's not genetic."

"Darling! So good to see you," his father said, standing to greet them. "How was the flight?"

His sister relaxed just a little. "It was good."

Then Dad turned to Malcolm. "I'm so glad you were able to make it for an early Christmas before heading up to Napa."

Mitch noticed his mother's face twitch and the slight glare she sent Lia's way. Obviously, she wasn't thrilled about being the second-choice family to spend the holidays with, but how could she blame Lia for wanting to spend Christmas Day with her husband's family?

Their home was on a beautiful winery, and Malcolm had six siblings along with their families that were flying in to be together. And there was less stress and judgment on his sister with the other family. As least he hoped.

The only thing was, without Lia there, his Christmas Eve departure wasn't going to go over very well. Which was why he hadn't told his family yet.

Noticing the stack of board games on the card table, he sighed. Obviously, it was family board game night, which meant he was probably going to be stuck there for a while. He'd skip out, but he was Lia and Malcolm's ride.

"Let's all sit and catch up," his mother said, serving tea in holiday-themed mugs and unwrapping the cookies on the tray shaped like an elf face. They all took their seats around the table.

These were the cookies he'd picked up from Jessica's bakery. Sigh. He couldn't go longer than five minutes without thinking about her. Bread and cookies existed everywhere. Would he be able to put her out of his mind once he was back on a plane? He'd be selecting pretzels as his free on-board snack from now on.

"So…I had an idea," his mother said, looking excited. She clasped her hands together and her gaze shifted between Lia and Malcolm.

Uh-oh.

"Ally…" His father's warning tone was ignored as his mother waved a hand at him to shush.

"Why doesn't your family come here for the holidays?" she asked Malcolm.

"Uh…" The poor guy looked completely put on the

spot. His already stern-looking features became even more contorted as he shifted on the chair and glanced at Lia for help.

"We already discussed all of this, Mom," Lia said tightly.

"Right. I know…I just thought our place can accommodate extra guests that can't book the inn…seeing how both of you choose to stay there."

So, she was still holding a grudge about that.

"Malcolm's grandmother is still not allowed to fly," Lia said, shifting awkwardly and glancing at Mitch now to help.

Oh right, she was friendlier *now* when she needed him to bail her out of an awkward conversation with Mom. He hesitated, wanting to let her squirm for the commitment-phobe comment before in the car, but of course, as always, he came to her defense. He cleared his throat. "Mom, you know all of this was already settled months ago. Plans this big can't be changed at the last minute. Probably best to just stick to the plan."

She didn't look happy about it, but she gave up and sat, biting the head off of a gingerbread man.

Gingerbread. Remembering the scent of Jessica's body lotion, it was now his turn to shift uncomfortably in his chair. His cell phone chimed on the table and, glancing down at it, he saw the photo of him and Jessica he'd snapped the night before lighting up the display.

Oh, thank God. He'd been wanting to text her all morning, but he was hoping she'd text first.

Jess: *Heard Lia was here. How's that going?*

His fingers flew over the keyboard, out of sight from everyone, under the table.

Mitch: *Just with the family now. Rather be with you.*

He set the phone down and his knee bounced. Was that too much? They'd had a hot make-out session the night before, so probably not. But how was she feeling about that today? Regrets? He certainly wasn't regretting it…

Another chime. He grabbed the phone, avoiding his mother's look of disapproval of him breaking her *no phones at the table* rule.

Jess: *Can I see you tonight or do you have plans with your family?*

He grinned. He'd bail on this bunch in a heartbeat, but that would probably raise some heavy suspicion. He'd already turned down dinner with his parents twice that week, claiming to be meeting up with some old friends in town. It wasn't exactly a lie.

Mitch: *Unfortunately, I think I'm stuck here tonight. Tomorrow?*

Jess: *Super busy day…*

His heart raced. Damn. The closer they got to the holidays, the busier her schedule.

Mitch: *Can I help?*

He waited as the tiny dots appeared while she was replying.

Jess: *Bakery delivery at six a.m. tomorrow morning. Don't be late. X*

He smiled. Bakery delivery at six a.m. the next morning it was.

Lia was eyeing him suspiciously when he glanced up. He tucked the phone into his pocket.

"So, Mitch says the inn is amazing," their mother said to Lia. "Is it decorated for the holidays yet?"

Lia turned her attention back to their mother and nodded. "Except for the tree. Sarah plans to keep her grandmother's tradition alive by inviting the community to do the decorating."

His mother sent Mitch a smile. "That Sarah is absolutely lovely."

Wow, no subtlety there at all. His mother made it no secret that she wanted nothing more than for him to find a nice person to settle down with and move home. Hell, she'd have him and his future family live with her and his father if she could. She'd be over the moon to discover that he was seeing Jessica. More reason to not tell her until the right moment.

"Sarah's also engaged," he reminded her. And most likely pregnant, if her throwing up the week before and the oversize sweaters she wore were any indication, but he kept that to himself. He didn't know for sure, and it definitely wasn't his place to tell anyone.

"She's also a million years younger *and* one of my best friends," Lia said as though the idea that Mitch could possibly be interested in Sarah was just absurd.

He didn't have to be a genius to figure out—she'd feel the same way about Jessica.

Which meant, for now, he'd be keeping his mouth tightly shut.

CHAPTER NINE

"Good morning," Jessica said as Mitch opened the passenger side door on her delivery van at five fifty-five the following morning. Playing it cool and not leaping directly at him took effort. In jeans and an old UCLA hoodie, one that actually looked like he'd worn it in his college days, his dark hair messy and a short stubble along his jawline, this new, not-so-put-together look had her practically drooling.

"Only because I get to see your face," he said, suppressing a yawn. "I missed you yesterday."

Oh my God. Her chest warmed at his words. She'd missed him, too. After seeing him three days straight, it had been almost weird not having him tag along the night before to her book club. Of course, she'd planned on bailing on book club—she hadn't read the book anyway—if he'd been available. "It was odd not seeing you, too," she said, hoping she sounded casual, light.

He reached for his seat belt. "Tell me you don't do these deliveries every morning, or I'm going to feel really guilty about having kept you out so late every night."

She laughed as she pulled out of her parking spot behind the bakery. "No. Only a few times a week."

Though it wouldn't have mattered. She wouldn't have called it a night any earlier even if these grocery store dessert deliveries were a daily part of her mornings. They'd spent a lot of time together that past week and it still didn't feel like enough. They were only scratching the surface of getting to know each other, but so far she liked everything she was discovering. His looks were a given turn-on, but his intellect and compassion were probably the sexiest parts about him.

Jessica had never dated anyone who checked off all the right boxes before. Unfortunately, his lack of a permanent home address put a red flag on his potential boyfriend résumé.

Not that he was applying for the job or anything.

He covered another yawn with his hand and she laughed. Early morning used to be tough on her, too, when she'd first opened the bakery, but now she woke without an alarm clock most days.

"You really didn't have to do this," she said.

"I told you—I want to experience small-town life. Your life." He reached across the seat and took her hand in his. "You don't need this to drive, do you?"

"Speed limit around here is only fifteen, we should be okay." The feel of his strong, warm fingers interlaced with hers was one she was quickly getting used to. Something she'd quickly miss as well.

He glanced out the window. "Not to mention, it's a ghost town at this time of morning."

"I like it. Feeling like I'm the only one awake. It gets so crowded during the day with tourists that I enjoy the peacefulness of dawn." Being one of the few people up so early on the empty streets made Jessica feel even closer to her hometown. Like she was experiencing a different side that others didn't get a chance to see. A rare glimpse into the twilight hours when the world was still sleeping.

"Once I can keep my eyes open, I'll probably agree," Mitch said with a grin.

"Really not a morning person, huh?" He was cute when he was tired and grumpy. What would it be like to wake up next to him? Would he still be adorably grumbly or would she be able to lure him into a better mood?

"Not unless there's a really good reason to be awake," he said, as though he'd read her mind, his gaze burning into hers. His expression said he wouldn't mind being woken up by her.

She swallowed hard and turned her attention back to the road before she swerved into the other lane.

A block later, she pulled into the lot of Supersave Groceries. Seeing old Mr. Parsons waving as he opened the loading dock door in the back of the store, she blushed at the inappropriate thoughts she'd just been having.

"First stop?" Mitch asked, unbuckling his seat belt and pushing his sweatshirt sleeves up to his elbows.

"Yep." She climbed out of the van and opened the back, then reached inside for the crate of boxed cinnamon rolls. Mitch joined her, and she stacked three crates onto his outstretched arms, enjoying the sight of the straining forearms just a little too much.

Damn, he was hot.

"Morning Jess, you have a helper today," Mr. Parsons said, approaching the van. Dressed in his grocer smock and his old L.A. Rams baseball hat on his head, the man could pass for fifty or eighty. It was impossible to tell his age. He'd run the grocery store since Jessica was a kid and he looked the same age now as he did back then.

Having Mitch around while she worked probably wasn't the most professional decision she'd ever made. But he was there to work. This wasn't a date. Even though he'd held her hand and flirted with her. "Yes, you remember Dr. Jameson?" she asked as he reached inside the van for a tray of cookies.

"It's just Mitch," he said, following the older man into the back stockroom of the store.

"I do remember you," Mr. Parsons said. "I believe you stocked shelves for me back in the late nineties."

"That I did…when Jess was still in daycare," he said.

She laughed as she grabbed the last crate of muffins and joined them inside. He'd asked her several times if their age difference was an issue, but it really wasn't. She could definitely vouch for Lia's relationship advice she'd given her a few months before about dating older men — Mitch was the most mature and centered man she'd ever dated. Also kind, caring, sweet, charming, sexy as hell… an amazing kisser…

She blinked as both men stared at her. She'd missed something. "I'm sorry, what?"

Mr. Parsons laughed. "My invoice?"

"Oh right. Here you go." She reached into her pocket

and handed him the invoice.

"Thanks, Jess." He tucked it into his smock. "Hey, did Amber come see you yet?"

She frowned. "Your granddaughter?"

He nodded and his chest even seemed to fill with pride as he smiled wide. "She's getting married on Valentine's Day."

Jessica's eyes widened. "Your granddaughter, Amber? Isn't she like seventeen?"

Mr. Parsons laughed. "It feels like just yesterday she was seven. But no, she's twenty-one now."

Seventeen. Twenty-one. Either way, a baby still. And getting married? That was ridiculous. "No, not yet." She paused. "How long has she known her fiancé?" she asked as they walked back to her van.

"About six months. They met at college. He's studying to be a dentist," Mr. Parsons said. "Nice kid."

"I'm sure he is, but six months? That's not a lot of time to get to know someone…before making such a huge commitment…" Feeling Mitch's gaze on her, she stopped. Her insecurity was showing. But damn, now even the next generation was getting married before her? Designing wedding cakes for people her age was tough enough. She cleared her throat. "I mean, I look forward to having her come by. Absolutely. I'd be honored to make her cake for the special day."

"Great. Thanks again, Jess," the older man said, waving as he walked back inside and closed the loading dock door.

Jessica climbed into the van and ignored the

expression on Mitch's face as she started the vehicle.

"So, do you not believe in marriage or just children not getting married?" he asked.

"Right? I'm right about this, though, they are too young to get married, aren't they? Twenty-one? They have at least five years of casual dating left to do first. Another heartache or two, at least. And six months? Can anyone know anyone that well?" Sure, she'd been ready to plan a future with some of the men she'd dated in less time than that. But she was almost thirty and she'd dated a lot of guys. She knew what she wanted and what she didn't...

"I agree on the age thing, but I don't know...I think when you find the right one, you know, you know?" He reached across and brushed the back of his hand along her cheek.

Heat rushed through her and she moved closer, Amber and her jealousy fading away. After only a week with him, her feelings were certainly growing stronger. But then, she'd known him practically her entire life. Or at least known *of* him. They may not have spoken much and their age gap had prevented a real friendship years ago, but he'd always been there in the background of her memories. At the Jameson house for parties, at community family picnics, at the local church at Christmas time and Easter when her family attended mass. Even all of Lia's complaining about him when they were kids had meant he was a focal point in Jessica's life, however small... So, it didn't feel like only a week.

He tucked a stray strand of her hair behind her ear and closed the gap between them, kissing her cheek. His lips were warm against her skin and her flesh tingled as his hands cupped the back of her head.

She swallowed hard when his dark eyes met hers. His gaze flitted back and forth between her lips and her eyes. He wanted to kiss her and it was about twenty minutes overdue, in her opinion. Their time together, their long talks getting to know each other, and the hand-holding were all wonderful, but nothing could reveal as much as a kiss, and as much as she'd learned from the first passionate one, there was still so much more she wanted to know.

She leaned closer and paused, shutting her eyes, waiting for him to make his move. Anticipation had her pulse racing. She'd been dying to kiss him as soon as he'd climbed into the van that morning. But this time she'd have to show some restraint as technically she was on the clock. Though she did make her own hours and set her own company policy rules. Nothing in the Delicious Delicacies handbook said she couldn't make out with her volunteers. Especially when they were smoking hot.

Where the hell were his lips?

She opened her eyes, just as he drew her face closer and the look of desire in his expression made her heart race.

Honk, honk!

Jessica jumped back at the loud blasting of the horn behind her van. "What the…?"

Mitch moved back to his seat, turning to see the intrusion. "A transport truck is waiting to back into the loading dock," he said, putting on his seat belt.

"And he couldn't wait another thirty seconds?" Jessica grumbled. She threw the van in reverse with a shaky hand and moved out of the loading zone. She waved at the truck driver, resisting the urge to give him a different hand gesture.

Mitch grinned at her. "Thirty seconds, huh? You think if I started kissing you, I'd be able to stop that quickly?" Taking her hand, he brought it to his lips.

Jessica cleared her throat, pulling her hand back and clenching the steering wheel. If she didn't focus on driving right now, she'd be dragging him into the back of the van and crushing all the baked goods. She drove along the back alley to Main Street. "Ready for the next delivery?"

"Yep. Let's see what else I can learn about you," he said.

"You've been taking notes, huh?"

"Maybe."

Her cheeks flushed and it took all her strength not to ask what he'd discovered so far and whether or not he liked the things he had.

· · ·

Two hours and an empty van later, she parked next to his rental car behind the bakery. "Want to come in for coffee?"

"I think I earned more than coffee," he said with a wink as he climbed out.

Holy hell. She took a deep breath as she got out and unlocked the back door of the bakery. He was so close she could feel his breath on the back of her neck, and her hand shook slightly.

I will not make out with him in my kitchen. I will behave myself. I will…

All coherent thought and good intentions vanished as soon as they stepped inside and Mitch's arms went around her. He lowered his head and his lips crushed hers without hesitation.

She wrapped her arms around his neck and pressed her body into his. He felt so good, smelled so good—a combination of strong, manly cologne and sugary baked goods. And his kiss was leaving her weak-kneed and breathless. His unshaven face was rough against her soft skin, and she shivered at the thought of beard burn on her flesh. It had been too long since anyone had her craving more…so much more.

Her hands slid into his hair, her fingers tugging gently as she ran them through the thick locks. Everything about him was perfect—his body, his mind, his heart. She'd found flaws in every man she'd ever dated, but no matter how deep she searched, the layers of Mitch just kept getting better and better.

And this kiss was everything.

He tightened his grip on her waist and moaned against her mouth before abruptly pulling away. "Sorry, I couldn't wait any longer."

She laughed, fighting to catch a breath. "No need to apologize."

"I could see you giving yourself a stern pep talk as you climbed out of the van, but I'm glad to see it didn't work," he said with a teasing grin, then kissed her softly again.

She slapped his shoulder playfully. "Well, if you weren't so tempting, it would help me hold strong to my resolve to take things slow."

The sound of the front doorbell ringing also helped.

She sighed. "Right. I have to open a bakery now." Reluctantly, she moved out of his embrace. "I'll start the coffee, help yourself to anything else you want."

"Anything?" he asked, reaching out for her hand and dragging her back toward him.

I will not have sex in my bakery. I will think of all the sanitary issues…

His hands sliding over her hips made her want to risk being shut down for a health code violation.

Ding dong!

"Oh my God! Someone better be having a diabetic crash right now."

He laughed as he released her.

Grabbing an apron from the back of the door, she pushed through with him close behind, then panic filled her chest. Turning back around quickly, she pushed him back out of sight. "Lia's out front," she whispered.

"Why are you whispering? She can't hear you."

"I don't want her to know you're here. Go out the back door."

He frowned in amusement. "She'll find out soon enough. We can't hide forever." He paused and took a deep breath. "I want you to come to early Christmas with me," he said, wrapping his arms around her again.

He what? Her mouth dropped and she continued to stare, speechless, at his smiling, gorgeous face.

Ding dong! Ding dong!

Jessica ignored the ringing. He wanted her to go to his family's early holiday celebration? With him? A date in front of his family? His *entire* family? Suddenly Lia finding out wasn't the most stressful situation facing her.

Air. She needed to breathe. A deep inhale didn't help.

"Jess? Will you come with me?" he asked nervously.

She wanted to, but she was terrified of his family's reaction. She knew them all so well, but they knew her as Lia's friend Jess, Delicious Delicacies Jess, fun, friendly neighbor Jess... Now they'd see her as Mitch's date Jess? She loved the sound of it—but would they?

He frowned. "Maybe it's too soon…"

"No!" She flushed as she nodded. "I mean, yes, I'll go with you, but right now, just sneak out the back. Please." She needed more time before Lia found out. They were so happy together right now and she wasn't ready to have anything ruin it.

He kissed her quickly. "Okay, but we're both going to need to find some courage between now and Saturday," he said, winking at her as he escaped through the back door.

Jessica fought to calm her thundering heartrate as she went to unlock the front door a few seconds later.

"Hi, Lia! Welcome home!" Too much. Over the top. Even she heard the forced enthusiasm that sounded more like anxiety in her voice.

Lia accepted her one-armed hug but gave her an odd look. "Hey, I thought you opened at eight?"

"Yeah, usually…but today I had deliveries around town. I assume you're here to go over any last-minute changes or additions to the early Christmas dessert menu?" An early Christmas Jessica would be attending as her brother's date. She wiped her sweaty palms on her apron, pushing all thoughts of Mitch from her mind.

Right now, she had to focus on Lia. Inappropriate thoughts about her brother or replaying their fantastic kiss or suffocating from the nervousness of them coming out as a couple to their family would have to wait.

"Yes!" Lia said, setting up her laptop on the counter. Her gaze landed on the open cake design binder on the counter and she raised an eyebrow seeing the three-tier cascade cake. "Still planning that dream wedding, huh? Is there a new man in your life I should know about?"

She hadn't meant to leave the book open to that page. Of course, Lia would recognize the cake as the one Jessica had always described as her own perfect wedding day masterpiece. She closed the book and ignored Lia's question. "Was there something you wanted to show me?" she asked, nodding toward the laptop.

Lia's attention returned to her mission. "I found some 'unique and trendy' desserts online that I was hoping we could try."

Tried and true favorites were apparently not an option. "Is your mom okay with this?" As much as Jessica wanted Lia to be happy—especially now—Ally Jameson was particular about her holiday desserts.

"Trust me. It will be fine. She's already pouting about the fact that we chose Malcolm's family to have, quote-unquote, 'real' Christmas with."

Jessica could definitely see the appeal of a holiday at a vineyard, and she could appreciate Lia's tough predicament of having to juggle two families who didn't live in the same place, but Jessica also felt a little sad for Ally. Christmas was the woman's absolute favorite time of year. By October, she was wearing Christmas sweaters and live-tweeting Hallmark holiday movies. Lia knew how important the season was to her mom. But the two had never really been close, so maybe it was just another slight.

Lia's phone chimed and she checked it, groaning before setting it aside.

"Everything okay?"

"Mitch. He's shopping and was wondering about the dress code for early Christmas."

Jessica hoped her flushed cheeks at the mention of him could be blamed on the heat from three ovens going in the kitchen at once. "How are things between you two?"

"Oh, fine, I guess. We're just not close like other siblings." She reached for a cherry tart from the basket on the counter and popped it into her mouth. The full tart.

"Those aren't vegan, Lia." Ally's order consisted of

specific directions to include vegan choices for her daughter. Did Lia know her mom was considerate like that? Would it matter?

"Neither am I," she said as she swallowed.

Jessica repressed a sigh.

She hesitated, then cleared her throat. "What is it about Mitch that bothers you so much?" After spending so much time with him, she still couldn't see Lia's disdain for him. He was smart and funny and considerate and kind...and his lips were absolutely the most delicious thing in her kitchen.

"It's that he acts so altruistic," Lia said, "but he's totally afraid of commitment. Temporary relationships, he can handle. That's why he likes to travel so much. Real, long-term, meaningful relationships, he sucks at."

Jessica swallowed hard. That assessment seemed harsh, but Mitch had admitted himself that he got bored in one place for too long. Did that extend to his feelings toward people, too? Was that why he was still single? There had to be plenty of other doctors, volunteers, women he met overseas who fell for him. Yet, he said his last real relationship was just after college, but even that one had only lasted a year.

"He's never going to settle down, so I guess it doesn't matter that we're not close. When he's traveling, I never hear from him. He calls between trips just to check in." She sounded less annoyed now and slightly sad as she said it.

Would that be their future correspondence once he left? Quick calls and messages and a few stolen days together whenever he was between trips? Would she even get that much? Maybe things would be over between them when he left.

"Hey, earth to Jess," Lia said, waving a hand in front of her dazed expression.

She blinked. "Sorry, what?"

"I asked what you thought about a lemon sorbet, to kinda cleanse the palate before dessert."

"I'm a bakery, not an ice-cream shop, Lia," she said, unable to hide a note of irritation in her voice. The things she'd said about Mitch had her on edge.

Was Lia right? Was Mitch unable to commit? Did she care? Was their connection strong enough over the last week for her to even be thinking about what happened when he left town again?

Unfortunately, she knew how she felt. She needed to know where Mitch stood.

Lia waved a hand. "You're right. Sorry. I'll get the lemon sorbet." She rested her head in her hand on the counter. "I guess I am feeling a little guilty about choosing to spend Christmas in Napa. I thought maybe a nice surprise dessert for my mom might ease the sting a little."

She sighed. She suspected she was being played, but she wanted Ally to have a nice surprise, too. Might help when Jessica showed up and crashed their dinner.

"Don't worry, Lia. Leave this to me. I won't let you down." At least not with the desserts. She suspected Lia might feel let down if she knew Jessica was spending almost every available minute with her brother.

Jess's phone chimed with a text message and she quickly read it.

Mitch: *I can't stop thinking about you and that kiss. Looking forward to seeing you. Your place at six?*

They'd decided on her place that evening so he could bring his laptop to show her pictures from his world travels. He led such an exciting life, and she wanted to get to know him better, on that level. Understand better the life that was so important to him. So much a part of who he was.

But now they also needed to talk. It was in her best interest to find out if what Lia had claimed was true. Was she just wasting her time and emotions on a man who would never be ready to settle down?

His kiss had held a promise of so much more…but that could also lead to so much more heartache if Lia was right.

Either way, she needed to know where they stood before they took things any further.

Jess: *Meet you at my place at six.*

...

Getting out of the shower, Mitch wrapped a towel around his waist and wiped the steam from the mirror. He hummed a Christmas tune as he applied shave gel to his face. He hadn't even thought he'd be breaking out the razor on that trip home. In such a short time, Jessica had him feeling more relaxed than he'd felt in a long time. She was a breath of fresh air in the small town where he usually felt claustrophobic.

And she'd agreed to go to his family's early Christmas with him. Of course, she was nervous about his family seeing them together. He was, too. He couldn't remember the last time he'd brought a woman home. It had to have been in high school. Hopefully, it wouldn't give anyone the wrong impression. Give Jessica the wrong impression.

He wasn't sure what was going on between them yet, but he did know he liked her a lot. More than he'd liked anyone in a long time. She said she was clear about keeping things casual…but he wasn't sure.

Hell, he wasn't sure his own emotions were so casual anymore. After all, he was risking his sister's wrath by taking her to Christmas. He couldn't understand why Lia would have a problem with him dating Jessica. Sure, they were friends, but they weren't best friends or anything, and it wasn't like they were all teenagers anymore. He was almost forty years old. He could date who he wanted to date.

He slid the razor across his cheek and down his neck, then checked the time on his cell phone. Just another hour until he got to see her. Not texting her that day while she worked took so much effort, but she was busy and he was already dominating so much of her time.

Though she didn't seem to mind.

Her request to see his videos and photos from his tours overseas hadn't completely surprised him. A lot of people liked to see his footage from his travels. Normally, he liked to share them. He hoped maybe watching some of those good memories on screen that evening would help remind him that most missions went well, they were a success...that life over in those countries wasn't always bad.

His phone chimed with a new text and his heart soared, reaching for it, but his excitement faded seeing his colleague Maria's number lighting up the display. They'd been in Cambodia together. They'd experienced this last mission trip as a team and his anxiety rose slightly just seeing her name on the display screen. Being in the trenches together bonded people.

The two of them had gotten close over the years. They shared things with each other, confided in each other, and had gotten physical from time to time. It had been casual at best, an intimacy formed out of convenience and a mutual respect and trust, but there were no real feelings there for either of them. And after the devastation they'd faced just weeks before, they'd both needed time to process. They hadn't spoken since they'd boarded the flight home from Cambodia.

Over the last week, he'd started to heal, but immediately, the tightness in his chest returned.

Maria: *Have you received your next assignment yet?*

Mitch: *Not yet. Have you?*

He held his breath as he waited. Over the years, he typically traveled with the same group of doctors, nurses, and volunteers. This had been the third mission with Maria on his team. If she'd gotten hers, his was coming soon.

Unfortunately, the need and desire to leave again for another mission wasn't so desperate anymore. He was definitely going to go, but the days didn't feel like torture, the way he'd assumed they would, and he wished he could stay a little longer. At least until New Year's.

Maria: *It just came in. Cambodia again. Fly out Dec 25th.*

That's the trip he assumed he'd be on as well, but he now wished they'd assign him somewhere different, with different people. A new team who didn't know what happened...

He sighed as he finished shaving. There was nothing he could do about it right now, so he'd wait until he received his own notification before stressing too much about next steps.

He brushed his hair and his teeth, then dressed in the jeans Jessica seemed to like and a black sweater he'd bought earlier that day, then he sat on the edge of the bed and put on his shoes.

His laptop open on the desk sounded with a new email, and he knew exactly what it was. Standing, he went to the computer but hesitated before opening the message from the Doctors Without Borders office in L.A.

Dear Dr. Jameson,

We are writing to confirm your next overseas placement, starting on December 26. Your requested location of Cambodia has been approved. All travel and accommodation details are attached.

Sincerely,

Alice Walsh

Director

This was what he'd been wanting, expecting…so why was his gut twisting? Was it just the thought of returning to Cambodia? Or was it also the idea of getting on a plane and flying a million miles away from Jess?

CHAPTER TEN

Mitch picked up their wineglasses and carried them into her living room. With a large bowl of buttery popcorn, Jessica followed him. Dressed in the pair of faded jeans she loved, a black sweater that hugged his chest and shoulders, and bare feet, he looked casual and relaxed. As hot as he'd looked in dress pants and button-down shirt the first day they'd met, Jessica loved this look the most. It meant that they were getting more comfortable with each other. She could picture him in her house—in her *life*—like this. Evenings binge-watching Netflix on the couch…

Getting way ahead of yourself.

She needed answers before she could let her fantasies run wild. In the living room, she set the bowl down on the coffee table, and when she turned to face him, he pulled her down on his lap. "I missed you today," he said, brushing her hair back away from her neck.

"You saw me just this morning," she said teasingly, though she'd suffered a similar ache for him. Especially after the discussion with Lia.

He touched her cheek. "Am I sounding too desperate?"

"Just desperate enough," she said, feeling her chest fill

with happiness. No guy had ever seemed this into her before. Never had she been with anyone who was as interested in spending so much time together as she was. At least not with their clothes on. She leaned toward him and kissed him softly. Or rather, she'd meant it to be a soft, gentle kiss, but the moment her lips touched his, she felt herself sinking into it.

His grip on her thighs tightened as she wrapped her arms around his neck and pressed her body closer. He deepened the kiss, and the passion from earlier that day seemed to instantly reignite. Her hands crept up his neck and into his hair, then ran over his shoulders and solid chest. Damn, he was smoking hot.

Reluctantly, she slowly moved away, breaking the connection of their mouths. "We should probably watch the video," she said, her voice sounding slightly hoarse.

Mitch's gaze was locked on her lips, and he nodded as he kissed her once again, quickly. "Probably a good idea," he said.

She went to stand, but he held onto her. "Stay right here."

Oh God…he was killing her. She snuggled in closer as he reached for the remote. He had the laptop cued to the first set of photos. "Should I hit play?"

"Yes." As much as she'd like to make out with him all evening, she really did want to see these videos and photos of his trips. "Where were these taken?" She was determined to focus on the slides. They had all night, so they could talk about other things later. Right now, she was eager to see what his life overseas was like.

"Africa," he said, hesitating. "And you're sure this isn't boring? You're not just saying you want to see these but really you'd rather watch paint dry?"

She laughed. "I want to see them. I've never been anywhere, remember?"

He smiled. "That's because you have everything you want right here."

Right at that moment she did, but would she feel a void in her fulfilling life after Mitch left? Thinking about the future was like running on a hamster wheel—it got her nowhere fast. What was next for them? Where did they go from there? Had their time together so far meant as much to Mitch as it had to her? Was he hoping things would fizzle out closer to his date to leave again?

Too many questions had her emotions in conflict, and she didn't want to waste any of their time together with thinking negative thoughts. They were together now.

"Hit play," she said.

He massaged her legs on his lap as he started the slide show.

The tiny gesture had Jess's heart racing, and she struggled to focus on what he was saying…something about immunizations and a new medical facility. Her gaze was locked on the photos scrolling on her television set, but her body was in tune to the way he gently massaged her thighs and calves.

This here was everything she'd ever wanted. The perfect guy. The perfect life.

"So, this was Zimbabwe," Mitch said as he forwarded to the next slide. "We were visiting an orphanage to vaccinate the children there. The medical resources in that part of the country are limited."

Her attention was now all on the images. "All of those children are orphans?" Jessica's heart ached as she stared at the happy, smiling faces of children who had very little.

A picture of Mitch sitting on the ground, surrounded by a group of young boys all giving the peace sign tore at her heartstrings.

He obviously liked kids. Did he want any of his own?

"Yes. It's so sad to see how they're living. Inside the orphanage, there's a room for boys and a room for girls, and they sleep on mats on the dirty floor. Food is quite basic and there's never enough of it…but they've never known anything else, so to them, it's just normal life and they appreciate everything they have."

Guilt over everything she took for granted filled her chest. No wonder Mitch lived such a minimalistic life— he was altruistic to his core. She could so easily fall for him if she wasn't careful.

"Children of Mary… Is that the name of the orphanage?"

Mitch nodded. "It's one of several in that area."

"And all of these kids, they're looking for homes?"

"Yeah. Adopting from overseas is a bit easier than adopting here in the U.S. actually. And unfortunately a lot of these children's parents have died from disease or famine, so there's no one to argue or intervene on the process of relocation to the United States. Babies and younger children tend to get adopted first, and the older kids continue to be overlooked and they often never find homes."

It was heartbreaking to hear. Mitch's stories had always been uplifting and inspiring, but she suspected there was also stress and a huge sense of responsibility that went along with what he did.

What kind of person would she be to ask him to consider eventually give up doing this great work? To expect him to?

Jessica studied him. "Spending so much time there, caring for them…have you ever thought of adopting one?"

He shook his head. "I fall in love with all of them and leaving is never easy. But then I remember the commitment I made to helping as many people in these third world populations as possible, and with my life requiring so much travel, it wouldn't really be fair to drag a child along."

Her heart melted, but his words served as a gentle warning. His life may not be set up for relationships to be possible, either. It made sense to her that a lot of the doctors he traveled with were husband-and-wife teams, either having chosen to embark on this life journey together or finding each other through their work with Doctors Without Borders. She wondered if he'd ever considered anyone he worked with in that way.

"But who knows?" Mitch was saying, his gaze locked on hers. "Maybe when this part of my life is over and I start a new chapter, then it might be something I would consider."

A new chapter. He hadn't exactly said when that would be, and she didn't think he meant anytime soon. Would *she* be motivation enough for him to consider that next path in life sooner than he'd planned? The idea was ridiculous, yet it plagued her all evening.

Despite her best efforts to push aside her insecurities and enjoy the photos, her mind and heart were locked in a conflicted whirlwind. She could understand why he loved his life. The places he visited were unique and exciting, and the challenges he faced on a daily basis were inspiring. Every day overseas was different. Unlike here. Hadn't she just spent a week showing him just how predictably boring life could be in a small town like Blue Moon Bay?

Unfortunately, she took comfort in the predictability and routine of her days. Mitch wouldn't. She held his hand tight, not wanting to let go as they reached the end of the slideshow.

"I think that's the last of them," he said an hour later.

"Wow, you've really led a fascinating existence," she said, slowly getting up off of his lap so he could put his computer away.

"I can't argue with that. I feel very fortunate to live this life. It's fulfilling on many levels…" He squeezed her hand before releasing it, and she didn't dare hope that maybe it wasn't fulfilling on every level, that some-thing—someone—might be missing.

Suddenly the air inside her house felt thick and heavy, and she definitely needed fresh air to clear the fog of uncertainty she seemed trapped in. "Why don't we go outside on the deck? I think the storm has finally stopped."

"I'll be right there. I'll get us some more wine," he said.

She watched from the living room as he went to her kitchen, opened the bottle of red, and poured two glasses.

He looked so at ease in her home.

Before he could bust her for staring, she hurried outside and sat on the porch swing, dragging a blanket over her lap.

"Your house is in a great location," Mitch said, joining her. He handed her a glass of wine as he sat next to her on the rocking swing.

She extended the blanket over his lap and moved closer so their thighs touched, then snuggled even nearer to him as he wrapped an arm around her shoulder. "I love this house. I bought it because of its location and view of the beach. The inside needed major repairs, but I did them slowly over the first few years, and now the place is perfect for me."

"You did the repairs yourself?" He sounded impressed.

She nodded. "I'm addicted to home repair shows." She laughed. "I did everything except the electrical. I learned my lesson the hard way on that one." She showed him the faint scar on her right forearm where she'd suffered an electrical burn when trying to install lights over her kitchen island.

"Ouch." He brought her arm to his lips and kissed

gently. "Full disclosure—I'm not very handy."

"Well, you're handsome, so that more than makes up for it," she said, sipping her wine.

He laughed, gently kicking his foot to move the swing back and forth. She stared out at the beach that was calm now after the violent wind and rain earlier that day. She loved the stillness after a storm. The smell of the humidity lingering on the air and the slight sway of the palm trees was calming.

This was home.

And it had never felt quite so right as it did in that moment, sitting there with him.

"You okay? You seem a little distracted tonight," he asked.

Obviously, she hadn't hid it very well. "I'm great. I'm having a wonderful time with you. I just have a lot on my mind. Sorry."

"No need to be. Is it about the bakery?"

Among other things. Sticking to that topic, though, seemed safer, easier for now. "It's a big part of it, yeah. A representative from Not Just Desserts came by this week. They increased the offer to buy."

"Was it significant?"

"A million dollars." She still couldn't wrap her mind around the money part, and she'd been so caught up in Mitch, she hadn't really even given Mr. Dorsey or the offer much thought. She lived comfortably. She had no debt, so money had never been a motivator for her. But if she could help her friend and have the freedom to figure out what she wanted for her future, it was tempting.

Mitch let out a low whistle. "That's not something to take lightly. Money like that could change your life."

"But that's the problem. I love my life. I haven't decided if I want to change it yet." Though the more time she spent with him, it was becoming even more clear than before that she longed for a relationship, to be with someone. Being with him made her feel like the missing piece was in place. But he was only temporary. She needed something long-term to feel this way permanently.

"I know it can't be an easy decision to make."

"I hate that my decision could affect my aunt's shop and Mrs. Barnett."

"You shouldn't feel guilty about making a decision that makes sense."

"Selling it and taking the offer makes sense? You think so?" She turned slightly on the swing bench to look at him, hoping all the answers were there on his face. All she saw was a fantastic, handsome man who gave her more uncertainty.

The fate of the business might be up in the air, but what about her feelings for him? She wanted to trust them. She wanted to believe that there was something real between them and that he felt it, too.

"I may be being selfish in my answer..." He turned her hand around until they could interlace their fingers.

"That's okay." Her heart raced and she wanted to know. She valued his opinion on the subject, especially if he was also thinking about what that could mean for the two of them.

"If you sell and the payout ensures that you could take some time off, you could look into that volunteer experience I mentioned." He stared at their interlaced hands.

Volunteering with Doctors Without Borders sounded like an amazing opportunity, one she'd never even considered. "Go overseas?"

He nodded.

With him. On a trip of a lifetime. She'd thought of it a few times over the last few days, but not seriously until that moment. "I'm not sure I'd be the best choice. I mean, I bake for a living. I'm not a doctor or a nurse…"

He shook his head, his eyes lighting up at the thought that she might actually consider it. "That doesn't matter. They accept all volunteers. We need people to do all sorts of things in the villages and around our camp. From getting water from the healthy streams and picking vegetables and cooking. We need lots of help building simple homes and you just admitted to being a closet carpenter."

She laughed, but it stuck in her chest. What he was asking would definitely be life-changing on an even bigger scale than she'd imagined, and she wasn't sure if it was the opportunity that appealed to her and excited her or simply the idea that she'd be with him. Their time together would be extended. It wouldn't be right to sign up for this mission if she wasn't doing it for the right reasons. Altruistic reasons.

"Trust me, your extra set of hands…" He turned hers around and took the other one in his. "These hands could do a lot of good for a lot of people."

Including him? Or was she just wanting to put the words in his mouth? He very well could be recruiting her because of his passion and belief in the cause.

"And it would be a fantastic way to start seeing the world."

She nodded. "It does sound amazing." She bit her lip. "But you leave soon, so when would I have to apply?"

"They have volunteer teams flying out every month. You're probably too late to fly out with me. There's a ton of paperwork involved with the application and you probably wouldn't be ready to go anyway so quickly, but you could fly out when you were ready and the application was approved. And meet me in Cambodia."

Meet him in Cambodia.

She'd never been outside of California. She'd been contemplating a trip to New York to visit Lia later that year. Could she take a leap that big?

"No pressure, Jess. Just something to think about," he said, kissing her palms.

A shiver of adrenaline coursed through her as his gaze lifted to meet hers.

Something *else* to think about.

CHAPTER ELEVEN

Why had they even invited him to lunch?

Sitting across from Lia and Malcolm at Surfboards Restaurant on the pier, it was a struggle to keep his salmon and roast vegetables down as they PDA'd all over the opposite side of the booth. It was bad enough watching his sister kiss the face off of her husband, but unfortunately, it only reminded him of the kissing he wasn't doing.

He checked his watch as he signaled the waiter for the bill. Only a few more hours until he was meeting Jessica at the bakery to help her decorate her window for some community holiday thing that evening.

The night before he'd allowed his hopes to rise about the idea of her traveling with him, but in the light of day, he realized how crazy it was to expect her to give up her life there for a missionary lifestyle that she'd never even thought of before.

But it had been nice to think about…

He scanned the restaurant decorated with surfing Santas on every available square inch. Fat Santas, buff Santas, young Santas, and old. Unique decor choice, for sure. The Beach Boys Christmas album played on the speakers, and he drained the last sip of his beer in the glass shaped like a Santa boot. Maybe he should just leave the cash on the table and split.

He wouldn't be missed.

He cleared his throat loudly and his sister reluctantly pulled her gaze away from Malcolm's face. "You two ready to go?" he asked.

Lia glanced at Malcolm. "Another round?"

He nodded, a grin on his lipstick-stained lips.

"Okay, well, you two enjoy. I'm going to head out," he said, reaching for his wallet.

Lia stopped him with a candy-cane themed mani-cured hand. "Actually before you go, there's something we should talk about." There was a note of seriousness in her voice that had him on edge.

Uh-oh. Had someone in town who'd seen him and Jess together ratted them out to Lia? Was she about to tell him to keep his hands off of her friend? Because he wasn't sure he'd be able to comply with that request. His heart pounded faster. "Oh? What's up?"

"I'm going to go to the restroom," Malcolm said, making a somewhat hasty exit. The man shot Mitch a look that said "good luck" before he kissed Lia's cheek and walked away toward the restrooms. His sister turned her attention back to him.

"What do you think about Dad retiring?"

Oh. That. He wasn't sure his father had told her yet, and it hadn't been his place to say anything. He shrugged. He didn't know what he thought of it, but his opinion wasn't really a factor in his father's decision. "I don't think it's what he truly wants to do, but he insists it is, so there's really nothing else we can do but support it."

She leaned her elbows on the table and lowered her voice. "You know it's Mom, right? Pushing this decision on him."

"They're making the decision together." His parents had always had a great marriage with clear lines of communication and boundaries. If his father was really resistant to the idea, he'd fight harder against it. Mitch had been shocked and a little uneasy when his father had initially told him, but that was because there had been a brief expectation that Mitch would take over. But that was settled…

"Dad's being bullied," Lia said.

Of course she'd take any side that wasn't their mother's. How much of her concern was really about their father's well-being and not just another thing she could disagree with their mother on? Mitch sighed. "Well, have you talked to him about it? Told him your concerns?"

"Yes, but he says the decision is made. He's even started transferring his clients."

Mitch nodded. He knew all of that already.

"And now, Mrs. P will be out of work."

Again, he nodded, not liking where he knew this was heading. "She says she was ready to retire five years ago." He didn't believe it, either, but he'd been pushing the issue out of his mind. It wasn't his decision or anything he had control over. He refused to let it have anything to do with him. Over the years, he'd kept in touch with his family, but he'd successfully distanced himself from any drama. This would be no different.

Lia leaned forward. "Dad says he asked you to take over running his practice."

"He did and I declined." His spine stiffened.

"You won't even consider it?" She frowned as though that was surprising.

"No. I gave up a private practice, remember? That's not what I want." The same thing day in and day out would make him restless. Same patients, same clinic, same office… He shook his head. He'd done that before. It wasn't for him.

But of course, his lawyer sister looked ready to argue her case. "Look, if you took over, Dad wouldn't have to give it up completely. He could still work part-time, or maybe after a year or two off, he could return to work."

Mitch frowned. "Did he say he wanted to do that?"

Lia's sigh was full of exasperation. "He didn't have to. This is his life. He's not going to know what to do with himself after he retires."

And that was suddenly on him? Mitch swallowed hard as he collected his jacket and slid out of the booth. Lia shot him a questioning look, but he kissed her forehead as he passed. "Dad's decision is his decision," he said in a tone that he hoped told her the issue was settled. "And my life is mine."

· · ·

Take the offer and travel the world with Mitch.

Maybe if she kept repeating the option to herself

over and over, it would feel right. It didn't feel wrong. But there was definitely hesitation on her part. Giving up everything she ever wanted, everything she'd worked hard for wouldn't be an easy decision. Knowing she'd be embarking on an adventure with him made the idea a lot more appealing than simply selling her bakery and venturing out on her own. But they'd only been dating ten days. Life decisions couldn't be made that quickly over a man.

She opened the walk-in freezer door and carried a cake shaped like an elf riding a reindeer inside. She placed it on the shelf and stared at the Jameson Nightmare Christmas Order. She'd started on their desserts the day before.

He'd invited her to the family event. That had to mean something. He never brought anyone home.

Mitch's arms around her waist made her jump as she turned to face him. She hadn't even heard the freezer door re-opening. He laughed as he pulled her in for a kiss. "Sorry. Didn't mean to startle you."

She moved closer and stood on tiptoes to kiss him. Would she ever get enough of these lips? He tasted better than any dessert in that walk-in freezer, and seeing him always helped to calm her frantic, overthinking mind.

"You're early," she said, checking her watch. He'd offered to help her with her window display for the Night of Lights that evening. She'd been so busy, she'd left it literally to the last minute.

"You're lucky I wasn't here at noon." He shivered

slightly. "It's freezing in here…"

"I know a way to warm it up," she said, surprising herself with the innuendo.

His eyebrow rose as he held her tighter. "Oh yeah?"

She nodded, slipping her cold hands up under his sweater. His breath caught. "So far, that's not working," he said with a laugh.

Taking his hands from her waist, she lowered them to her ass.

He massaged gently, then with more force. His fingers digging into her flesh beneath the thin fabric of the skirt she wore. "Okay, now I'm heating up a little," he said.

Jessica slid her hands around his back and massaged the thick, solid muscles there as she kissed him again. He felt so incredible. It had been a long time since she'd been with a man as sexy as Mitch. She didn't want to think. She just wanted to feel.

She slid her tongue between his lips and savored the taste of him as she pressed her body to his. The cinnamon and coffee combination had never tasted so good.

She could feel him harden under his jeans and her pulse went wild. She loved that she had this effect on him. Their attraction was mutual, and giving in to these sensations felt right. Overdue.

His hands moved to her breasts and she moaned against his mouth. The hardened buds grew tauter at his fondling. Despite the freezing air around them, her body was on fire.

He pulled back slightly, his gaze burning into hers as he gently bit her lip and murmured. "I want you, Jess."

"I want you, too," she said, nearly panting. She'd never wanted anyone so badly in her life.

He still hesitated, searching her expression. "You sure you want to do this?"

There was no hesitation in her nod, as she forced his mouth back to hers.

He lifted her up onto the shelf and wedged himself between her thighs, never breaking contact with her mouth. Unzipping his jeans, he lowered them down over his ass, exposing his erect cock. Taking a tiny step back, he yanked a condom from his wallet, tore it open, and slid it over the length of himself. "I've been dying to do this," he said.

"Believe me, so have I." Jessica lifted her skirt and moved her underwear aside, ignoring the cold wooden shelf beneath her ass. Wrapping one arm around his shoulder, she moved her body closer until she felt the tip of him press against her. She rocked her hips forward and closed her eyes as he plunged inside her body. So deep, so thick, he filled her completely.

The cool air around them made their shallow breaths come out like smoke rings around their heads as he fucked her hard and fast. Desperate, frantic movements causing the shelf to bang against the freezer wall. All the sexual tension between them that had been mounting for days was culminating in the most intense sex of her life.

"I can't get enough of you, Jess," he said, his head

cradled into her neck. He kissed and sucked along her collarbone and shoulder, and the sensations were almost intoxicating. She tossed her head back, letting her hair fall away from her shoulders, allowing him to kiss everywhere along her skin.

"The feeling's mutual." How had she ever lived without this? Since meeting him, he was all she thought about, the only person she wanted to be with, craved him…every single inch. She'd always enjoyed sex, but it was never this satisfying, this fulfilling. She barely knew Mitch, yet when they were together, it felt like she was where she belonged. There was no doubt that they were good together. What the hell was she going to do when he left?

She held tighter, and he seemed to sense her apprehension as he clung to her as well. Pumping in and out of her body, he pulled back to look at her. His expression full of desire, longing…questions…ones she had no answers to, reflecting in those eyes she could stare into forever.

Her breathing was labored as she felt the first ripples of pleasure mounting. His hands on her body held tighter as he moved his hips faster and she felt him grow even harder. They were both so close.

"I need you, Jess," he said, his voice husky and deep, and she knew he meant more than just physically. She could feel his need for her in his touch, his kiss, his gaze. There had been a different energy coming from him when he'd entered the freezer, obviously on a mission.

She wasn't sure what he was working through that

holiday season, but she knew she was helping him through it.

She just hoped that wasn't all this was. This chemistry, this connection wasn't just because he was needing to fill his heart with something other than pain. And that he would still need her once he outran whatever holiday ghost was haunting him.

CHAPTER TWELVE

"You're really good with that spray can." Jessica stood back to admire Mitch's handiwork with the snow-in-a-can an hour later. It took a certain level of finesse and just the right amount of control to apply the white frosting to the windows. But then again, she was quickly learning Mitch had just the right amount of control and finesse in everything he did.

She'd had sex in her walk-in freezer. It still didn't feel real. She was expecting to wake up any moment passed out in the freezer from a frozen cake falling on her head. The rush of heat that warmed her every time she thought about it had her feeling like she needed to go back in there to cool off. Though, she'd probably never be able to walk in there the same way ever again.

Mitch grinned. "I may have used my share of paint cans in my more delinquent years."

Jessica feigned shock. "You did graffiti?"

His grin turned into laughter. "As much as I'd love to let you believe I was a bad boy, the truth is, I was on the cleanup crew. I was part of a community volunteer program that turned the less appealing graphics into something more appropriate."

"So, you've always had a charitable spirit," Jessica

said, applying a penguin wearing skates decal to the window next to a polar bear family building a snowman. Hers might not be the most unique or impressive design on Main Street that year, but at least she wouldn't be the Grinch without a display.

But she *was* cutting it close with the last-minute dash to get it done. The sun was setting fast and the Night of Lights was scheduled to start in twenty minutes. Already she could see families making their way toward Main Street. Luckily, the tree lighting was first to launch the event, so that would buy them some time.

Either way, she didn't regret getting "delayed." In fact, she'd probably abandon this right now and head back to the freezer if Mitch was into it.

"I think it's in my blood. Dad does a lot of community volunteering," he said. "And he offers a lot of free services at the clinic."

"Sad to hear about your dad retiring," Jessica said. Dr. Jameson had been her family doctor when she was a kid, too. In adulthood, she'd moved to a female gynecologist, but he was always great at accommodating a quick walk-in antibiotic request.

Mitch leaned on the ladder to apply more snow to the corner of the window. "Yeah, it was actually a shock to me, too."

"Do you think he wants to retire?"

"I think he wants to do the right thing for my mom, but I think if he could continue working, he would."

"Well, a lot of people will certainly miss him and the practice. His clinic always accommodated early patients and stayed open later than the others in town. And Mrs. P was always so wonderful with the kids. I wonder what she'll do now. I know she can't afford to retire yet with her husband's failing health…"

"Yeah, look, it's not a great situation all around," Mitch said, a harshness in his voice Jessica had never heard before.

She frowned up at him as she secured the second penguin to the window. "Did I say something wrong?"

Mitch sighed as he climbed down from the ladder. A look of remorse crossed his features as he ran a hand through his hair. "No. You didn't. I'm sorry."

"What's going on?" she asked, gently, touching his shoulder.

"Dad asked me to take over running the clinic. To replace him."

Jessica's heart raced. That would be amazing if that was what Mitch wanted. She'd love it if he stayed in town, and it would obviously make everyone else happy and alleviate Mrs. P's work dilemma. But Jessica knew it wasn't the plan Mitch had for his life. "That had to put some pressure on you, I imagine," she said.

"Little bit," he said, sounding torn. "It was never something I was considering. I never thought Dad would retire this early and I thought I'd made it clear that living here full time and owning my own practice wasn't for me."

Her gut twisted, but she knew that already. Mitch had never made any promises about staying longer than the holidays. He talked about leaving all the time and he'd even asked her to consider leaving with him. Another decision that she was running out of time to make. "But your dad must understand that, right?"

"He does, but I'm just struggling with this guilt of wanting to do the right thing, but not quite sure what that even is."

Jessica stepped toward him and took the spray can from his hand. She wrapped her arms around his neck and stared up at him. His gaze was still pained and full of conflict when his eyes locked with hers. She wished she could make this easier on him, but all she could do was offer him the same advice he'd given her.

"You need to do what makes you happy. If that's traveling the world, then that's what you should do. Your dad followed his dream. You should keep following yours." Even if it was going to destroy her when he left again. How quickly these feelings had spiraled into something real and strong…something she'd lost the fight against. She hadn't even had a chance.

Mitch was everything she wanted in a man—kind, caring, compassionate, funny, sexy as hell and the way he made her feel was unlike anything she'd ever experienced in a relationship before. He made her feel special without doing much at all. The way he looked at her set her pulse racing. The way he touched her had her craving him when he wasn't around, and the way he made love to her, she knew she'd never again find a partner as loving and passionate as he was. Their short time together had her imagining what a future with him could look like…if she was willing to let go of the direction it was headed in now and take a chance. But could she do that after only being with him for a couple of weeks? Could she take a leap that far based on feelings that very well could be one-sided?

He kissed her softly and rested his forehead against hers. "You really are amazing. You have this way of calming me, helping me keep my overthinking in check and stay focused."

She forced a smile. Now if only she could figure out a way to have that effect on herself.

Her cell phone chimed in her pocket and she recognized Sarah's tone. "It's Sarah. They're all meeting us for the Night of Lights tonight."

She'd forgotten to tell him that the outing was a group thing, and she hoped he wouldn't mind hanging out with her friends that evening. It was a tradition for her and Whitney and Sarah to do the walk along Main Street together, bundled in warm clothing and drinking hot chocolate. This year, they'd all be together with plus-ones and a kid.

Mitch smiled. "That's great."

Jessica's heart warmed, but then it pounded in her ears as she read the message from Sarah. "Uh-oh…Lia and Malcolm are coming, too."

Mitch looked unfazed. "Great. The more the merrier."

"Only not great, because I'm still not sure about her knowing about us." So far only Sarah knew. Wes and Trent suspected, and she really needed to tell Whitney. Her best friend would be pissed if she was the last to know…but Lia- eek!

Mitch sighed. "Well, I could bail?"

She shook her head. "No. I really want to share this with you. Especially since you haven't done it in ten years." She bit her lip. "Can we keep things…us…on the down low?"

He grinned. "Like keep it a secret? Pretend we're not looking forward to ripping each other's clothes off again soon?"

Thank God he was on the same page regarding that. "Exactly."

He laughed. "I can do that." He stepped forward and cupped her face between his hands. "But it won't be easy."

• • •

True to his word, Mitch hung back as the group left their meeting point at the bakery, hot chocolates in hand, and made their way south along Main Street a half hour later. Seeing Jessica with her friends only had him liking her even more. They all adored Jessica. She was the glue holding the threesome best friendship together, and her inclusion of his sister when the other two could have easily done without Lia's overbearing, overcompensating, desperate for love ways that made her unbearable, had Mitch's heart growing like the Grinch's.

Not being able to hold her hand or wrap his arm around her or kiss her as they made their way down the lit-up, magical-looking Christmas display show was torture, but it made him feel slightly better knowing she was feeling it, too.

The women walked ahead with an excited Marissa leading the charge and the men lingered behind with him. Trent had seen them together already, and that evening, the guy seemed more accepting of the fact, so Mitch relaxed a little. Sarah would have told them all they were keeping things under wraps with Lia around.

Unfortunately, he knew his sister would be more pissed to learn they'd been keeping the secret, but he was honoring Jessica's wishes with his silence. And besides, he was still annoyed at Lia for messing with his resolve earlier that day. He'd put his father's clinic out of his mind, but that day she'd gone and made him second-guess everything and feel guilty for not wanting to take over.

Arriving at the bakery and seeing Jess in that sexy skirt had been the only thing that made him feel better again. And damn, she'd certainly made him feel incredible. He couldn't believe they'd actually had sex in her freezer. It was admittedly one of the most impulsive things he'd ever done in his life, but once she'd started kissing him, there had been no turning back. Despite the cold, he'd been red hot, and he'd never wanted anyone so badly in his life. Thank God she'd been up for the wild, impromptu sex.

Which only made her that much more fascinating.

He watched her now as she skipped alongside Marissa, pointing at different displays. Her cheeks rosy and her joyful energy was like a drug for him. One that was bringing him back to life. One he couldn't get enough of.

She obviously loved kids. She'd make a terrific mom…

"I hear your little girl is a bit of a tech genius," Trent said to Wes.

The newly engaged, formerly single dad smiled proudly. "I have no idea what she and Sarah are saying most of the time. Coding this…server that." His tone suggested he didn't mind.

"Believe me, that's typical of any house with women in it," Trent said.

"How's she feeling anyway?" Mitch asked, feeling compelled to join in the conversation with the other men.

"Who? Marissa?" Wes frowned under the brim of his L.A. Rams cap.

"No, Sarah." She'd looked slightly green around the gills again when they'd first arrived at the bakery. She'd disappeared into the bathroom for a while. No one else seemed to notice, and call it doctor's instincts, but Sarah wasn't feeling great that evening and there were no scented candles to blame this time.

"Sarah's good. Why? Was she sick?"

Mitch shook his head. "No, just the night I checked in she was…" He waved a hand. "It was nothing. Just some strong-scented candles." And if he were a betting man, about a ten-week pregnancy.

Wes nodded. "Right, those candles. We've had to get rid of all of them, even from the guest rooms," he said, sipping his spiked hot chocolate. "In fact, she can't even handle the smell of food cooking, either. I've taken over all the breakfast prep at the inn and it's safe to say we may need to hire someone."

Mitch waited for the man to clue in. After all, he had witnessed one pregnancy…albeit ten years ago. Instead, Wes turned back to Trent. "How'd you do in your fantasy football stats last week?"

Mitch tuned out as the other men talked about fake football teams and trading players he knew nothing about. He was never really into sports, except soccer, and right now, his attention was on the pretty brunette with the red knitted scarf and hat, stopping to peer into the Chocolate Confessions store window while the others moved on to the bookstore.

"Hey, pretty girl," he whispered, stopping next to her.

She shot a quick glance toward Lia, but she was preoccupied, pointing out a book on mountain climbing to her husband. "This is torture," Jessica hissed.

Mitch turned his body to block the others' view and secretly slid his hand beneath Jessica's hair, gently caressing her neck. "I could kiss you right now and the secret would be out," he said, staring at her beautiful pale pink lips and flushed cheeks.

"So tempting," she said, sinking toward him.

She still smelled like the bakery—cinnamon spice and ginger combination that made his mouth water. The scent of chocolate from the shop couldn't even dare to compete. He wasn't sure how he was going to keep this up. A memory of her fiery passion in the freezer had him hardening again, and he longed to explore every inch of her. The first time had been quick due to the sexual tension that had been building between them all week, but the next time he wanted to take his time… savor every second…

"Mitch! Check this out for Mom for Christmas," Lia called out.

Because of course she had to interrupt. He sighed. Jessica took a quick step away from him and raised her hot chocolate to her mouth. "Your sister's calling out to you," she said, taking a devilish-looking sip from the cup. The way she licked the rim was definitely on purpose.

Damn, this Night of Lights couldn't end fast enough. He wanted to move on to the next activity, a night of passion that didn't include the rest of her gang or any of his family members.

CHAPTER THIRTEEN

With the inn off-limits because of Lia, Jessica unlocked the door to her house two hours later with enough pent-up sexual energy, she was hotter than those old-fashioned seventies Christmas tree lightbulbs.

"I thought headaches were an excuse that women use when they want to get *out* of sex," Mitch said as he reached for her sweater, sliding it down over her shoulders and arms as soon as she'd closed the door behind them.

Jessica laughed. "I had to give a valid excuse to get out of drinks." She lifted the base of his shirt up over his body. He raised his arms to allow her to remove it. The others were heading out to Trent's Tavern after bringing Marissa home, but for the first time ever, Jessica had bailed on her friends to be alone with Mitch. Not her usual M.O. to abandon friends for a guy she was dating, but he was on borrowed time and she had to take any free time they had together.

"My excuse was valid," he said, pulling her into his bare chest.

"You said you would go, but you really didn't want to," she said, cocking her head to the side.

"It was the truth," he said against her lips. He kissed

her gently as his hands slid inside her tank top. His fingers tickled her waist, then moved higher over her rib cage and then over her lacy bra. "Should we have gone?"

"Hell no," she said, removing the tank top and reaching around her back to unclasp the bra. She let it fall to the floor, and Mitch's gaze drinking her in had her even more turned on than ever. His obvious appreciation for her curves made her feel sexy as hell. She reached for the waistband of her skirt and shimmied out of it, then kicked her legs free.

"You are so incredibly sexy, Jess," Mitch said, roaming his hands over her shoulders, down the front of her body, around her waist and hips.

She unbuckled his jeans and slowly removed them. His erection was already visible beneath his underwear. She pressed her body to his and, wrapping her arms around his neck, she kissed him hard. "Give me thirty seconds, then come in the bedroom," she said.

He squeezed her waist and kissed her again before releasing her. "Thirty seconds?"

"Thirty seconds," she said, hurrying away from him and into her bedroom. She quickly collected the discarded clothes on the floor and stuffed everything into her closet. She threw all her decorative throw pillows and favorite Build-A-Bear stuffed toy onto the chair near the window. Then she plugged in the strand of white Christmas lights she had bordering the room. A warm, romantic glow illuminated the space and she was suddenly nervous.

"Twenty-eight…twenty-nine…thirty," she heard

Mitch count down as he approached.

She turned and, seeing him standing in her bedroom doorway, she thought her heart might explode.

"Can I come in?" he asked.

She nodded, and within two big strides she was back in his arms. Kissing, they made their way to the bed and fell onto it. Mitch's body covered hers as he deepened the kiss, tilting his head to the side and exploring her mouth with his tongue.

Her body trembled with anticipation as she broke away to climb higher onto the bed. Mitch removed his underwear and joined her. His naked body was warm and she moved closer to him. He lay on his side, dragging his fingers down over her face, down her neck, between the hollow of her breasts, down her stomach and lower to her mound. She closed her eyes, enjoying his touch.

Quietly, sensuously, she arched her back and opened her legs for him. Silently demanding what she wanted. He grazed the inside of her thigh, drawing circles as he moved closer toward her opening.

She swallowed hard as his fingers slid along her folds, then inside her body. Reaching for him, she stroked the length of his erect cock, desperate for the feel of it inside of her.

Mitch moaned at her touch and slowly removed her hand from his body. "That feels too good and I want to be inside of you." He rolled his body onto hers and wedged himself between her legs. Taking her hands, he lifted them overhead on the pillow, entwining his fingers with hers as he pressed his cock against her wet body. He kissed her neck and shoulder and his breath against her skin drew goose bumps to the surface. He ground his cock against her until she was almost panting. "Mitch, I want you," she whispered.

"Condom?" he asked.

"Bedside table," she said.

He reached for one, tore it open, and slid it on over the length of himself. Jessica swallowed hard as she watched. She'd never wanted anyone so bad before. Mitch was absolutely everything she'd ever desired.

"Turn over," he said, gripping her hips and rotating her body on the bed in front of him.

On all fours, she glanced back at him over her shoulder, tossing her dark hair over to the other side. His lust-filled gaze was intoxicating when it met hers. He knelt on the bed behind her and gripped her waist, pulling her back toward him. She raised her ass higher into the air as she lowered the top half of her body back to the bed. Her hands gripped the fabric of the pillow case as he slowly entered her from behind. Her vulnerability was empowering. Surrendering to him while knowing she had full control had her body begging for release.

"Damn, Jess, you're so tight."

She pushed her hips back farther, taking him deeper within her body. She moaned and her fingers gripped the pillow tighter.

He rocked his hips, thrusting in and out, reaching around her body to grip her breasts. He squeezed and massaged and pinched the nipples tight as he continued to take her from behind.

She cried out from the pleasurable intensity and he quickened his pace. She was so close to the edge. Her entire body screamed for release. "Mitch, faster, harder…" she begged. His cock buried itself deeper and her orgasm erupted. Waves of desire so intense she shut her eyes and held tight as they overtook her.

Mitch plunged a final time, his hands digging into her flesh, and then his body fell limp on top of her. His breathing was hard and labored as he slowly removed himself from her body and discarded the condom.

Jessica pulled back the comforter and slid in between the soft, fleece Christmas-themed bedsheets and held it open for him to climb in next to her. He pulled it over them as he moved closer to her. He opened his arms and she snuggled into him. "That was incredible," she whispered, glancing up at him.

He kissed her forehead, her eyes, her nose, and then her lips. "You are the most unexpected gift this holiday season."

She sighed, her contentment only dimmed by the knowledge that this was one holiday gift with an expiration date.

. . .

Sleep wouldn't be happening. Not lying there next to the most fascinating woman he'd ever met. He was painfully aware of the ticking clock counting down his time in Blue Moon Bay suddenly far too quickly. Once he left, it could be years before he took any extended time off to visit again. Being with him wasn't a choice of whether a woman could live with a long-distance relationship with long periods of time apart. He was always gone.

Never before had he wanted to stay.

He trailed a hand over Jessica's bare arm as she lay sleeping with her head on his chest. Making life decisions based on a woman he'd only gotten to know over the last few weeks was ridiculous, but he couldn't ignore the tug in his chest that told him these feelings ran deeper than any others he'd ever had and they wouldn't fade once he left town. This connection with Jess was physical and emotional. She'd kept him calm and grounded when he'd arrived in town, feeling lost and uncertain. But more than that, she made him happy. He loved his career, loved traveling, loved the knowledge that he was making a difference in the world, but could he say he was truly happy? He hadn't questioned it before, but now it was impossible not to. This true joy of being with Jess, spending time with her, getting to know her and liking her more and more everyday was foreign to him.

He sighed, and the motion of his chest rising and falling made her stir. Her eyes flitted open and she turned to look up at him. "Am I crushing you?" she asked.

"Not at all." Even if she was, he wouldn't want her to move.

"Can't sleep?" she asked.

"Rather not waste time with sleep," he said with a smile.

She wiped her sleepy-looking eyes and sat up.

"You can sleep," he said, feeling bad. She had to work early the next morning.

She propped several pillows against the headboard and reached for her television remote. "I have a better idea." She turned on the TV and scrolled through the channels until she found an old black-and-white holiday movie, *It's a Wonderful Life*.

She moved closer to him and rested her head against his shoulder. "This okay?"

"This is perfect," he said, kissing the top of her head before turning his attention to the movie.

Unfortunately, it was unexpectedly too perfect. Somehow in a matter of weeks, this breathtakingly beautiful brunette had him questioning the life he'd thought he had figured out.

CHAPTER FOURTEEN

Absolutely nothing could destroy Jessica's mood the next morning. Not the last-minute cancellation of a cookie order she'd spent five hours on the day before, or the voicemail from Mr. Dorsey reminding her the clock was ticking. The night before with Mitch had her practically floating across the bakery floor at five a.m. even though she'd only gotten an hour of sleep. Having to pretend they weren't seeing each other in front of Lia had made her feel guilty as shit, but it had also been the most incredible foreplay. The element of secrecy and danger...

Leaving her house with him finally sleeping soundly in her bed had been hard, but also a little exhilarating. Her vivid imagination had obviously gone full throttle, and she couldn't fight the thoughts of how wonderful it would be if they lived together and could wake up together like that every morning.

She refused to let the reality of the situation bring her down or spend time overthinking what really came next.

She was even in a good enough mood that the next order on her list made her smile for the first time in the ten years she'd been making it. The Jameson Nightmare

Christmas order… She'd be enjoying those desserts that year, too.

Mitch's family were nice, open, caring, friendly people, even if his mom was a little over the top when it came to Christmas. And it was the season of goodwill. Lia really couldn't be that upset, could she?

She tied her apron around her neck and gathered the ingredients for the chocolate Panettone. It was one of the harder desserts on Mrs. Jameson's list and it lasted longer than some of the others.

Turning on the radio to the local festive holiday channel, she got to work. There was definitely more love going into this cake this year.

Love.

Sigh. How close she'd come the night before to telling Mitch that she was falling for him. She'd wanted to say it. The moment couldn't possibly have felt more right, after an incredible night of passion, cuddling in bed, watching Christmas movies, the warm glow of the season all around them…but she needed to be careful. Already, the damage to her heart once he left might be irreparable.

Two hours later, a loud crash from next door made her pause her dough kneading.

What on earth was that noise?

Another *bang* as though something had fallen against the wall she shared with her aunt's shop, then voices had her straining to hear better. Her aunt was at work already?

The voices grew even louder, her aunt's and another

woman's. Then another loud thumping sound had Jessica abandoning the dough and running out of the bakery, her hands sticky with the mixture. Using her shoulder, she pushed open the door to Frankie's Fabrics and ducked just in time as a roll of silk flew past her head.

Racks of material were tipped over and reams of fabric stretched out across the floor. A bucket of loose buttons had been scattered all over and her aunt's life-size antique Mrs. Claus decoration was lying facedown near the door. Her recording of "Have a Holly Jolly Christmas" stuck skipping, so that the lyric "Have a ho…" played over and over on repeat.

It might have been funny if the scene in front of her didn't have her panicking. Was her aunt being robbed? Why hadn't she grabbed a rolling pin or knife on her way out?

Jessica's head snapped right and left and her eyes widened as she saw Mrs. Barnett poised and ready with a mannequin arm. "Just admit you lied!" she was saying to Frankie.

Lied? About what?

"Put down the mannequin or so help me…" Jessica had only seen her aunt Frankie this red-faced once before. When Trent and his sisters had snuck out and drove to Santa Monica for an outdoor concert when they weren't of legal age. Her aunt was normally calm and rational in her dealings with everyone, even her neighbors.

Positioned between the two stores, Jessica often felt

like a mediator between the two women. They'd had their share of disagreements over the years, like when Mrs. Barnett had created some heinous smelling oil that was so strong, it had seeped into Frankie's fabric and she'd had to send it all out for cleaning before she could sell it, or when they'd both dressed up as Elvira for the local businesses along Main Street's Queens of the Dark Night Contest and had had to share the first place prize.

But she'd never seen the two of them get physical.

Mrs. Barnett wouldn't actually attack her aunt with the hard, plastic limb, would she? She'd done quite a bit of damage to the store.

Jessica stepped in between them as Mrs. Barnett advanced toward her aunt, holding the mannequin arm like a baseball bat. Her aunt held a glue gun in each hand. Unplugged but still slightly menacing and completely out of character for a passivist.

"Stop!" she said, holding bread dough covered hands out toward each of them. "What is happening in here?"

Mrs. Barnett still held the arm, but her grip relaxed slightly as she said, "Your aunt here sold out." She jutted her chin toward Frankie.

Jessica turned to look at her aunt.

Frankie glared at Mrs. Barnett behind her cat-eye glasses. "I did not."

"You did!" the fiery older woman said, readjusting her grip on the arm.

"I didn't. You have no idea what you're talking about, you old bat, and I've had enough of your accusations."

Oh my God. "Stop! What are you two talking about?"

Jessica asked, looking back and forth between them.

"Mr. Dorsey paid me a surprise visit this morning," Mrs. Barnett said, her angry tone mixed with a hint of hurt. "He told me Frankie took their buyout offer."

Jessica frowned. There was no way Frankie would do that. Definitely not without talking to her first.

Frankie shook her head. "Wait a sec, Mr. Dorsey told me that *you* accepted their offer," she told Mrs. Barnett.

Mrs. Barnett's nostrils flared. "I did no such thing!"

Could a person's red hair get more red with anger?

A quick glance at the woman's mood ring had Jessica quickly retreating behind the counter with her aunt and accepting one of the glue guns. Then she sighed and put it down. "Okay, everyone lower their weapons."

Her aunt put down the glue gun and Mrs. Barnett reluctantly lowered the mannequin arm.

"Look, it's obvious what's happening here." Jessica turned to her aunt. "Let me guess, he told you both that *I* had accepted their offer?"

He aunt nodded. "He's playing us all," she said with a sigh.

Mrs. Barnett raised the arm again. "Next time I see that sniveling little snake…"

"Hey…it's okay. At least we all know what he's up to now. I'll grab us some tea and we can all talk this out, okay?" Jessica said, making her way to the front door. "No one kill each other or destroy the place further while I'm gone?"

The two women nodded, but still avoided looking at each other as Jessica left the shop.

Breathing a deep sigh, she pushed through the bakery door and washed the dough from her hands in her kitchen sink.

"Drama, drama, drama," she muttered. That Mr. Dorsey was something else. How he thought he could get away with trying to trick them all like that and setting them against one another was just shady.

Could she really consider selling her bakery to a company like that?

Pouring three caffeine-free teas, she flipped the sign on the door to BE BACK IN AN HOUR and then re-entered a much calmer shop, where the two women were putting everything back where it belonged.

Suddenly, Jessica was the one on edge. Clearly, neither of them had accepted the offer from Not Just Desserts, meaning the fate of the businesses was once again completely on her shoulders.

. . .

"Was Lia too busy to come shopping today?" Mitch asked as he and his mother entered Petals and Gifts on Main Street later that morning. He'd almost forgotten about his plans to meet her that day after sleeping at Jessica's place the night before. She'd already left for work when he'd woken up, and he'd been analyzing his feelings all morning. It was definitely a new sensation. Waking up in a woman's bed wasn't something he did often. Waking up in a woman's bed in his small home-town was something he'd never done, but he'd caught the slightest glimpse of what spending a night with her and waking up with her could be like.

He didn't hate it.

"She has all her shopping done," his mother said. Dressed in a red and white candy-cane striped dress and green tights, she looked like an elf as she perused a display of snow globes she certainly didn't need any more of.

Mitch took her arm and gently led her away. If she brought home another one, his father would lose it. "You mean you didn't even ask her," he said.

His mother avoided his gaze as she picked up a scented candle, sniffed it, and shoved it under his nose. "Does this smell better than the pine one I was burning the other night?"

How on earth would he know? He sighed. "They all smell like pine." He paused. "You know who'd be great at picking out candles? Lia."

His mother huffed. "Look, it's no secret that your sister and I don't particularly get along."

Whose fault was that? As the adult and curator of the relationship, he'd bet his mother was the one who should be to blame. His sister had even hosted a family reunion that fall to bring everyone together. His mother had to see the efforts she was making. She'd purposely held the reunion at a time she knew Mitch couldn't make it, but if he didn't hold that against her, why should his mom? "You need to stop pouting about Christmas. For the first time in years, Lia and I are both home."

Both of them were leaving before Christmas Day, but he still hadn't grown balls big enough to tell her that. He'd focus on the positive for as long as possible.

His mother waved a hand. "I'm over it. It's fine."

She was absolutely not over it, but Mitch had already exhausted enough energy on trying to get through to either of them over the years. His attempt to bring them closer always just ended up with both women being pissed off at him.

Can't win. Don't try.

And there was actually something else he wanted to talk to her about that morning. He stopped in front of a display of personalized tree ornaments and pretended to peruse them as he said, "Hey, Mom, is it okay if I bring a plus-one to early Christmas dinner?"

His mother dropped the snowman diamond necklace she was looking at and turned to face him. "Like a lady friend plus-one?"

Wow, he wasn't that old that he'd refer to Jess as a "lady friend," but it was all semantics, so he nodded.

Intrigue was all over Ally's face, her holiday decor shopping completely forgotten as she hurried to his side. "Is it someone your father and I know?" she asked in a conspiratorial whisper.

He nodded again.

"Well, obviously it must be someone in town." She bit her lip, thinking. She loved this twenty questions game. Loved solving puzzles and mysteries, so he didn't ruin her fun by just telling her who it was.

That. And he was a little freaked out. What would

she think about him dating one of Lia's friends? Someone a lot younger? He hadn't been worried about it until that moment. Even when he'd invited Jess, it hadn't caused him any conflict, but after the night before, the idea of bringing her home terrified him slightly. Not enough not to do it, though.

"Is it Shirley from the tourism office?" she asked.

Shirley from the tourism office was fifty-five years old. He better tell her before his self-esteem took a hit as she guessed all the newly divorced cougars in town. "No. It's Jessica."

His mother frowned. "Jessica who?"

"Connolly."

Still no recognition.

"Delicious Delicacies Jessica Connolly. The woman who is making all the desserts for early Christmas dinner?" She was so much more than that to him that he almost felt guilty describing her that way.

His mother's eyes couldn't possibly get any wider. "You're dating little Jess?"

She wasn't exactly "little Jess" anymore. "The last few weeks we've been hanging out." Okay that sounded even worse than lady friend. "We've been seeing each other. Just casually," he said quickly before she envisioned him settling down.

Her beaming smile was brighter than all the holiday decor in the store. "Darling, that's fantastic."

"You think so?" Relief flowed through him. That wasn't as tough as he'd thought it would be. Of course his mom would be okay with it. She'd been pushing him to "find a nice girl," "settle down," "start a family" for years. Not that any of that was happening, but obviously she saw it as a step in that direction and she wasn't opposed.

"Absolutely, I do," she said, taking his arm as they made their way through the store. "Of course, your sister's going to kill you."

Right, there was still that.

CHAPTER FIFTEEN

She could totally do this. Spend an evening with her friends at the inn that night, including Mitch's sister, while he was there somewhere and keep pretending like they weren't seeing each other, that the day and night before they hadn't taken things to the next level. They could be in the same place together without Lia suspecting something. She hoped.

Maybe he'd go out that evening, since he knew she'd be there. They'd both been disappointed that she had alternate plans that night, but this was good. She couldn't avoid spending time with her friends because she was completely wrapped up in a guy.

He'd invited her to his family's early Christmas, so they wouldn't be able to hide this for much longer, but Jessica knew Lia was going to freak out once she did find out, and she hoped that wouldn't be this evening. She really liked Lia, but the way her feelings were growing for Mitch, she never wanted to be in a position to have to choose between them.

Climbing out of her van, she straightened her dress and carefully made her way up the B&B steps, where Sarah, Whitney, and Lia were already seated on the outdoor furniture.

Good. Staying outside was a good idea.

"Wow! You look amazing. Hot date tonight?" Sarah said, eyeing her dress and strappy sandals with a slightly mischievous grin.

Her cheeks flushed and she hoped the glow could be blamed on the reflection of the holiday lights above them. Sarah was obviously having too much fun being the only one to really know what was going on with Jessica and Mitch. She'd tried telling Whitney earlier that day, but lately her friend was busy whenever she tried to schedule a lunch or just call to chat. She was there that evening, which was a relief, but now wasn't the time to say anything.

"I thought I'd dress up a little," she said. And spend two hours curling her hair and applying more makeup than she usually wore for a night with girlfriends.

"For me?" Lia said. "I'm honored," she said, standing and wrapping Jessica in a one-armed hug while she held her wineglass with the other.

"Red or white?" Whitney asked, holding two bottles for Jessica's choice. Her cell phone was pressed between her shoulder and ear, and the distinctive sound of "hold music" could be heard on the line.

Hopefully, her friend wouldn't be taking work calls all evening. Whitney's ability to multitask was superior to anyone Jessica had ever met, but her friend needed to take some time off now and then. A concept that seemed lost on her.

"I'll have the red, please," she said as she sat in a plush chair facing the window looking into the den.

Whitney poured, then handed her a glass. She turned to Sarah. "White?"

Sarah shook her head. "Actually none for me."

Whitney laughed at the perceived joke and poured the white. But Sarah shook her head again. "No, really. I'm just trying to cut back. Holiday season and all…"

Whitney frowned but nodded and Lia took Sarah's unwanted glass. "Waste not, want not," she said, sitting back on the porch swing, one glass in either hand.

"I brought dessert," Jessica said, retrieving a box of pastries from her oversize purse. She opened the box and the smell of cinnamon filled the breeze.

"That smells like Christmas in a box," Lia said, reaching for one of the chocolate cinnamon treats.

"These are Sarah's favorite," Jessica said. Or at least they used to be. Right now, Sarah looked slightly green as she covered her nose and mouth against the smell. "You okay?"

Sarah nodded. "Yeah…strong smells—even delicious ones—are just getting to me lately. Some weird allergy I've developed or something maybe." She shrugged and moved her chair back a little away from the desserts.

Whitney disconnected her call and glanced at her phone. "Fifty-two minutes on hold with the printer and I just got disconnected." She sighed as she set her phone under her leg on the chair. She was polite enough to turn off the ringtone, but Jessica knew it was on vibrate in case they—or anyone else—called back.

"Do you ever take a night off?" Lia was the one brave enough to ask.

Whitney frowned, looking as though she didn't understand the question. "I think I have a holiday booked in April."

Lia laughed, but unfortunately Whitney wasn't kidding. And Jessica knew it wasn't a holiday, it was a doctor's appointment for a breast exam and pap smear. She had the date marked in her calendar, too. They'd been going together for mutual support since they were twenty.

"This time of year is so busy," Whitney said, sipping her wine. Dark circles seemed to have formed under her friend's eyes overnight and she looked thinner than the last time Jessica had seen her.

"Aren't all of the town's holiday festivities already planned and organized?" Sarah asked, rejoining the conversation from a distance, still holding her hand over her nose.

"Yes. Now we're onto budgeting for the spring promo. Always a season ahead." Whitney checked her phone and looked irritated that it wasn't ringing.

"Must make it hard to enjoy the season you're in," Lia said, shoving the pastry into her mouth.

Whitney shrugged. "I prefer to plan and let others enjoy." She twitched, feeling her cell phone vibrate beneath her. Grabbing it, she stood as she answered. "Daisy…tell me you got those new designs approved." Her voice trailed as she moved farther away from the deck, holding up a finger to indicate she'd just be a minute.

"Wow. I thought I worked a lot," Lia said. She turned to Jessica. "I assume Whitney will be working and

Sarah will be celebrating her first Christmas with Wes and Marissa. Do you have any special plans for the holidays?"

Jessica shrugged casually and avoided Lia's gaze.

Only crashing your early family Christmas.

"My parents are traveling through Europe right now and won't be back until February, so I'll most likely be with Aunt Frankie and the family." It was true. Once Mitch was gone, she would be spending Christmas Day with her extended family. Like always. The idea had never depressed her before, but that year when she was enjoying the season more than usual because of having someone special to share it with, being single for Christmas Day was going to hit harder.

"So there's no one special in your life?" Lia asked.

"Um..." Damn, it was easy to lie by omission, but now that Lia was asking her directly, what did she say? Mitch was someone special. Very special. "I...uh..."

Sarah looked to be holding her breath, waiting to see if a train wreck was about to occur. This evening could go sideways very fast.

Her cell phone chimed on the chair next to her leg and, seeing Mitch's face on the display screen, she picked it up and quickly hid it from Lia's view.

Mitch: *I'd like to know the answer to that as well.*

Jessica's gaze flew upward and she caught Mitch grinning at her from the library. Dressed in a pair of jeans and white T-shirt, his hair messy and his face unshaven, he looked comfy and cozy sitting in a leather armchair with a mystery novel in his lap. Obviously eavesdropping.

"That expression of yours says yes," Lia said, intrigued.

Jessica forced her gaze away from the window, feeling Mitch's still on her. "I've been dating someone casually. Nothing serious," she said. Damn, this was going to make it even more awkward if she didn't confess to Lia right now…

Her phone chimed again.

"Well, looks like Mr. Nothing Serious is missing you," Lia said.

Mitch: *That is one fantastic dress.*

Repressing her smile was nearly impossible as she texted back.

Jess: *You're making this secret relationship a lot harder.*

Mitch: *So let's tell her.*

Her heart raced, and when she glanced back toward the window, Mitch was gone.

She cleared her throat and stood. "Excuse me for a sec. I just have to…"

Lia waved at her. "Go ahead. Go call him," she said with a laugh. Then turning to Sarah, she sighed. "Young love."

Jessica moved past Lia and slipped inside the inn. Several guests were checking in and Wes was struggling to explain the keyless, cell phone room entry option to them. Poor guy, technology really wasn't his thing.

She made her way to the den, but Mitch wasn't in there. She dipped into the dining room and kitchen but couldn't find him. Oh no, had he gone outside to talk to

Lia? The other woman wasn't raging through the B&B looking for her yet.

Her phone chimed and her heart quickened as she read.

Mitch: *Seaview Room. Third Floor. Door's unlocked.*

She glanced outside. The women were still all on the deck, laughing and talking. They wouldn't miss her or notice how long she was gone, would they? Shit. Could she really do this?

Apparently, her body thought she could as she found herself sneaking past Wes at the check-in desk and up the staircase to the guest bedrooms. She paused outside the Seaview Room, her heart beating so loud Mitch had to be able to hear it from inside.

Jess: *Behave yourself. A quick kiss and that's it.*

As she reached for the handle, the door swung inward and Mitch dragged her inside.

Wearing only a soft, plush towel, his hair wet from what was obviously the fastest shower in history, water droplets still on his body, he pulled her into him. His mouth crushed hers with an intensity she'd never felt from anyone before.

His kiss was long and hard and full of desperation, and he was breathing heavy when he pulled back. "Damn, I needed that," he mumbled against her lips.

"I know the feeling," she said, wrapping her arms tighter around his neck and pressing her body close. He was getting her dress wet, but she didn't care. This body of his was definitely top of the list of things she was going to miss about him.

"You were driving me to distraction out there in this sexy dress and those heels…"

At least all the prep that evening to get ready hadn't gone unnoticed or unappreciated. She swallowed hard as his hands slid the length of her sides, down over her hips. Tingling danced down her spine.

"You're so incredibly tempting, Jess." His hands found the bottom of the fabric and he slid it higher over her thighs. "Can I have you?"

Right now? Right here? With her friends waiting for her?

His mouth found her neck and her entire body craved him as he placed a trail of kisses from her earlobe to her collarbone.

"What do you say, Jess? You don't even have to get undressed," he whispered in her ear.

Her body was practically vibrating as she nodded quickly. "Yes. I want you." Understatement. She needed him. "We have to be fast." Which only added to the insanely intoxicating moment.

"No problem," he said. Lifting her legs and wrapping them around his body, he pinned her to the wall. He lifted her dress up around her waist and let his towel drop to the floor. Grabbing a condom from the dresser, he quickly tore the wrapper and put it on, then he moved her underwear to the side.

"Ready?" he asked, his gaze burning into hers with a desperate intensity unlike ever before.

She nodded, not trusting her voice to speak.

He entered her fast, plunging deep inside her ready,

wet body and there was no muffling the scream that escaped her lips. Immediately Mitch's mouth covered hers again as he moved his hips frantically, plunging in and out of her body fast, desperate.

She clung to his shoulders as she rode his cock up and down, her back sliding against the wall, feeling the sensations growing stronger. She could barely breathe as she hung onto him tight and they fucked against the wall. His hips slamming into hers and his chest pressed against her body had all her wildest fantasies coming true. No man had ever wanted her this badly before. No one had taken her right there on the spot because they couldn't wait a second longer. Mitch's craving for her rivaled hers for him. A long-distance relationship would never be enough with this kind of chemistry between them. Skype sex or phone sex would pale in comparison to the real thing.

"I want to come together," he said, breaking contact with her mouth.

Holy shit. He'd better be close, then. She nodded and his gaze locked and held with hers as he thrust in and out a few more times. "Jess…"

"Yes, I'm right there with you," she said breathlessly.

"Look at me," he said when her eyes closed.

She opened them as her orgasm toppled over and he moaned his own release. He held her tight as she pulsated around his throbbing cock. She took a deep breath and her shoulders sagged.

He rested his forehead against hers. "That has to be some kind of record."

She laughed. "Well, I appreciated the quickie. Very much."

He slowly moved out of her body and set her down on the floor. She straightened her clothes and fixed her hair as he went to the bathroom to throw away the condom.

"Sneaking around like this is kinda fun," he whispered against her lips when he returned.

For him, maybe. She was having a heart attack. "Lia is going to be even more pissed that we kept this a secret. I almost told her a few minutes ago."

He took her hand and started to leave the room. "Okay, so let's tell her now."

She pulled him back. "No!" She eyed him. "And I'm calling bullshit—you don't even have clothes on." Obviously he'd been counting on her to stop him.

He laughed. "Look, Jess, I'm a grown man and you're a grown woman. We can date who we want to date," he said softly, but she sensed his apprehension as well.

She swallowed hard. It should be that easy, but it wasn't. If Lia wasn't happy, maybe Mitch would pull away to keep the peace, and she selfishly didn't want that possibility. "We will wait until your family's early Christmas."

And hope that a Christmas miracle saved both their asses.

CHAPTER SIXTEEN

"You're sure Lia and Malcolm aren't here?" Jessica asked, hiding behind the large Christmas tree in the foyer of the inn the next day. She scanned the group of families all entering through the double doors.

Mitch nodded, taking her shoulders. "I'm positive. Relax. And time's running out. There's only a few days until Early Christmas Dinner. Sure we shouldn't tell her before then?"

Jessica bit her lip. They probably should. He was right. But she was terrified of Lia's reaction. She liked Mitch a lot, but she also worried about upsetting her friend. She didn't want Lia to feel as though Jess preferred Mitch, when the other woman struggled with that feeling among her own family members. When they did tell her, Jess was desperate to find the right way so that no one got hurt. "I'll think about it." That day, she just wanted to enjoy decorating the inn's Christmas tree with him.

He kissed her quickly as Sarah joined the group and welcomed everyone. Wes and Marissa followed behind with trays of hot chocolate and cookies she'd supplied from the bakery.

"This was something her grandmother did?" Mitch

whispered next to her, as Sarah explained the tradition.

Jessica nodded. "Sarah wanted to continue tradition."

"Is that her grandmother's Christmas sweater, too?" he asked.

Jessica eyed Sarah's holiday sweater with the reindeer with the red nose on it that had to be three sizes too big. "Maybe." She'd never seen it before.

"So, how does this work?" he asked, watching families open the boxes of ornaments.

"Everyone is welcome to bring a special ornament of their choosing and Sarah supplies the regular bulbs and garland to fill in the rest."

"Sounds like it will be a very mismatched tree."

Jessica laughed. "I take it your family Christmas tree was all matching bulbs and tinsel strategically placed?"

He shook his head. "Tinsel is tacky."

Her eyes widened. "Do not let my Aunt Frankie hear you say that. She thinks it's the essence of the holidays."

Mitch reached for her hand and a warm sensation flowed through her. She didn't care who saw them together, holding hands. Except Lia, of course. "Thank you for agreeing to do this. I know it isn't exactly your thing."

He nodded as he slowly glanced her way. "It's a lot less not my thing when I get to do it with you."

Oh God. She was falling hard and fast and she needed to put the brakes on. Keep it casual. He had no intentions of staying in town and the minute she fell in love with him he'd discover his soul mate on his next tour overseas. "Well, I suspected you didn't bring your own ornament, so…"

"Oh you did, did you?" He reached into his back pocket and retrieved a tiny bag from the holiday shop on the boardwalk.

Her eyes widened. "You bought something?"

"I suspected the tradition went along those lines and I had to participate if I was going to decorate, right?" he said with a grin that had her emotions completely toppling over the edge of casual into the deep depths of torturous, unrequited love territory.

He'd promised not to fall in love that holiday season. She needed to remember that. Not that the knowledge was helping her control her own developing feelings.

He handed her the bag and she opened it. Reaching inside, she took out a personalized holiday ornament of two snow people wearing chef hats and holiday aprons, baking cookies. Mitch had their names written on them, with that year's date. It was one of those family collectibles. This one was clearly meant to be for a couple's first Christmas together.

Her heart pounded so loud in her chest, he had to be able to hear it above the holiday music playing around them as the families got to work on the tree. She stared at it in her hand.

What did it mean? Was he trying to tell her something?

He cleared his throat in her silence. "Hey…I just thought because we baked together the day we met. I didn't mean for it to be…"

Right. Of course. It meant nothing. Just a cute reminder of how they'd met. She waved a hand and laughed awkwardly. "Oh, I know. Don't worry, I wasn't reading anything into it," she said as painlessly as possible.

Mitch studied her but he nodded slowly. "Should we hang it before all the good spots are gone?"

Jessica smiled. "Definitely. I have the perfect spot."

• • •

He was such an asshole. How could he not have realized that Jessica would think the ornament meant something? It was clearly a couples' ornament. When he'd bought it, he'd just thought it was the perfect way to summarize their holiday time together. It was cute. He was trying to be thoughtful.

He may have gone too far. The look on Jessica's face when she saw it had spoken volumes. His chest was tight as he watched her hang it on a branch near the front in the very middle of the tree.

Problem was, he wasn't so sure it didn't mean something anymore. His feelings for her were growing stronger each minute they spent together and there was no one else he'd be doing this for. That meant something in itself.

He felt horrible for basically implying that the ornament didn't reflect his growing attraction or how he saw them together, but he couldn't commit to something he still wasn't sure about. His feelings were confusing the hell out of him, and until he sorted them out, he didn't want to mislead her.

But now he'd gone and hurt her. This was why he avoided relationships. His chosen lifestyle didn't give him a chance to be good at them.

She turned to face him. "How does it look?"

He stared into the eyes that terrified him with their ability to make him envision a different future for himself, a different path. "It looks like it belongs right there."

But where did he belong?

That holiday season, he wasn't quite as sure.

And he refused to believe that his ringing cell phone at that moment was a sign of anything other than bad timing. Maria's name was lighting up his call display when he took the phone out of his pocket, and he hesitated.

Jessica glanced at it. "You can go ahead. I'll keep decorating," she said.

"You sure? It's…a colleague." It was true, so why did he feel guilty? Probably because there were times overseas that Maria was more than just a colleague. Though he knew that wouldn't be happening on this upcoming mission.

"Absolutely," she said.

"Okay. I'll just be a minute." He walked away from the crowd and the tree and found some quiet in the den. "Hey, Maria," he said as he answered.

The distinct sound of sobbing on the other end of the line simultaneously made him wish he'd sent the call to voicemail and that he was where she was to comfort her. "Hey…you okay?" Dumb question. Obviously, she was spiraling. The way he probably should and would be if Jess hadn't saved him from himself that month.

"I...don't...think...I...can...go...back." The words came out on short, raspy breaths as though she were struggling to breathe.

He hated hearing her this way. Maria was one of the most positive and upbeat nurses he'd ever traveled with. She was mild-mannered and soft-spoken, but tough and resilient when she needed to be. She was a damn good nurse—compassionate, smart, quick thinking. They'd become fast friends during their first mission together overseas and then over the years, they'd gotten really comfortable with each other. They weren't in love. They were friends who relied on each other in a lot of different ways.

"It's okay," he said steadily. "Take a breath. Start counting...one, two..."

"Three...four..."

They counted up to ten and he rubbed a hand over his face, feeling her anxiety being transferred through the phone. It was almost another full two minutes before she was able to speak. "I'm not sure going back is the right thing."

"I understand." He'd had similar thoughts when he'd first left the country.

"But I think if I don't, the last mission...what happened will continue to plague me."

"I agree." It was definitely one of the driving forces behind him wanting that placement, too.

"You're coming, too, right?" she asked, sounding

relieved by that at least. "I saw your name added to the team list online."

Mitch stared out through the den doorway toward the tree. His gaze landed on Jessica and his heart had never felt so conflicted. It wasn't that he was considering not going and staying in Blue Moon Bay, it was that he knew leaving wasn't going to be easy.

"Mitch? You were assigned to Cambodia on the 25th, weren't you?" Maria asked again in his silence. "You did accept, right?" She sounded slightly panicked again.

"Yes, I did. Don't worry, I'll be there," he said reassuringly, even though his own feelings on it had gotten so much more complicated.

"Promise," she asked softly, and the hair on the back of his neck stood up. She no longer sounded like she was asking as a colleague and someone who needed his support professionally...but something more personal. His gut twisted, but he was going to go and he would be there for her. Not in every way she might need, though.

"I promise."

Jessica turned and glanced his way as she selected a shiny, plastic gold ball to hang on the tree, and her smile was unsure when she caught his stare.

"See you soon," Maria said.

He disconnected the call and took a breath as he returned to the tree.

"Everything okay?" Jess asked, concern in her voice and expression.

Glitter and sparkles from the decorations covered

her beautiful, soft cheeks and he didn't need to force a smile as he took her hand in his. "Yeah…everything is great."

Their time together would end way too soon, but for now, everything was great.

CHAPTER SEVENTEEN

DECEMBER 17TH...8 DAYS UNTIL CHRISTMAS...

Mitch couldn't remember the last time he'd felt refreshed upon waking up, but that morning when his eyes opened, he didn't immediately want to shut them again. The last few weeks, his sleeping had gotten longer, deeper, and less riddled with nightmarish memories.

Definitely had to do with the gorgeous brunette lying on his chest, sleeping peacefully. He held her tighter as he took a deep breath. He'd never been so happy being confined to one spot as he was that morning. There was no pressure to get up right away. No desire to, either.

He twirled a piece of Jess's hair around his finger and she stirred, cuddling in even closer. Damn, he loved the feel of her body lying next to him. One leg draped over his, her arm resting across his stomach, her soft cheek against his chest. When was the last time he'd felt this at peace and so comfortable with a woman? Jess had the most amazing calming effect on him.

The night before was the first nightmare-free sleep since leaving Cambodia.

That meant something.

Unfortunately, it also made him feel guilty that Maria was still having a rough time. He'd found something—someone—to help him heal that holiday season.

He hoped she'd be okay…

Luckily, he'd been able to convince Jess to stay over-night at the inn with him. After his tree decorating blunder and ill-timed phone call, he'd thought maybe she'd be upset or disappointed that he hadn't exactly given the best response over the misunderstanding or been very forthcoming about the situation with Maria, but she'd just as eagerly climbed the B&B stairs with him to his room after the tree was lit, and that's where they'd stayed all evening. She hadn't asked any questions and, not really knowing any answers, he hadn't tried to give any.

He held her tight and her eyes flitted open. She looked up at him, her sleepy but happy expression filling his chest with a warmth he hadn't experienced in years.

In too long. He hadn't realized he'd missed this personal connection, this intimacy. He'd never allowed himself to slow down long enough to realize the void was there or allow any loneliness to enter.

"Hey, good morning," he said.

"Did you sleep okay with me crushing you?" she asked, attempting to get up, but he held her to him.

"Best sleep I've ever had," he said.

She smiled and snuggled closer. "You're so warm."

He grabbed the blankets and pulled them up around her body. "Better?"

"Yes." She kissed his chest and he immediately felt his attraction turn to a more desire-filled sensation.

She shifted her body and continued her trail of kisses lower across his stomach and along his obliques. He closed his eyes and rested his head against the mountain of soft pillows as her hands traced the path of her mouth down his body.

She knelt between his legs and her hands massaged his thighs as her kisses went even lower. His cock was immediately at attention, and when her hand wrapped around its base, he swallowed hard. She was tender, yet strong. Her control of her own passion was intoxicating control over him.

She stroked slowly up and down as her other hand cupped his balls. He moaned and clutched the bedsheets on either side of him. When her mouth lowered and her lips wrapped around the tip, he was already close to the edge.

How could he give this incredible sensation up in less than a week?

He glanced down at her, and he knew this was far more than just physical. Their connection went so much deeper. He'd never met anyone quite like Jessica. Her commitment and dedication to her hometown and her friends was not so unlike his own commitment to the greater cause he believed in. They were alike in a lot of ways.

The fact that she was considering giving up everything she loved, her own comfort zones to try something new with him only made her that much more irresistible. He reached for her and she gently released him from her mouth and glanced up at him.

"Come here," he said, gripping her around her rib cage and lifting her higher on the bed. She straddled him, her underwear pressed against his straining cock. He could feel her wetness and the thought that she was just as turned on and eager for him was even more of a turn-on.

Gripping her face between his hands, he kissed her. Softly at first, then harder. His tongue separated her lips and he savored the taste of her. She pressed her pelvis forward against him and began rocking her hips back and forth, grinding her body against him.

He could barely breathe, his mouth never leaving hers as their actions grew more desperate, more frantic. She clung to his shoulders as she moved up and down against him.

When was the last time he'd dry-humped a woman? High school?

This was killing him. The need to be inside her, to feel her tight body wrapped around him, submerge himself in her warm wetness. He couldn't get close enough to her. Too much clothing between them.

Pulling away, he reached for the base of her tank top and quickly lifted it up over her head. He tossed it onto the floor and reached for her underwear. One quick yank had the thin lace falling away from her body.

Her laugh was a slightly shocked sound, and he immediately sobered, realizing his actions. "Shit…sorry, was that okay?"

Placing her hands against his chest, she pushed him back onto the bed. "It was hot as hell," she said before her mouth connected with his again.

He put on a condom in record time and then,

grabbing her hips, he lowered her body down over his cock. He moaned against her lips as he felt her take him completely into her body. Damn, that felt so incredible.

Sitting up, she gripped the head board and moved faster, up and down. The friction between their bodies growing stronger…building to an intense sensation.

Jessica moaned in pleasure as he pressed deeper into her body, and the quick rocking of her hips slowed.

"I'm so close Jess," he said, trying to hold off the orgasm threatening to explode. He came so fast with her. There was no effort at all.

Looking at her breasts just inches from his face, the curvy, sexy shape of her waist and hips and thighs…the long dark hair cascading over her beautiful soft, round shoulders and sexy collarbone. She was breathtaking. She was everything he hadn't realized he'd been missing out on.

The world had a lot of amazing things to discover, but he'd yet to find something so precious and unique as Jessica Connolly.

Would he ever find anything like her ever again? Something worth giving this up for?

"Mitch, I'm coming," she said, almost breathless as she pressed her pelvis forward. Her body spasmed around him and he felt her throbbing with the intensity of her orgasm.

He pushed himself in farther, as deep and hard as he could go, feeling his own orgasm topple over. He stared up at her gorgeous, satisfied expression as his body rippled in waves of pleasure and an immediate new longing and craving that made him feel like he could never possibly get enough. He released a deep breath, relaxed his tight grip on her body, and sank deeper into the bed cushions.

Jessica climbed off him, and he removed the condom and placed it in the trash can next to the bed. She snuggled into his side and rested her head against his chest. "I'm not sure I can live without that anymore," she said. "You've spoiled me with amazing sex and now you're planning on ditching me." Her tone was playful, but he heard the note of seriousness.

He felt the same conflicted emotions. He traced a finger along her arm. "Have you given more thought about coming with me?" He didn't want to push or put any pressure on her, but he was dying to know.

She nodded. "I have. I still don't know."

"Anything I can do to help the decision?" he asked, kissing the top of her head.

"I think you already just put your best case forward," she said with a laugh that warmed his core, and he held her tighter.

. . .

"The coast is clear," Mitch said an hour later. He stood in the open bedroom door, glancing up and down the hallway of the inn.

Sneaking out of his room without Lia noticing would only be fun for so long. The nervousness she'd felt all evening, just waiting for Lia to drop by the room for some reason or another had only been extinguished by Mitch's passion. They'd barely slept all night and it was a blessing that Sarah hadn't put brother and sister in neighboring rooms.

As awkward as the tree decorating had started out, they'd had a lot of fun, and no matter what meaning was behind the ornament, it was still so very special. Despite whatever happened, there was a memory of their holiday together and she'd always cherish that.

She'd be lying if she said she wasn't curious about Maria, his colleague, but it was none of her business. Mitch traveled the world and met lots of different women all the time. Being with him now, for however long, would have to be enough. Unless, she decided to sell the bakery and go with him. His asking her about it that morning had surprised her. It did put a little pressure on, but it had also filled her heart with hope that he wasn't exactly excited about leaving her. He wanted her with him.

The sound of kids in the main dining room drifted up the stairs. Laughter, joy, and tiny voices that had Jessica's maternal clock kicking into overdrive, especially after that morning's sex.

Mitch would make beautiful babies…

"What's going on down there?" he asked, pulling a light blue sweater on over his still-wet-from-the-shower hair. He looked so freaking good all the time, it was hard to keep her hands and her true feelings to herself. She was definitely falling in love with him. In fact, she may have already fallen so hard she'd hit the ground.

"Breakfast with Santa," she said. "Dove used to host one for the kids every year, so Sarah is doing it." She couldn't have been more thrilled when Sarah had decided to keep the inn and move home that fall. Using the B&B as an event center throughout the year was a genius idea. The money Sarah and Wes made from the inn's event revenue was funding both of their own businesses— Sharrun's Construction and Sarah's App Development.

Mitch studied her.

"What?"

"I just haven't seen that particular expression on your face before."

"What expression?"

"That slight look of longing when you spoke about the kids. Do you want kids? I know you asked me about it the other night, but I don't think we explored your feelings on the subject."

What the hell was the right answer to that? She didn't want to freak him out or scare him off if there was potential for a relationship after the holidays, but she wouldn't lie to him, either. She did want kids. Eventually. And that eventually time frame was drawing closer with each passing year. She didn't want to be an old mom. She wanted kids while she was still young, healthy, and energetic enough to enjoy them. "I think so, yeah."

"You'd make a great mom," he said, and she had to look away for fear of revealing too much. Afraid her feelings for him would be written all over her face.

She cleared her throat. "I should get going. I have deliveries."

"I'd offer to help, but I have to meet my dad today for golf."

She waved a hand. "Absolutely! You're here to spend time with your family, not work."

He pulled her in for a soft kiss. "I'd rather work with you. I'll walk you out before we both end up back in that bed," he said, a slight hoarseness to his tone.

• • •

Downstairs, he reluctantly walked Jess through the foyer toward the front door. "Can I see you tonight?" he asked. He'd given up any pretense of playing it cool, and he was thrilled when she nodded eagerly.

Noise from the dining room caught his attention, and he turned to look at the Breakfast with Santa event. He spotted a little girl smiling and laughing with several other children at the table, and his mouth went dry. Dark hair in a long braid down her back. Dark brown skin. Light gray eyes. Thin nose. He squinted and a sharp pain radiated across his forehead.

Ava?

He moved into the dining room, oblivious to the sights and sounds all around him. He thought he heard his name, but it sounded distant…unreal.

All of a sudden, he was back there in Cambodia.

Seeing the little girl laughing and smiling and playing. Healthy, happy…safe. Then the sound of the bullets ringing in his ears. The screams, the blood, the limp, lifeless little body…

He touched her shoulder and as she slowly turned to face him, Mitch's pulse skyrocketed.

Not her. Of course it wasn't her. This was Blue Moon Bay. And Ava was gone…

"Hey," the little girl's mother said, slapping his hand away. She stood abruptly and glared at him. Everyone stopped to glare at him.

Jesus. He'd lost it for a brief second too long.

"Sorry…so sorry," Mitch said, turning and leaving the dining room as quickly as possible, brushing past Jess on his way out. Whispers and stares followed him out. He must look crazy. His heart thundered in his chest and his mouth filled with saliva. He was going to be sick.

Racing back up the stairs to his room, he made it just in time.

When he lifted his head from the toilet bowl and stood, his hands still trembling slightly and the nausea in the pit of his stomach still lingering, Jessica was standing in the bathroom doorway.

"You okay?"

His gaze met hers through the bathroom mirror reflection and the concern on her face had his pulse racing even faster. She deserved an explanation for that, but he wasn't sure he could talk about it. He wasn't really sure what had happened. Trauma had a callous way of hitting hard and unexpectedly. It rewired a person's brain and seemed to fire at the synapses at will. He thought he'd been doing okay, moving past it. He nodded. "Yeah, sorry…that must have looked really weird."

"Did you recognize her?"

"I thought I did," he said, splashing a handful of water on his face, then turning off the tap.

Jess handed him a towel and he took extra-long drying his face. He hung it on the rack and released a deep breath. "For a second there, I thought she was a young girl I'd…treated overseas."

Jess nodded.

He followed her out into the bedroom and they sat on the edge of the bed. He'd replayed all of this over and over in his mind for weeks after it happened, his recurring nightmares never missed a detail, but vocalizing it wasn't going to be easy. Telling Jessica might help relieve some of the heaviness from his chest, though.

"You don't have to tell me if you don't want to," she said softly, touching his shoulder.

He took her hand in his. "I do." He forced a deep breath. "We were treating children with malaria in a drug resistant area with a new combination therapy vaccine. The existing strains become resistant to the most effective drug, artemisinin, but societal constraints cause most people to buy their drugs from local dealers, pill by pill, and therefore they never truly get better. So we were combining it with chloroquine, a longer lasting but slower affecting drug. It was going well. Really well. The success rate for recovery was amazing." He paused.

Jessica squeezed his hand, encouraging him to continue.

"We met Ava when we found her on the street outside our clinic setup. She was thin, pale, and very sick. We brought her in and started treating her. She got better. She was so smart and funny. She wrote stories and she'd sit next to the other sick kids and read to them or tell them jokes. She had a vibrancy about her even though she was sick and recovering." He paused again, gathering his thoughts.

"Then her parents took her from the clinic. They didn't believe in Western medicine and said we'd violated their rights." He ran a hand through his hair. "Unfortunately, one of the side effects of the chloroquine is hallucinations, and because they'd only ever taken artemisinin, the family was scared when Ava started experiencing them. They accused us of poisoning their daughter, of witchcraft..." He swallowed hard.

Jessica wrapped her arms around him and nodded for him to continue.

"I tried talking to them, but they wouldn't allow us to keep treating her. She got sick again and she came to us, begging for help. We couldn't turn her away." His hands shook in his lap and he clenched them tight. "Unfortunately, her hallucinations returned." His mouth filled with saliva again and he swallowed several times. The image of that day returning clear in his mind. "One day as we were leaving the clinic, we saw her. Her parents had dumped her body outside the tent, there was a... bullet hole in her chest...with a note blaming us for her death." He would never be able to fully erase that from his mind. From his conscience.

Jessica inhaled sharply. "I'm so sorry, Mitch. That had to be devastating."

He nodded slowly, letting the emotions come back.

No longer repressing them. No longer trying to forget. He needed this to process. "I've seen children die overseas, but this one got to me in a way no others had, because I knew we could save her. I knew she could have survived if we could have continued to treat her. She didn't have to die. And the guilt I feel for going against her family's wishes and having her instead die the way she did." He choked on the lump in his throat, feeling the first tears burn in his eyes.

Next to him, he heard Jessica swallow hard. "It's heartbreaking," she said sadly. "But you were doing what you thought was right. The thing you were there to do—save these kids whenever possible. They wouldn't even have a chance at survival without your team."

He knew that. For every person they couldn't save, there were hundreds that they did. Statistics didn't help him sleep at night, though. Nor did distancing himself or keeping his emotions in check. He cared about the people he met and treated. He wouldn't be a good doctor if he didn't. But Ava had been special to all of them. "I've seen some terrible things, but parents allowing their child to die like that...for killing their child." The horrors of the world no longer surprised him, but they still had a soul-crushing effect.

Jessica hugged him tighter.

He sighed. "My colleague who called yesterday, Maria. She was there, too. We found Ava together," he said, feeling as though he needed to tell Jessica everything.

She nodded quietly.

"She was having a hard time dealing." Maybe it was

hearing Maria's breakdown that had triggered him. Not being able to release those intense emotions himself and having them build to a breaking point.

"Understandably."

He turned to face her and her sympathetic, caring gaze filled his chest with something other than pain. "Thank you, Jess."

"Of course. I'm here anytime you want to talk," she said.

He touched her cheek. "You've done more than you could ever know," he said. And to say he wasn't falling for her would be a lie. Now, he just needed to figure out what to do about that.

. . .

Jessica reached forward and turned off the holiday music in her delivery van an hour later. Somehow, the cheery music didn't feel right that morning. The sights and sounds of the fast-approaching holidays were slightly overwhelming as they held new meaning for her that day. The season of joy and goodwill toward man. She'd always loved the holidays for the events and the family gatherings and the festive fun, but so many others didn't get a chance to enjoy this time of year. War, sickness, and pain and suffering stole joy from so many every day of the year.

Jessica sighed as she turned into the lot behind her bakery. Mitch's story that morning had her so conflicted inside. Her heart ached for him and his team and for that poor little girl who hadn't been given a chance at a healthy, happy life. His story had terrified her and made her wonder if she could handle those harsh realities. If she could mentally and emotionally be strong enough to witness the things Mitch had.

But then, it also gave her a sense of humanitarianism so strong that as soon as she entered the bakery she opened her laptop on the counter and logged onto the Doctors Without Borders website. She still didn't know what she'd do with them, but she could at least research the application process.

The site for volunteers reiterated all of the need for assistance that Mitch had vocalized. She didn't need to be a doctor or nurse, just someone willing to help. She read through various available positions and spent a long time reading testimonials from other participants who'd had their lives changed by the experience.

An hour later, she'd filled out the volunteer form application and printed it. She stared at it, no closer to a decision but feeling as though she'd taken the first steps toward one. Hearing the door bell chime and customers entering, she took the form and carried it into the front. She opened the drawer under the cash register and placed it on top of the buyout offer from Not Just Desserts, then closed the drawer. That's where it would stay for now until she was certain.

Then she smiled as she turned her attention to the family perusing the display case. "Hi, happy holidays," she said.

Mitch's story was never too far from her mind as she went to work that day.

CHAPTER EIGHTEEN

The harbor was always pretty at night, but that evening it had an extra glow as Jessica strolled along the wooden boardwalk with Mitch. All of the docked boats in the marina were illuminated with Christmas lights and decorations as far along the coastline as she could see. The boat owners handed out eggnog and mulled wine to the adults and cookies to the kids. They were both quiet, and she sensed he was in as much of a pensive mood as she was. But she had been thrilled to get his text earlier that day suggesting they do this. It was one of her favorite holiday activities, and enjoying it with him was even better.

"Now, this I remember," Mitch said, squeezing her hand as they reached the first decorated boat.

A tingle ran the length of her arm. The simplest gesture from him set her pulse racing. Her attraction to him was off the charts, and keeping things casual and uncomplicated was becoming very complicated. Especially after his confiding in her and opening up that morning. His vulnerability had just given her yet another side of him to fall in love with. He'd trusted her with something deep and personal, and she valued that for the sign of the depth of their connection. "I was surprised you even knew about it," she said.

"It was my dad's favorite thing to do when we were kids. I figured they still did it."

Jessica laughed. "That is a safe bet." Not much changed in Blue Moon Bay. Traditions were sacred.

"There used to be an old pontoon decorated with red and green fish hooks…I remember the man had one of those singing fish on the wall, but this one wore an elf's hat and sang Jingle Bells."

"That one right over there," Jessica said, pointing to the one at the end.

Mitch shook his head and laughed. "I probably shouldn't be surprised that he still participates."

"It's a yearly tradition." She stared up at him. "You must find it so hokey, though."

"Why's that?"

"The fact that every year it's the same thing. Life doesn't change much around here," she said.

It was actually the thing she enjoyed most about small-town life. Things didn't change too quickly. There was a security in the familiar, knowing there were things—like these holiday traditions—that she could depend on. But after their discussion that morning, she was starting to wonder if maybe security in the familiar and never experiencing the world beyond her front door wasn't the right way to live. She didn't think she buried her head in the sand and ignored what was happening in the world, but maybe by being so removed from it all, she was essentially living in a privileged oblivion.

At first, the idea of traveling with Mitch had been

solely based on him, her attraction to him, the idea of being with him. But the more she thought about it and researched it, the more her motivation had changed.

"I'm starting to see the appeal," he said, bringing her hand to his lips and kissing it.

They continued to walk in comfortable silence, enjoying the lights, pointing out funny decorations, and sipping their mulled wine. But when they reached the fishing pontoon boat, Mitch stopped.

Jessica laughed. "This one really is your favorite, huh?"

"Follow me," he said with a grin, heading down the dock toward the boat.

She hurried after him. "Where are we going?"

"You'll see." He tossed a wink over his shoulder.

Captain Eli nodded in greeting as they reached the boat. Dressed in his usual fishing gear—overalls and large rubber boots—but he'd added a Santa hat to the ensemble. "Jameson?" he asked with a welcoming smile.

Mitch nodded. "That's us."

Us? What was he up to?

"Great, climb on board," Captain Eli said.

Jessica frowned. "We're getting on the boat?"

"I may have reserved a private marina tour. Hope you don't mind." Mitch looked slightly panicked. "Shit, you don't get seasick, do you?"

Lovesick was the only illness she had right now. She shook her head. "No, this is great." More than great. It was an unexpected surprise. Something he'd arranged for her to make the evening even more special.

She accepted Captain Eli's hand to climb aboard, and he handed her a life jacket. She slid into it and Mitch zipped it up, his fingers gently grazing her chin. Then he put on his own as the captain started the boat.

"Best place to see the lights is in the stern. Feel free to use the blankets under the seats," Captain Eli told them.

Jessica's sea legs adjusted to the sway of the vessel as they made their way toward the back. Mitch opened the seat and retrieved a thick checkered blanket and then sat, motioning for Jessica to sit next to him. She cuddled into his body and he draped the blanket over them. "Comfy?" he asked, his breath warm against her cheek.

She nodded. "I can't believe you did this."

"What better way to see the lights?" He kissed the side of her head. "Sometimes for the best experience you have to leave the safety of the shore."

She heard the double meaning loud and clear. She turned to face him and his expression searched hers. In that moment, she knew she wanted to explore more of these opportunities with him. She'd stayed safe on the shore long enough. Being there in his arms was making her feel like that might be where she belonged. The old saying "home is where the heart is" may have some merit. Her heart was definitely with Mitch. In such a short time, she'd fallen hard and fast and he'd opened her eyes to different possibilities. A different future. A different happiness.

"What's going on in there?" he asked gently, and she sensed he knew exactly where her thoughts were.

"If I wanted to come with you…when would I have to decide?"

He brushed her hair away from her face and kissed her forehead. "There's no pressure. We leave December twenty-fifth, but you can join us over there anytime."

The note of hopefulness in his voice had her confidence in her decision rising. He wanted her with him. She wanted to be with him. So why not take the leap?

"I was worried I'd completely scared you off this morning," he said, searching her expression.

If he was looking for any sign of her losing interest in him, in them, he wouldn't find any. "The complete opposite actually," she said as the boat picked up speed and a mild wind blew her hair across her face. Mitch brushed it back. "Your story this morning was heartbreaking, but I guess it made me realize that maybe there are parts of the world that I'm not experiencing. Things I've been unaware of. Things I could help change."

His affection for her nearly stole her breath away. "You are the most incredible woman I've ever met," he whispered against her lips before kissing her gently.

Soft, romantic holiday music started to play from the radio on the boat, and the moment felt truly magical. She held Mitch's hand and cuddled into him as they enjoyed the view of the harbor lights in silence. Jessica took it all in, knowing this may be the last holiday season she enjoyed her hometown's traditions.

CHAPTER NINETEEN

"Fresh, hot-from-the-oven cookie delivery for my favorite aunt!" Jessica pushed through the door to Frankie's Fabrics at 9:05 a.m. the next morning. She'd been pacing the bakery, waiting for her aunt to arrive and open shop and get settled...but she hadn't been able to wait longer than five minutes before heading over.

She needed her aunt's advice...or maybe her blessing.

"Hi darlin'," her aunt greeted from behind a stack of holiday-themed material. She was rolling out a red-and-green tartan pattern and cutting the lengths.

"Whatcha doing?" she asked as she approached.

"End of season cut-offs," Frankie said, expertly sliding the shears through the fabric, then rolling it into a smaller piece to sell in her off-season sale bin. By now, crafty shoppers had moved onto Easter or spring-themed prints.

Jessica set the bag of cookies on the edge of the counter and pulled up a stool. She opened the bag and extended an oatmeal raisin cookie toward her aunt. Frankie opened her mouth and Jessica laughed as she shoved it in, allowing her to take a bite as she continued to work. "How is it?"

"Your best yet," Frankie said as she swallowed, but she eyed Jessica over her cat's eye glasses. "But I know your whiteboard is full of orders that need to be done today, so I feel like this cookie delivery visit is meant to soften the blow of a certain decision?"

Man, her aunt knew her far too well.

Jessica sighed as she slumped forward on the stool. All morning she'd stared at the contract from Not Just Desserts. One minute she thought she could definitely do it. The next, absolutely no way. The indecision was killing her and making it impossible to move forward one way or the other. "I still don't know what to do…" she said slowly.

"You're considering it more seriously now, aren't you?" her aunt stopped working to give Jessica her full attention.

Jessica handed her the rest of the cookie.

"A month ago, I hadn't thought I could actually accept. But now…"

Things were different. Her feelings for Mitch were undeniable, but she couldn't make major life decisions based on a relationship. And she had no idea how he really felt about her. She could feel love in his gaze, his touch…but what if all that faded or disappeared completely once he was back living the life he loved.

But if she didn't go with him, there'd be no chance.

"Would this conflicted state of heart be because of a certain handsome doctor I've seen glued to your hip the last few weeks?"

Her aunt had noticed? "Mitch Jameson has definitely been opening my eyes to new possibilities." She wouldn't deny he'd been the catalyst in her change of heart. "He wants me to travel overseas with him as a volunteer."

"Wow."

Jessica frowned, staring at her aunt. "Wow good? Or wow bad?"

"Just wow," Frankie said, but this time she smiled and touched Jessica's hand. "It would be an amazing adventure."

She nodded. "Yeah, but shouldn't I start small? Like a trip to Arizona or something? Cambodia, helping Doctors Without Borders seems like a big leap for small-town bakery owner."

"Don't sell yourself so short, sweetheart. You have such a big heart. You could really make a difference over there."

"That's what Mitch says, too," she said.

"You really like this one, don't you?" her aunt said, reaching into the bag for another cookie.

"I do. I may even be falling in love with him."

"Is he falling in love with you?" Her aunt's concern mirrored her own. Jessica was known for having her share of heartaches.

"I'm not sure," she said honestly. "Things feel different with him. There's definitely a connection."

Her aunt raised an eyebrow. "I thought I heard some odd noises coming from that walk-in freezer of yours."

Jessica's cheeks flamed. She'd forgotten the freezer

wall was connected to her aunt's shop.

Her aunt squeezed her hand. "I think it's wonderful, sweet girl. I love seeing you happy and you know I want you to do what your heart tells you."

Her heart was telling her to go with Mitch. See where this adventure could take her. If it didn't work out she could reopen a bakery with the money from the sale. She'd miss Blue Moon Bay and her family and friends, but she didn't need to constantly travel the way Mitch did. She could just do one mission a year with him... There were options. One step at a time. It would actually be one of the safer risks she'd taken financially. Emotionally, it was her biggest gamble.

"Why don't you do it?" Aunt Frankie said.

Jessica's eyes widened. "Like now?"

"Your heart's made up, now let your head follow. Call Mr. Dorsey and accept their offer."

"What about you and Mrs. Barnett?"

"We will be fine. Let us figure that out." She nodded toward Jessica's cell phone. "I'm here for moral support," she said, but she did reach for a third cookie.

What would she do without her aunt? Her continued love and support had always been there when she'd needed her. And if she thought this was a good idea, confirming Jessica's own desire, then maybe it was the right thing to do.

She picked up her cell phone and scrolled through the contact list for Mr. Dorsey's cell number. She stared at it for what felt like an eternity.

A text message chimed and she jumped, nearly

sending her off of the stool.

"Sweet baby Jesus," Frankie muttered, hand to her heart. "That was intense."

"It's Sarah." She fought for a calming breath as she opened the message.

Sarah: *S. O. S. Come right away! Bring those chocolate cinnamon cookies.*

Jessica frowned. An emergency that required baked goods?

Maybe she should call for clarification, but she was actually ahead of schedule that day, and she really could use her friend's advice on her own emergency. Having her aunt's support was just one opinion, albeit an important one, she should consider before making this huge, life-changing decision.

She climbed off of the stool. "Sarah has some sort of emergency. I have to go." She reached across the counter and hugged her aunt quickly. "Thank you."

"Anytime, honey," her aunt said, her mouth full of cookie.

In her bakery, Jessica packed up Sarah's favorite cookies, locked the bakery door, and jumped into the van. Ten minutes later, she pulled into the lot of the inn and parked next to Whitney's yellow convertible.

Damn, Sarah had called in all reinforcements. Something was going on. She climbed out and ran to the door.

Sarah paced the foyer as she entered. Whitney leaned against the staircase railing, typing an email on her cell phone. "What took so long?"

"You texted ten minutes ago. What's going on?"

Sarah looked slightly pale as she paced the foyer of the inn, dressed in yoga pants and a loose-fitting tank top. "Did you bring those chocolate cinnamon-filled things I love?"

Jessica nodded, retrieving the pastry box from her purse. "Right here. Now, what's wrong?" She glanced at Whitney, but her other friend shrugged a thin shoulder. One that suggested she'd lost more weight. Concern for both her friends had her anxiety rising.

Sarah took the box and opened it. She took a huge bite of a cookie and closed her eyes to savor the flavors. "Mmmmm...I desperately needed this."

"Sarah! Do not tell me your emergency was a sweet-tooth craving."

Sarah swallowed the pastry and took a deep breath. "Sort of."

"Sarah! I was kinda in the middle of something."

Whitney looked unimpressed as she folded her arms and huffed. "And I need to get back to the office."

Sarah inhaled and released a slow deep breath as she glanced back and forth between her friends. "This sweet-tooth craving is just one of the million cravings I've been having lately."

Jessica frowned. "You okay?"

"I'm pregnant."

Jessica's eyes widened and her mouth dropped. "Oh my God!" She rushed toward Sarah.

"Shhhh..." Sarah said, pulling her into the den. She motioned for a stunned silent Whitney to follow. "Wes doesn't know yet," she whispered.

"When did you find out?"

"About thirty seconds before I texted you both." She suddenly looked exhausted as she collapsed into the oversize plush chair near the fireplace. "I'm kinda freaking out," she said, shoving the rest of the pastry into her mouth.

"Are you happy about it? Was it planned?" Whitney asked the practical questions. Though her own feelings about it were completely undecipherable. Probably she wanted to make sure it was what Sarah wanted first.

"Yes and no. To both."

"You two were trying?" Jessica asked in a high-pitched whisper. So exciting. She'd been so caught up in Mitch, she hadn't paid any attention to her friend's slight weight gain in recent weeks. She thought it was just that relationship weight most couples put on. Technically, she guessed it was.

Sarah nodded. "Only half-heartedly. I just went off the pill last month and we thought it might take a while." She shook her head. "Grandma always said we were a fertile bunch."

Whitney looked ghostly pale and she'd yet to smile or show any sign of excitement over the news. But their practical friend was probably just wondering how Sarah was going to juggle the new businesses and a new baby. Whitney worried first, celebrated later.

Well, she could be the excited one for all of them. "Wow," Jessica said, forcing Sarah to shove over to make room for her in the chair. She took her friend's hand in hers. "This is incredible."

Sarah nodded, but she appeared to still be in shock.

"I'm honored that we are the first ones to know," Jessica said. "When are you planning on telling Wes and Marissa?"

"I don't know."

"Why not on Christmas? I can't imagine a better gift."

Sarah nodded. "That's a good idea."

"Hey, Sarah, I have to go. I've got a meeting in ten minutes," Whitney said. "But this is great news. Congrats."

Her smile seemed forced as she quickly leaned down to hug Sarah. But only Jessica seemed to notice.

"I'll talk to you both later," Whitney said with a quick wave before making a hasty exit. Definitely not the response of a friend that was happy for a friend. Jessica really needed to talk to Whitney soon. Her friend's workaholic ways were obviously damaging to her health and it wasn't helping her in the friendship situation.

Sarah squeezed Jessica's hand tight. "I'm terrified, Jess. I've only known for an hour and already my life is completely turned upside down. I'm afraid to move in case I hurt the baby. I needed this sugar like it was a life preserver, but now I'm guilty about extra weight gain or prenatal diabetes."

Jessica laughed softly. "That's totally natural. This is definitely going to take some adjusting and your body is going to change obviously, but you'll do just fine. Wes and Marissa are going to be thrilled and they will be here throughout the whole thing to help you."

Sarah turned to face her. "That's fantastic. And no offense to Wes, but at a time like this, a woman needs her best friends. Whitney may not be available very much, but you'll help me through all of this, right?"

Jessica's heart stuck in her throat. Normally, Sarah wouldn't even need to ask. Of course she'd be there—emotionally, physically, whatever her best friend needed. But her conversation with her aunt made her hesitate. Nine months of pregnancy and then helping with the baby…all stuff she wanted to do, but it meant staying in Blue Moon Bay for at least a year. The offer from Not Just Desserts would have long expired by then.

And would Mitch's offer have expired by then, too?

But this was her best friend. She couldn't just abandon her.

She sighed inwardly. The timing wasn't great…or maybe it was just another sign that she couldn't give up her life, her bakery, her hometown for a man she'd only been falling in love with for a few weeks.

Sarah was staring at her expectantly. Fear and uncertainty in her eyes.

Jessica swallowed hard and forced a reassuring smile as she nodded. "Of course. You know I've got you."

Sarah's relief made her feel even worse. Could she keep her promise to her friend? Or was she secretly hoping that by the time she needed to make her own life decisions, Sarah would have stopped freaking out?

...

As his feet pounded the pavement, Mitch fought the feeling that he may have completely messed this up with Jessica, despite their conversation on the boat the night before. He had to have come across a little screwed up the day before with his complete meltdown in the dining room, and he'd probably also scared her off the whole idea of traveling overseas.

Truth was, the missions could be dangerous sometimes. Their work wasn't for the faint of heart or squeamish or people who liked stability and safety…

Damn, what the hell was he thinking even asking her to come along? It had been his own motivation and dreams talking. He'd gotten caught up in the moment and the idea of showing her the world. *His* world. It had excited him.

It had only put pressure on Jessica. Her life was here. He was selfish to think she should give it all up. For him.

He ran along the boardwalk, the loud music in his headphones not helping to drown out his overthinking. That day was his family's early Christmas dinner and he was starting to feel Jessica's pressure. Not because of his sister, but because of the fact that when he'd invited her, he'd been doing so under the pretense of having a friend—a hot, interesting, fun friend with benefits—come to dinner to make it more enjoyable for him.

But in a few weeks, things had changed. Feelings had developed. For both of them. Bringing her home to an important family event could be misunderstood or lead her on, or confuse things…

But damn, he wasn't even sure that was the case. Maybe he wanted something more, too. Maybe he wanted to be bringing her home for the holidays with his family because she meant a lot more to him than just friends with benefits or a distraction he'd needed to get through the season.

He couldn't quite define the feelings he had for her. He liked her more than any other woman he'd ever dated. She was by far the most attractive woman he'd ever met. She ticked all the right boxes that he'd look for in a potential partner...if he was looking. He missed her when they weren't together and he counted the seconds until he could see her again. That would be a lot of counting once he left again.

He had fun with her, but he'd also connected with her on a serious, vulnerable level the day before. Something he'd never have expected to happen. He liked who he was with her and he'd seen his hometown in a different light when experiencing it with her. It wasn't dull or boring when he was doing the everyday life things with her.

But would that last? Or was it the high of a new relationship that would fade in time?

He reached his father's clinic and he slowed his pace, struggling to steady his breath. The small white office building with his father's name on the faded awning held so many memories for him. As a kid, visiting his dad and Mrs. P at work had fostered his own dedication to helping others and his decision to go into medicine. He'd volunteered there as a teen, learning more from his dad than he had throughout his medical school training. His own broken bones had been set in the clinic. Most of the town's babies were born there.

The clinic meant a lot to so many people. The services it provided would definitely be missed. His dad's compassion and love of the community would be, too.

He sighed. Mitch had never planned to stay and live in Blue Moon Bay. But he hadn't planned on falling in love that holiday season, either.

CHAPTER TWENTY

This had to be an anxiety attack, because she was far too young to be having serious heart palpitations. Yet, she could certainly understand why people confused this feeling with an attack. Her palms were so sweaty her liquid eyeliner kept slipping out of her hand, and the sweat pooling on her skin made her too clammy to put her dress on yet. She'd applied press powder to her forehead three times already. Not her best makeup job.

Her hair in curlers and one eye made up, she stared at her reflection in the mirror. Could she really do this? Go to Mitch's family Christmas with him, come out to Lia that they'd been seeing one another and potentially cause family drama? For what? Was it really worth it?

All night, she'd tossed and turned. Sarah needed her here now for support with the pregnancy and the baby, and Whitney definitely needed her—she just hadn't figured out exactly what was going on there yet. Selling the bakery could potentially drive her aunt and Mrs. Barnett out of business. She was terrified about the idea of traveling overseas.

Although she'd been fooling herself into thinking otherwise, the obvious choice was to say no to Mitch's offer and enjoy the next few days with him. Not go to the family Christmas and ensure that the vibe between them remained casual and uncomplicated. It had been foolish to contemplate any other outcome.

So why was her heart twisting so much at the idea of doing what her head told her was the right thing? The practical thing.

Her aunt had advised her to follow her heart.

She sighed as she applied makeup to her other eye and slid red lipstick across her lips with a slightly trembling hand. She might bail on the overseas trip, but she'd told Mitch she'd go to his family's dinner that evening, and she wouldn't back out at the last minute.

She stepped into her dark green velvet long-sleeved dress and stood in front of her air conditioning unit as she stepped into her high heels.

Hearing Mitch's car pull into her driveway, she checked her reflection one last time before heading outside. He stood at the passenger side door waiting for her, and her heart felt like it might actually explode in her chest.

Dressed in dress pants and a red sweater that hugged him in all the right ways, his hair gelled to the side, his face cleanly shaven, and those damn sexy glasses on, he was absolutely killing her slowly. Only a few more days together. She'd do well to start putting a little distance between them, building up a wall to help the inevitable crumbling of her emotions, but she wasn't sure she wanted to. She'd never felt like this for anyone before and she wanted the feeling to last as long as possible.

He let out a low whistle as she approached, and she

forced a smile that didn't give away just how terrified she was. "You are stunning," he said, his gaze drifting over the dress and heels. "Far too beautiful to spend the evening with my family."

Panic set in again. "Oh my God, am I overdressed?"

"You're perfect," he said, leaning in for a kiss, but seeing the lipstick he paused. "Can I ruin that lipstick?"

She instantly felt a little better as she nodded. "I can reapply it in the car."

He pulled her into him and kissed her. It felt different somehow. It wasn't the soft, quick peck when they were in public or the intense passionate ones when they were completely alone. It was gentle, yet purposeful, as though trying to convey something he couldn't say with words.

She closed her eyes and savored it, really embracing every second they had left. Every touch, every kiss, every smile…it all meant so much more as they were coming to the end of those moments. They'd still talk and keep in touch, but it wouldn't be the same. Eventually, it would get too hard.

He moved away reluctantly and studied her. "Stop worrying. You know everyone there."

"That's part of the problem." Once he left, she would be the one still there garnering the sympathetic looks from his family and friends. She'd be the one answering their questions: How's Mitch? How are things between you two? When's he coming home next?

He kissed her once more before opening the door for her. She climbed in, and when he got in the driver's seat, she immediately reached for his hand. Sweaty palms or not she wasn't missing any opportunity to hold his hand.

They drove in silence, each lost in their own thoughts, the short distance to his family home. She'd been there so many times over the years when they were younger, but not in recent years. It still looked the same, and the over-the-top holiday decorations outside made her smile. "I love how your mom loves to decorate."

Mitch laughed. "Compliment her on her decorations and you'll have her adopting you as a second daughter." Then realizing what he'd said, a slight look of panic crossed his features.

Jessica squeezed his hand. "Don't worry, I didn't read anything into that." She reached for the doorhandle but he stopped her.

"It's okay if you did."

Damn. By the end of the day she might actually have a real heart attack.

"Why don't you reapply your lipstick and we will head inside."

Right, time to face everyone. It made her feel a bit better knowing that his mother knew she was coming. She hadn't told anyone else. Mitch said he suspected she wanted to keep it a secret for their sake. Respect their privacy. Jessica appreciated that, but her cowardly side might have appreciated Ally telling everyone in advance to save them from having to.

She took her time putting on the lipstick and then took a deep breath. "Okay. Ready."

He climbed out, opened her door for her, and held

her hand tight in his as they walked up the front steps and went inside. Holiday music played through the surround sound system in the house, and the Kenny and Dolly Christmas album warmed her. It was her all-time favorite holiday album, too.

"Is there an inch of space not decorated?" Jessica whispered as they entered the large, impressive foyer, her gaze falling to the collection of trees. A white one, a pink one, a green one, and a blue one—all different sizes, decorated with glass bulbs. "That's a lot of trees."

Mitch laughed. "There's a total of nine trees through-out the house."

Her eyes widened. "Nine?" She surveyed the garland on the staircase railing and admired the snow globe collection in the living room. She was stalling.

He turned to face her and placed his hands on her shoulders. "You ready?"

"No." She thought she might throw up.

"Me neither," he said, taking her hand in his and practically dragging her uncooperative legs toward the dining room, where the sounds of laughter and voices grew louder the closer they got.

Her heart echoed in her ears. This was it. Moment of truth.

Lia's laugh quickly faded as she saw them enter and her eyes immediately dropped to their joined hands.

Shit. Jessica tried to pull her hand out of Mitch's, but he held firm.

"This has nothing to do with her," he whispered. "It's you and me."

Damn, in any other situation those words would have her swooning. At that moment unfortunately, they didn't make Jessica feel the least bit better.

She felt like she'd betrayed her friend. Not because she was dating Mitch or falling for Mitch—the heart wanted what it wanted and she'd never regret the past few weeks or their growing connection—but the fact that she'd hid it from her. Instantly, she realized that was a mistake.

"Mitch! Jessica!" his mother said, noticing them. "Come on in." She hurried toward them and gave them both a one-armed hug as she balanced her wineglass in the other hand.

"Sorry we're late," Mitch said, kissing his mother's cheek.

"Nothing starts without you anyway," Ally told her son.

Lia shot an exasperated look at her mother as she slowly approached. "Mitch? Jess?" She glanced back and forth between them. Her perceptive lawyer gaze burning a hole in Jess's forehead as she made the connection. "You two are…?"

Mitch was nodding, so why was Jess shaking her head no? Must have been an instinctual defense mechanism.

Mitch nudged her and took a deep breath. "Yes. Jess and I are dating," he told his sister confidently.

Ally tensed, watching and waiting, and Mitch's father hung back, just outside the room. They were on their own for whatever Lia's reaction would be.

Jess stilled and waited for the attack, the anger, the disbelief. But Lia just stood there, staring at them in surprise…then she smiled?

Was she actually smiling or was Jess passed out cold on the Jamesons' floor from holding her breath so long?

"Oh my God, this is fantastic!" Lia said excitedly.

Jess's mouth dropped. "It is?"

Mitch squeezed her hand. "Yes, it is," he said teasingly, but she could hear relief in his tone as well. His shoulders had relaxed and a genuine smile had spread across his handsome face.

Jessica was still on edge, refusing to let her guard down so quickly. Lia approved? Hadn't she been the one to warn Jess that Mitch had a fear of commitment? That he didn't do so well with relationships? She cleared her throat. "You're okay with this?"

Lia folded her arms across her chest and forced a stern look. "The keeping it a secret part? No. But the fact that you two are together? Yes. I'm not a monster," she said, linking her arm through Jess's. Leaning closer, she whispered, "I've always wanted a sister, and now maybe I might have a chance at getting to know my brother."

Jess's eyes widened. Wow, that was suddenly a lot of pressure she hadn't been expecting. Maybe annoying Lia would have been easier.

"Drinks, you two?" his father asked, approaching with two wineglasses.

Drinks. Yes, good idea. The last thirty seconds had been one hell of a rollercoaster of emotions.

"Thanks, Dad," Mitch said, accepting them and handing one to her.

"Welcome, Jessica, it's so nice to have you here this year," the older man said, and she heard the meaning in his voice. Her being there was helping their son enjoy the season.

And obviously Lia was seeing her brother's new connection as a good sign as well. That maybe he was starting to be ready to settle down...be more committed to family?

"Thank you, Dr. Jameson." It took all her concentration and energy to keep her hand steady and not spill the dark red liquid, as the unexpected weight of the family's expectations combined with her own hopes about the future of their relationship.

"So, we thought we'd start with the most fun part — the gifts!" Ally said, clapping her hands together in excitement. Her flushed cheeks and sparkling eyes made her look so much younger.

But Jessica's heart stopped for a quick second. Gifts. Mitch hadn't said anything about gifts. Though she must be the dumbest person on the planet not to have thought to bring any. In her nervousness, she'd even forgotten the bottle of wine she'd meant to bring.

Mitch squeezed her hand and lowered his voice to a whisper. "Don't worry. I put 'from Mitch and Jessica' on all of mine."

Oh God! Now she was sure to melt into a big lovesick puddle. A man actually putting her name with his on presents for his family? How many holidays had she longed for joint gift-giving with a man in a steady, committed relationship? Mitch had practically just sealed the deal on her feelings for him.

In the living room, Ally sat next to the Christmas tree to hand out the gifts, and Jessica took a seat next to Mitch on the sofa. She took a deep, calming breath and sank into him, into this experience, into these overwhelming feelings. For the first year in a long time, she was celebrating Christmas with a man she adored and his amazing family.

As she watched them exchange gifts and thankfully accepted a beautiful hand-knit scarf and mitten set from his parents, her chest filled with happiness. Lia accepted them. His parents accepted them. Everything was perfect.

"I think that's the last of them," Ally said from somewhere buried beneath a large pile of discarded wrapping paper.

"I actually have one for Jess," Mitch said, turning on the seat to face her.

Her eyes widened. "I thought we were exchanging gifts on Christmas Eve?" They'd discussed spending that last night together and exchanging presents then. She hadn't brought one for him.

"This one was time-sensitive," he said, handing her an envelope with her name on it.

With his entire family watching in anticipation, she took it and opened it slowly, glancing up at him nervously. She still hadn't made up her mind about going overseas with him. She was still confused and conflicted, so she hoped this wasn't a plane ticket...

Instead, she found a hotel confirmation slip inside and frowned as she read it. Her gaze shot up to his. "Mountain Top Resort in Big Bear?"

"A reservation for three nights. We leave tomorrow morning. What do you say, Jess? Take that road trip with me?"

Take a road trip with him? Not a life-changing journey overseas, but a three-day vacation in a winter wonderland with a man she was falling in love with. How could she possibly say no to that?

"Yes! Of course she'll go!" Lia said in her prolonged silence.

Mitch shot his sister a look and Jess laughed, feeling tears burning the back of her eyes. "Yes. What Lia said," she said, taking Mitch's hand in hers.

He breathed a sigh of relief as he pulled her in closer and held her tight. His mother turned on the holiday music, and his father lit a fire. Across from them, Lia and Malcolm looked blissfully content as Lia examined the beautiful bracelet her husband had given her.

Jess smiled as she observed the family scene around her, feeling as though her heart might explode out of her chest. Not only was she falling hard and fast for Mitch, but the acceptance from his family, especially Lia, was the best Christmas gift ever. No more hiding anything from anyone. Including each other.

Maybe this trip to the mountains would be the perfect opportunity to tell him exactly how she felt.

CHAPTER TWENTY-ONE

DECEMBER 21ST...4 DAYS UNTIL CHRISTMAS...

Parked in Jessica's driveway the next morning, Mitch was sweating despite the mid-December chill in the air.

When was the last time he'd gone on a vacation with a woman? His overseas trips didn't count. This one was all about relaxing, enjoying the holidays, connecting on an even deeper level.

He didn't regret asking her. Not one little bit. But he knew this trip could change things, and he wasn't sure he was ready for what those changes might be.

When she exited her house, her overnight bag in hand, his heart raced for a completely different reason. Dressed in jeans, low-cut leather winter boots, and a thick cable-knit sweater, her new red winter jacket over her arm, he suddenly couldn't wait to get to the mountains. He just hoped he'd have the strength to pull himself away from the lodge to actually enjoy the outdoor activities. Knowing their time together was getting shorter each day had him craving every second of touching, kissing, holding her...

Climbing out of the vehicle, he met her on her step and took the bag. He leaned in to kiss her cheek, and she wrapped her arms around his neck, drawing him closer for a more passionate kiss.

He closed his eyes and suppressed a moan as she sunk into him. She tasted like cinnamon-flavored lip gloss, and her kiss held all the passion he felt surging within himself. She reluctantly pulled away. "I missed you," she said softly.

He swallowed hard. He'd missed her, too, and it had only been twelve hours since he'd dropped her off after early Christmas dinner with his family. How was he going to survive the next trip overseas? "Well, we have three full days and nights together," he said, taking her hand and heading toward the car.

He opened the door for her, then put her bag in the back next to his. Seeing the two bags together created an involuntary tug at his chest.

Man, he needed to pull it together. Otherwise, it was going to be impossible to leave his hometown in a few days.

• • •

"Snow! It's snowing!" She must sound like a four-year-old, but she didn't care. She couldn't remember ever being this excited over the weather, but as she sat staring out at the big, soft-looking flakes falling outside the window, her eyes widened. The beautiful scenery of the snow-capped mountains in the distance was breathtaking.

Mitch laughed as he squeezed her hand quickly, then resumed gripping the wheel on the slightly slippery roads. "This is really the first time you've seen snow?"

"Yes." She sat back in the seat and glanced at him. "I always talked about making this trip someday, but Christmas being one of my busiest seasons, I never did." She didn't add that a romantic, Christmas trip to the mountains wouldn't have been as magical alone. She'd only ever spent one holiday season with a significant other, and the relationship hadn't lasted long after the new year. "I'm happy that I waited," she said.

Taking this trip with him made it that much more special.

"Me too," he said, glancing at her quickly before turning his attention back to the road.

They drove in comfortable silence up the rest of the mountainside, and when he pulled into the lodge's valet parking area, her pulse raced. Three full nights together. All night.

This was going to be a whole new level of intimacy. One she hadn't shared with someone in a very long time. But she was more than ready to take this next step with Mitch. She wouldn't think about what it meant or where the relationship was headed beyond the next few days.

She'd focus on the moment and this incredible time together.

"This place is amazing," she said as they climbed out of the vehicle. She shivered in the cool mountain breeze, then laughed. "That wind might take a little getting used to."

Mitch handed the keys to the valet and wrapped an arm around her as they headed into the resort. "Don't worry. I have plenty of ways to keep you warm," he whispered into her ear, and she shivered again for a different reason altogether.

Ten minutes later, the ride in the elevator to the third floor felt like an eternity, and when she stepped inside the luxury suite he'd booked for them, any hesitation or apprehension she'd been holding onto evaporated.

The rustic yet posh five-star accommodation was something she'd only ever seen in travel magazines. Dark, open-beam interiors with a loft-style bedroom, a large jacuzzi tub near the ceiling-to-floor windows overlooking the snow-covered mountains. A seating area with plush off-white leather chairs and a bird's nest for cuddling near a stonework fireplace that was already blazing.

An ice bucket with champagne sat on the small two-seat table next to a plate of chocolate-covered strawberries.

"What do you think?" Mitch asked, closing the door behind them and wrapping his arms around her waist. He buried his head into the crook of her neck and kissed softly.

Jessica sighed in complete contentment. "I think you may want to cancel all of those activities you planned, because I'm not sure I want to leave this room." She turned within his embrace and wrapped her arms around his neck. Standing on tiptoes, she kissed him.

He gripped her tighter and held her close. "I think I'm completely okay with that."

• • •

Turned out, Jessica was a natural on the slopes. Despite their claim of not wanting to leave the room, they did eventually venture outside onto the ski hills, and Mitch was having the best time watching Jess experience all that northern California had to offer. She'd stepped out of her comfort zone to join him on the road trip, and she seemed to be enjoying every minute of it.

Snow blew up around him as Mitch weaved his way down the side of the snow-covered mountain. The sun reflected against the surface and the wind cooled him as he made his way to the base of the hill. He hadn't skied in years, and he'd forgotten how much he enjoyed it.

Of course, the day was even more fun because he was there with Jess. Experiencing this with her. He couldn't believe they'd only been seeing each other a few weeks. It felt like much longer. Early Christmas with his family and their open acceptance of her had only further solidified his feelings. Contrary to his claim, he was definitely falling in love that holiday season.

If only he knew what to do about it.

He rotated his hips and slowly came to a stop near the lodge, then turned to see Jess not too far behind.

"Again?" she asked, stopping at the base of the mountain, her cheeks flushed from the cool air.

Dressed in a form-fitting pale pink ski suit and matching hat and gloves, her dark hair in a loose braid over one shoulder, and dark ski glasses on, she looked like a pro and so incredibly beautiful, she'd been a major distraction to him on the hills that day. He'd barely been able to take his eyes off her.

He pulled her in for a quick kiss, then checked his watch. "I think there's time for two more runs, but then we need to get ready for dinner." The night before, they'd ordered room service and ate in bed naked, and while that had been the highlight of...well, probably his entire life, he wanted to take her out that evening. Blue Moon Bay had nice restaurants, but the view from the steakhouse in town couldn't be beat.

He wanted to make this trip as memorable for her as possible. Show her how amazing life could be outside of their small hometown. With him. Of course, this was just a short vacation, not too far from home, but it was the first step to potentially opening her horizons.

"Race?" she asked, a fun note of challenge in her voice.

"You think you can take me?"

"I know I can take you," she said, leaning toward him for another quick kiss.

And she had no idea just how right she was.

They headed toward the chair lift, but an out-of-control skier to their right caught his attention. A small kid was sailing down the steep mountainside and not slowing his pace as he neared the bottom. His ski poles were flailing at his sides, and Mitch could see the look of fear and panic on the kid's face even from that distance.

He headed toward him, no real plan in mind, just on instinct as the kid lost his balance and crashed down against the slope. He started to tumble, his skis coming overhead and his body hitting hard as he continued down the mountainside. He finally came to a stop several feet from the base of the mountain and lay motionless on the snow.

Mitch's heart raced as he unclicked his skis and ran across the snow-covered slope to kneel next to the child dressed in a blue ski suit and matching helmet. "I'm a doctor," he said, staring into the child's face for any sign of consciousness. He was awake, but barely, and his expression contorted in a grimace of pain as he moaned. He might be eight or nine years old and definitely too small to be skiing the bigger hills.

Jessica was suddenly next to him, a concerned expression on her face as she flagged down the emergency services on sight. "Hey! Help!"

Ski patrol was instantly on the move, grabbing their first aid kit and a litter as they approached. They were trained to deal with emergencies on the slopes, he should let them handle it. Still...

Mitch moved closer to the injured child. "Hello... Hey there, can you tell me your name."

The child blinked, tears freezing on his eyelids. "Dy... Dylan..." He sounded frightened and in shock.

"Hi, Dylan. I'm Mitch and this"—he motioned Jess forward—"is Jess."

"My leg..." the kid said, wincing.

Mitch's stomach turned at the sight of the twisted limb bent underneath the child in an unnatural angle. Definitely broken. "Do you have any pain anywhere else?"

Dylan shook his head.

"What can I do?" Jess asked, kneeling on the snow

next to them.

"Hold his hand, maybe… Just provide comfort." He quickly examined the child for signs of other injuries. He was conscious and there wasn't any sign of concussion. No obvious fractures anywhere else.

Jess took the child's hand between hers as he studied the leg and sighed. He glanced toward Ski Patrol, who were still making their way toward them, at least a few minutes away. "I'm going to straighten the leg." They wouldn't be able to get the child onto the litter like this. And he wasn't confident leaving this up to the mountain emergency team. He'd done this a million times. Better to act quickly before the injury had time to swell even more.

Dylan's eyes widened in fear. "Is it going to hurt?"

"A little." He was honest. The child needed to be prepared for the pain. "I'll make it quick and in a minute it will all be over," he said. He turned to Jess. "Can you support his upper body and try holding him still?"

She looked nervous as hell, but she maneuvered herself into a better position to support the child.

"You okay?" he asked her. She looked slightly pale, the color having drained from her cheeks. Not everyone did well in an emergency situation. He didn't need her passing out on him as well.

But she nodded confidently as she cradled the boy's upper body and held tight. She leaned closer to offer soothing words, and Mitch's heart lurched in his chest at the sight. Jess was caring and compassionate, and in these situations, that went a lot further than anyone realized. Calming the patient, helping keep their heart rate low, was crucial.

Ski Patrol stopped next to him and he quickly explained his position and intent. They didn't argue, visibly relieved to have a more advanced medical team member for assistance. They moved back to give him space and held back the crowd that was gathering around.

"Are the parents here?" he asked.

"No one's stepping forward yet," one of the Ski Patrol members said, scanning the crowd.

Mitch glanced at Dylan. "Ready?"

The child nodded quickly, then buried his head into Jess.

Mitch glanced at her and she nodded. He took a deep breath and carefully gripped the child's wounded leg. Another deep breath later the leg was straight. Dylan let out a yelp and clung to Jess, but relief spread across his features as he opened his eyes.

"Oh my God! He wasn't supposed to be on this hill," a woman's anguished voice said as she approached.

Obviously the mother. She was followed by two smaller children who looked just as worried. Mitch stood and turned to her. "It's okay. He's okay. A broken leg for sure, but I think he's through the worst of it." He'd need to be brought in to the medical clinic in town for further examination, but the child hadn't complained of any other pain and his quick assessment hadn't revealed anything else of immediate concern. "He was lucky to be wearing a helmet," he said.

She looked appreciative at the kind reassurance. "I

only left him for five minutes to take these two to the restroom." She looked distraught as she approached her oldest child, now on the litter, being attended to by Ski Patrol.

Mitch suspected snowsuits and five-year-olds took a lot longer than five minutes, but he sympathized with her. Children didn't always listen and, left unattended, they could get into trouble. "He's going to be okay."

She smiled tearfully down at her son and sent Mitch a grateful look. "Thank you."

"You're welcome," he said, aware of Jessica's gaze on him.

They left the boy with emergency services, and Mitch forced several deep breaths as they headed back toward the lodge. The boy was lucky. With the speed he'd been traveling down the slope, things could have been much worse.

"That was incredible," Jess said when they stopped, a look of admiration and respect reflecting in her gorgeous eyes. "*You* were incredible."

He turned toward her and took her face between his hands. "Believe me when I say this—what you did, your part in that, was the part that mattered most."

• • •

That night she was going to tell him she'd go to Cambodia with him.

Her hand shook as Jess curled her hair in the hotel room bathroom hours later, getting ready for dinner.

That day had been exhilarating, and seeing Mitch in action with the injured kid had opened her eyes to another side of him. A quick-thinking, resourceful, confident side.

One that was impossible to resist.

She'd been so nervous out there on the mountainside, but she'd been more intent on helping, on playing a part, and the high from helping the child was unlike any other she'd ever experienced. She wanted to take this plunge. Go on this new life adventure with him. It meant making big changes, possibly disappointing people she cared about in the process, but this was her life to live and she knew what she wanted. She'd regret it if she didn't at least try.

She swallowed hard as she set the curler down and applied a thin coat of pale gloss to her lips. No sense taking the time to put on real lipstick. Mitch would kiss it off within minutes anyway.

She hoped the restaurant had a nice, romantic, secluded booth where they could get wrapped up in each other. She smiled at her reflection, feeling happier and lighter than she had in weeks. Her decision had been made, and she was excited to tell Mitch.

There were also those three little words she wanted to say.

She was in love with him. There was no denying it. The emotions she felt for him were unlike any she'd ever had for anyone. Mitch made her happy, they connected physically and emotionally. Her heart raced when she was near him, but there was also a sense of peace and calm, as though she could rest easy in his arms, knowing he'd never hurt her.

It was fast the way these feelings had come on, but she knew they were real. And she suspected he was feeling the same. Either way, she wanted him to know where she stood.

Her cell phone ringing in the pocket of her dress made her jump. Still smiling, she retrieved it and answered the unknown number on the second ring. "Hello?"

"Jessica Connolly?" an unfamiliar voice spoke clear and sharp.

"Yes, speaking."

"There's been an accident."

The cell phone nearly slipped from her hand. Aunt Frankie? Her parents?

"Your friend Whitney Carlisle is here in the hospital," the woman continued. "You are listed as her emergency contact."

Still? She had been for years, since Whitney's mother had gotten ill, but Jess had assumed Whitney would have changed it to Trent by now.

"Hello?" the woman said.

"I'm here," she croaked.

"We need you here right away."

Her knees nearly collapsed beneath her as she nodded. "I understand."

"Ms. Connolly?"

"Yes?"

"Your friend is in bad condition," she said more

gently, which made everything a million times worse. "Can you get here soon?"

Jessica's heart pounded in her ears and her mouth was bone dry. Three hours away. "I'm out of town, but I'll be there as soon as I can," she managed to say.

After providing the nurse Trent and Sarah's numbers, she disconnected the call and tears of fear gathered in her eyes. She opened the bathroom door to Mitch.

His happy expression faded fast, seeing her expression. "What's wrong?"

Her body trembled as she stepped quickly out of the bathroom and reached for her bag to pack. "We have to go. Whitney's been in an accident."

CHAPTER TWENTY-TWO

DECEMBER 22ND...3 DAYS UNTIL CHRISTMAS...

Her mother always said daylight made things better.

But as Whitney opened her eyes and a look of confusion mixed with fear registered on her friend's bruised, bandaged face, Jessica couldn't agree. The hospital room's bright lights and the beeping of a monitor had made her nauseous all night, sitting in the hospital chair near the bed, while her friend was in an induced coma. In her hand was an IV and she had a cast on her right leg, another one on her left wrist. Her breathing sounded labored all night and Jessica had teared up more than once as she'd stayed awake by her side.

"Hi... Look who's finally awake," she said gently. Quietly.

Sarah stirred in the chair on the opposite side of the bed, where her exhaustion had finally taken over about an hour ago. Raccoon-eyed from smudged mascara, she sat up seeing Whitney awake.

"Jess. Sarah." Whitney cleared her throat, but it sounded raw and dry, as though she hadn't drank anything in a long time. She moved her head back and forth between them, but then she shut her eyes tight as though the motion had made her dizzy.

"Just relax…you've been out for a while. The doctors said it might take a little while to fully regain consciousness," Jessica said.

"Fully regain consciousness? What time is it?"

The sunlight gleaming through the open blinds of the hospital room window suggested it had to be morning, but Jessica had lost the concept of time. Mitch had driven as quickly as possible and she'd arrived at the hospital just before ten p.m. the evening before.

"It's ten a.m.," Sarah said, moving closer to the bed.

Whitney's eyes widened. "What happened?"

"We were hoping you could tell us," Jessica said. The paramedics said police had been called to the scene about five minutes away from Rejuvenation Seniors Center where Whitney's mother was living under medical supervision for her Alzheimer's. Her Miata had gone off the windy road and over the embankment. It had flipped and Whitney had been unconscious when they found her.

"The last thing I remember is visiting Mom, then driving along the coast away from Rejuvenation. My vision went blurry…my eyes had closed, but just for a second," she said quickly. "Then the vehicle was spinning…then falling. As the car hit the guardrail, I thought for sure I was going to die."

Her friend had fallen asleep at the wheel. All the overtime and stress had obviously caught up to her.

She shut her eyes tight, then they snapped open again. "Mayor Rodale…work. I have a meeting scheduled today. I can't be lying in this hospital bed."

"We already called and told her you wouldn't be there this week," Sarah said.

"This week?" She shook her head. "No, I can't be in the hospital that long. My injuries can't be that severe. What did the doctors say?"

"They said you need to rest," Jessica said. "So, stop worrying about work right now and just take it easy."

"What are my injuries?"

"You broke your right leg, left wrist, fractured three ribs on the left side and your right collarbone. You have a concussion," Jessica said.

Whitney looked like she didn't believe her. "I can't feel any of that."

"A small silver lining," Sarah said. "It's the pain meds."

Whitney slumped back against the pillows, looking more concerned about being trapped in the hospital bed than about actually recovering, and Jessica wanted to shake some sense into her. She'd given them all a fright. Trent was away in Boston on a trip to visit a brewery, but he was on a flight back now. Her cousin must be going out of his mind. She wished there was a way to update him.

"How's my car?" Whitney asked, wincing.

"You'll need a new one," Sarah said. "Preferably one that handles better on slippery roads."

"Trent's on his way back from Boston and the nurses called your mom…but she…" Jessica's voice trailed and she cleared his throat. Fresh tears threatened. Whitney's mother was battling her own illness. Whitney couldn't rely on her for support through this. She'd need her friends, though.

"Yeah, that's fine. I'll explain all of this to her some-how eventually."

"Jess and I will go see her while you're recovering, so don't worry about that. We've already confirmed it with the staff at Rejuvenation," Sarah said.

"Thank you," she said. "Did I snore?" she asked, smiling weakly.

Sarah smiled, sitting on the edge of the bed and covering Whitney's hand. "Yes. Yes, you did. I'd forgotten how horrible you are to sleep with," she said.

"Hey, before you turn back into Wonder Woman and jump out of this hospital bed in record time, we need to chat," Jessica said.

"The accident was my fault," Whitney said. "I fell asleep. I've been really tired lately and honestly, I'm more embarrassed than anything for having put you both out like this."

"You can cut the bullshit anytime now, because it's actually insulting."

Her mouth gaped. "Sorry, I…"

"First, you are not putting us out. We are your best friends. You have the biggest heart of anyone I know, even though you try to act tough, as though things don't affect you like they affect everyone else. You almost died last night, so this brave act you're faking right now, you can stop. I'm not buying it anymore, Whitney." Jessica gestured toward Sarah. "*We're* not buying it. You're working too hard and it's killing you. It almost did kill you."

Sarah nodded her agreement. "You are human, Whitney, and you're allowed to be stressed out and overwhelmed and have moments when you just can't keep going. It's okay. And I promise, your secret's safe with us."

A tear slid down Whitney's cheek and her shoulders sagged, the dark circles under her eyes even darker against her pale complexion. "I know what you're saying is true, but Sarah, I don't know how to slow down. And life is so busy with work, my mom, and Trent pressuring me about marriage and kids…"

Pressuring. The word hadn't gone unnoticed.

Whitney sighed. "Not pressuring me, but just expecting answers and decisions and right now my focus is elsewhere."

Sarah's voice softened. "I'm not saying you should quit your job or forget your responsibilities, but just recognize that if you need to take a moment to just breathe, it's okay to do it."

"Thank you. I appreciate you both being here for me last night, and now…"

"And every day since we were six years old and every day going forward until we're in adult diapers," Jessica said, reaching out to wipe the tear from Whitney's cheek.

"We're not leaving your side until you are out of this hospital bed," Sarah said.

Whitney shook her head. "You can't keep sleeping here. You have your own lives, your own businesses to think about."

"Sure we can. We'll buy earplugs, right Jess?" Sarah

said, hugging her tight.

Jessica nodded. "Absolutely." She wanted to be there for her friend just as much as Sarah did. Not just that day, either. Obviously, Whitney was struggling and going through some things and hadn't wanted to reach out for help. She'd pushed herself to a breaking point and Jessica needed to be there for her. Just like she'd made a promise to be there for Sarah.

What had she been thinking to believe she could actually leave Blue Moon Bay, her career, her friends, her responsibilities? Weight of that reality settled on her shoulders, bringing her back down to earth.

Whitney's eyes widened as she turned to Jessica. "Oh my God. Did my accident interrupt your road trip with Mitch?"

"It's okay." Suddenly, she wasn't so sure if things were okay. The drive back to Blue Moon Bay had been silently tense as she'd been filled with worry. He'd been there for her, holding her hand, but she'd sensed he knew this had changed things. She'd been wanting to tell him she loved him, but the moment definitely hadn't been right after receiving the heart-stopping news about her friend.

He'd texted that morning to ask if she needed anything and how Whitney was, but that was their last contact. Right now, this was where she needed to be and she couldn't focus on Mitch. Or what happened next.

Or more realistically, what didn't happen.

• • •

JENNIFER SNOW   267

"Are Jess and Sarah still at the hospital?" Lia asked as Mitch entered the B&B. She and Malcolm were packed and waiting for him to drive them back to LAX for their flight to Napa that day.

"Yes. I just brought coffee to them. I couldn't see them because they were in with Whitney and her doctor, but she's awake," he said.

His sister's shoulders sagged in relief. "Good. That's good. Did Jess say how she's doing? What the injuries were?"

"Lots of broken bones and a concussion. I guess she fell asleep at the wheel after visiting her mother in a senior home." He took a gulp of his coffee. He hadn't gotten any sleep after dropping Jessica off at the hospital the night before. He'd stayed in the waiting room for a while, but then when it was apparent that she was needed by the other woman's side, he'd reluctantly headed back to his family's house. Though the mood there had definitely turned somber as they all worried about Whitney.

"I'm happy Sarah and Jessica are with her. With Trent away..." Lia's voice trailed.

Mitch nodded, draining the contents of his cup and immediately craving more caffeine. "Yeah, I've never seen two next of kin guard dogs quite like your friends."

Lia hesitated. "They're your friends, too. In fact, I think you might be a little closer to one of them in particular." She studied him closely, and he knew it was about the relationship.

"About that...I'm sorry I didn't tell you. I just didn't

know where it was going and we knew it might upset you."

She gave a weary sigh. "Your life is your business, and from the short time I saw you two together, there definitely seemed to be a genuine connection. I've never seen you so caught up in a woman before, and I hate to think that you both thought I'd be an asshole about it."

"Thank you," he said, collapsing into an armchair in the foyer. His sister's words meant a lot, but it didn't help to clarify the conflict in his heart and mind. Jessica hadn't yet said whether or not she planned on accepting the offer from Not Just Desserts and coming overseas, but his gut told him she wouldn't. Not now. And he had to accept that.

He did accept that, even if for a brief moment he'd allowed himself to get his hopes up. When she'd assisted him with the injured child, there had been a moment where he'd thought she, too, could see how exhilarating and rewarding a life traveling and doing good for others in need could be.

But she was already doing that by being here with her friends who also needed her.

Lia sat across from him. "But as Jess's friend and your sister, someone truly invested in this relationship, I need to ask—where is it leading? Was this just a holiday fling for you? Or is it something more?"

Mitch removed his baseball hat, ran a hand through his disheveled hair, and put it back on before answering. "It's definitely something more."

She studied him. "But?

"But you said yourself—I don't do well with relationships. Settling down somewhere wasn't in my plans yet. Settling down here was never the intent."

"Hate to break it to you, brother, but life doesn't give a shit about your plans. Things happen when you're not expecting them. Are you willing to trust in these feelings you have for Jess or are you determined to see through your own path?"

"I honestly don't know. I really care about her, but life here…"

She nodded. "I get it. I love it here, but the pace would kill me. New York gets me, just like traveling overseas is your calling. You're doing amazing work, Mitch, and Jess sees the great heart in you—that's why she's falling for you. And I think you see a little of the stability you're lacking in her. It makes sense."

He laughed. "You should have been a therapist."

She shook her head as she reached across and touched his knee. "I enjoy arguing too much," she said with a laugh. "Anyway, I know you'll do the right thing."

He wished he was as sure of that as she sounded. But he didn't even know for sure what the right thing was. "Thanks for the talk, sis," he said, meaning it. A heart to heart with his sister was long overdue and he hoped there were more in their future.

Malcolm descended the stairs and Lia stood. "Well, if you do decide that Jess is The One, let me know and I'll let you in on a little secret."

CHAPTER TWENTY-THREE

Knock. Knock.

Jessica glanced up from the magazine she was reading in the chair next to Whitney's bed, and her heart raced at the sight of Mitch standing in the hospital room doorway. Dressed in jeans, a hoodie, and a baseball hat, he was both a sight for sore eyes and a tear straight through her heart. He was leaving the next morning at three a.m. They only had twelve hours left together.

"Hi, come in," Jessica said, standing and straightening her sweater.

"Is she actually working from her hospital bed?" he asked, nodding toward a much better-looking Whitney who had her laptop on her lap, on which she was typing with her one good hand, and her cell phone pressed between her shoulder and ear.

"She is, but she's limited to three hours a day. Doctor's orders," Jessica said, shooting her friend a pointed look that said her time was almost up.

"Trent here yet?" Mitch asked.

"He should be any minute." They'd been switching off hospital duty with Whitney for the last several days, each taking a shift so she didn't have to be alone.

It was making the bed-ridden woman a little cranky,

but she was being released that evening to be home for Christmas. Whitney covered the mouthpiece on her cell phone. "You can go. Y'all are pissing me off being here twenty-four seven," she hissed.

Jessica laughed. "She's really appreciative," she told Mitch sarcastically, grateful for the moment to break the tension surrounding her all day, knowing she'd have to tell Mitch that she wouldn't be going away with him. She couldn't leave Blue Moon Bay for six months when she was needed there. Her decision not to sell the bakery had become a much easier one to make, knowing Whitney and Sarah both needed her right now.

Mitch smiled at her, the expression in his dark eyes unreadable. Longing and apprehension…remorse? Only that they didn't have much time left together. He was flying out that evening. The last few days she'd barely seen him—only when he'd stop by the hospital with food or coffee for her and Sarah. It wasn't enough. They needed more time. They needed more talking and kissing and other things they hadn't gotten a chance to do in the mountains…

"Hey, seriously, you two, get out of here. You don't want to spend your last few hours in Blue Moon Bay with me," Whitney told Mitch, before returning her attention to her call.

"I can't imagine why not. She's so delightful," Mitch said with a grin as Trent entered the hospital room.

"Hey! Sorry I'm late. Hectic day at the bar, being Christmas Eve," Trent said, rushing forward to give

Whitney a hug. He checked his watch and took her laptop away.

She went to argue, but when he reached for the phone, she clutched it tight. "Two more minutes," she said.

Trent turned to Jessica and Mitch. "Thanks for hanging out. You two have anything special planned for tonight?"

Jessica swallowed hard. Did they? Part of her wanted to go back to the inn with him and make love and snuggle until he had to leave. The other part wanted to try to preserve any piece of her heart she could still salvage and walk away that evening before she fell apart in front of him.

"I had some thoughts…" Mitch said, avoiding Trent's gaze.

He did? Well, she'd let him take the lead, then. Her heart and mind were too conflicted to be trusted to make wise decisions anyway. Jessica hugged Whitney quickly. "I'll see you tomorrow for Christmas at Frankie's." She was happy her friend wouldn't be spending the holidays in the hospital. "Bye, Trent."

"Safe travels, man," Trent said to Mitch.

Leaving the hospital room, Mitch took her hand in his. It felt so natural. So right. As though they'd been holding hands forever. She almost couldn't remember what her life was like three weeks ago.

Three weeks.

Was that really enough time to fall in love with somebody, or was this just lust?

No one had ever made her feel the way he did, and the thought of him boarding a plane in a few hours without knowing she'd be boarding her own in a few weeks to meet him overseas made her chest hurt.

They walked in silence to his rental car and he opened the door for her to climb in. She watched as he passed in front of the car to the driver's side, the tension causing her shoulders to ache. She had to tell him now.

"Mitch…" she started as he climbed in behind the wheel.

He turned to face her, pulling her closer. "Shhh…it's okay. You need to be here. Your friends need you."

She searched his expression. But did *he* need her? She couldn't go with him, but she still wanted him to want her to.

Needed that.

"Believe me, I want to be selfish. I want to drag you all over the world with me, but I want you to fall in love with me, so I can't be that guy," he said with a sad laugh.

She cupped his face in her hands. This intense desire to be near him, hold him, kiss him, plan a future with him had to be love. "I am falling for you, Mitch. Hard," she said, kissing him softly. She could never get enough of those lips. How would she survive without them?

"I'm so glad you said that. I was afraid maybe I was moving too fast, thinking this was something it wasn't," he said.

She rested her forehead against his. "It's real."

Adrenaline ran through her body from her fingertips

to her toes. She wanted to get as much physical close-
ness as possible in the time they had left, even though
she knew it would ultimately be harder to let him go.

He cleared his throat. "I'd like to spend my last
twelve hours here with you. Will you come back to the
inn with me?"

She hesitated, biting her lip. Saying goodbye to him
would be torture whether she did it now or at three
o'clock in the morning, and she wasn't ready to yet, so
she nodded. "Yes."

He drove slightly above the speed limit the entire
way and then, taking her hand, they entered the inn and
made their way up the guest staircase to his room.

He unlocked the door and inside, he reached for her,
pulling her closer to remove her sweater. He carefully
draped it over the back of the armchair in the room,
then continued to slowly, quietly remove all of her
clothing. Then his own.

Emotions strangled her as they lay side by side on
the bed, and he wrapped his arms tight around her body.
This was the only place she wanted to be that Christmas
Eve. "Is this okay? Not too much?" he whispered into
her hair.

"It's not enough," she said, smiling sadly. She wouldn't
worry about the future. Right now, this moment with
him was all that she had and she'd take it.

He slid his hands into her hair and stared deep into
her eyes, his own desperate uncertainty mirroring her
own. He brought his lips to hers and kissed her long and
soft, holding her face close as though afraid she'd stop

kissing him. Holding on tight like he was afraid to let go, like he wanted to disappear into the kiss so that he wouldn't have to say goodbye.

Within hours, the sun would chase away the moon and they'd be facing a new day. One without each other.

She lay back and pulled him on top of her, wanting and needing him more than ever before. Trusting in the feel of their bodies together, she let go of preserving any remaining pieces of her heart and gave it all to him, quietly, passionately, deeply…until there was nothing left.

He pulled back slightly and brushed her hair away from her face. He stared into her eyes, searching, longing for something she wasn't sure how to give him. "I'll miss you, Jess, and I haven't had someone to miss in a very long time. It's going to make this mission a lot harder."

"I'll be here when you get back," she said. Home, where she belonged, even if her heart was across the world with him.

• • •

Sometime hours later, in the darkness of the room, she felt the bedsprings shift and Mitch's soft breath against her bare shoulder. His lips were soft, gently pressed against her skin as they lingered for a long beat. She heard him struggle with a decision he'd already made as his hesitation was thick in the air around them.

She couldn't, wouldn't ask him to stay. Tears burned

the back of her tightly closed eyes, and she steadied her breathing to control her spiraling emotions.

"Merry Christmas, Jess," he whispered as he moved away, and then she heard the distinct sound of him walking to the door.

She kept her eyes closed. They'd already said the best version of goodbye either of them was capable of. So she pretended to be asleep as he slipped out of the room and back out of her life.

• • •

Once he was on a plane, he'd be fine.

This wasn't the first Christmas Eve he'd spent in an airport. The last five years he hadn't even celebrated or acknowledged the holidays, so why was the thought of being on a plane, getting farther and farther away from eggnog and Christmas-shaped cookies and the big evergreen tree in the inn's foyer making him depressed as hell?

Deboarding the plane three weeks ago, his entire body had been filled with dread, his head was a mess, and his chest had been filled with a thick fog of anxiety that had threatened to destroy him. Similar emotions overwhelmed him now.

Leaving Jessica in the middle of the night while she slept had to be the hardest thing he'd ever done. Lying there next to her in the dark, he'd gone back and forth a million times about what it was he really wanted. Three weeks with her had left him questioning everything.

He ran a hand through his hair as he slumped into an empty seat at the nearly empty boarding gate. He was more rested and regrouped for this trip than he'd been for any other in a long time, yet he was also more on edge. He was eager to get back to work, but this time he was also going to miss something here. Badly.

He stretched his legs out in front of him and set his suitcase down on the floor. Across from him, a young family—mother, father, and two small kids—huddled around a cell phone.

"Delayed again," the father said, looking exhausted. "We know… We will be there soon."

"Under the Christmas tree on Christmas morning like the best gifts you are," he heard a friendly older female voice say on the other side of the connection.

The kids blew kisses as they disconnected.

Mitch glanced away. Other people were trying to get home to be with loved ones for the holidays. Other people needed those important connections in their lives. Cherished them. Mitch loved his family, but he'd never felt that pure need to be surrounded by their love. He was always okay on his own, among strange faces in strange places. He'd found his comfort in the unfamiliar. No ties, no attachments, no obligations.

That wasn't the case anymore.

Maybe he'd just never before found someone who'd wedged themselves into his soul so deeply and completely. Until Jess.

He sighed as he checked the time on his phone. Six a.m. She'd probably be waking up now to go spend the day with Trent and her aunt's family like she did every year. He could call or text…

He stared at her picture on his phone as the boarding announcement was made for pre-boarding. That was him. Always the first one on the plane. Always the most eager to leave. Now, the decision to get on the plane felt like the worst one he'd ever make.

He tucked his phone away, gathered his things, and boarded the plane before he allowed three weeks of unexpected happiness to derail his life.

Once he was on the plane, he'd be fine.

CHAPTER TWENTY-FOUR

DECEMBER 25TH…CHRISTMAS DAY…

Christmas morning at her aunt Frankie's house had always been Jessica's favorite day of the year. Brothers, sisters, aunts, uncles, and a million kids all excited and boisterous. It was impossible not to catch the spirit of the holidays surrounded by the love and happiness and good-will.

That year her heart felt heavy as she sat in the corner of the couch in the matching reindeer onesie pajamas her aunt always bought for the entire family, coffee cup cradled in her hands as everyone gathered around the tree at seven o'clock in the morning to open presents. The same tradition every year for as far back as Jessica could remember. The decorations in the home, the ornaments on the tree, the holiday music playing, and the smell of her aunt's famous Christmas morning bake of bacon and eggs and hash browns were all exactly the same.

But something was different this year. *She* was different.

Mitch would be on a plane now, an hour into his flight. He hadn't called or texted since leaving the B&B and she hadn't had the courage to reach out. They'd talk again soon, but today was too soon. Emotions were still too raw.

A part of her had really thought he'd stay. That their time together had made him want to be here...or at least not want to leave so soon. A silly part of her had thought maybe he'd realize this was where he wanted to be and he'd come back. Show up for her in those final minutes. Like some romantic movie...

Who left on Christmas Day anyway? The day *after* Christmas made sense. Her pain had her switching between wanting to cry and being irritated with him. The irritation was better. It eased the ache in her chest for a little while.

Unfortunately, it didn't last. She knew for Mitch it was as though he didn't want to experience this joy and season of giving, knowing it wasn't happening in other parts of the world. She couldn't fault his kind and generous heart. Hell, it was part of the reason she'd fallen in love with him.

Hadn't Lia warned her about falling in love with someone who wanted to save the world? And that was something she loved about him. She'd never want him to change.

And he *had* asked her to go with him. So she couldn't put this loneliness all on him. She'd had a choice to make as well.

"Jess, this one's for you," her cousin, Kara said, placing a large gift on her lap. Jessica smiled and set her coffee cup aside, then opened the gift from her aunt.

"Tear it open!" her cousin said excitedly.

"Yeah, don't save the wrapping," Trent said, his arm draped around Whitney on the loveseat across from her.

Her friend was home and feeling better that day, and Jessica knew that was the best gift any of them could have gotten that year. She was so grateful that Whitney was okay, and seeing the two of them together didn't invoke any jealousy, just increased the dull longing for that kind of love and commitment in her own life.

Tearing through the candy-cane themed wrapping, Jessica took out an army-green, multi-purpose backpack with a sleeping bag and thermos attached. A compass and a housekey that she knew was meant for her aunt's front door hung from the side. The tightness in her chest grew even thicker as she read the card.

For all your life's adventures…May they always lead you home.

Adventures she'd decided not to take. She fought back new tears and swallowed the lump in her throat as she smiled at her aunt. "Thank you. I love it."

Aunt Frankie beamed at her, pride and happiness on her face, and Jessica knew eventually she'd have to tell her aunt about changing her mind, but this wasn't the right time. She sat back on the couch and tried to force thoughts of Mitch and Cambodia and Not Just Desserts out of her mind for one day with her friends and family to celebrate all the amazing things she did have in her life.

The things that three weeks ago she thought were enough.

• • •

December 26ᵀᴴ…Cambodia

They were at least in a different camp this time.

The tents lined up along the dirt ground, already set up by volunteers, and the sights and sounds of the hustle around establishing a new site they'd call home for the next three months usually gave him a sense of comfort. This was what he knew. This was the environment he thrived in. Living with few amenities and hard laborious days were what made him feel alive.

He waited for that feeling to rush back.

Anything to distract him from the thoughts of Jessica and Blue Moon Bay. Thoughts that had never before plagued him. He was the *moving on* guy. He didn't want to be in one place for too long. But he couldn't deny the pang in his chest whenever he thought about what he might be missing out on, back in his small hometown.

He needed to roll up his sleeves and get busy. Work wouldn't leave any opportunity to ponder decisions already made.

He headed into his personal tent at the end of the long row and dropped his bag onto the tiny cot that he'd maybe get four hours of sleep on a night. He set up his laptop on the tiny makeshift desk and hooked everything up to the generators and servers that would power his equipment for the duration.

His cell phone had been searching for service since he'd landed, and the farther inland they'd driven, away from civilization, he'd lost hope of it finding one.

"Hey…didn't see you on the flight," a female voice said from the doorway of the tent.

He turned to see Maria standing there, dressed in tan shorts and a white tank top, her hiking boots on her feet and a light scarf around her neck. She too was a familiar sight that should have had him feeling like he was back where he belonged, but seeing her only made him more anxious. Remembering her desperate call the week before and the softness in her tone when she'd made him promise to come had his pulse racing.

What was she expecting? From him? From them?

They'd never defined what they were doing, so he'd assumed it was nothing. Casual friendship with the side benefits of limited options and mutual stress relief through a physical connection. They didn't even really talk or stay in touch between postings.

"How are you?" he said, walking toward her for the customary hug in greeting.

She held a little too tight and too long. "Good to see you. Did you enjoy the time off?"

He nodded. More than he could ever tell her. "It was what I needed, I think. How are you doing?" he asked again. He needed to know where her head was. For more reasons than just his fear that she might be clinging to him and their connection in a different way now.

She sighed, her chest rising and falling. "I'm better. I'm sorry I was such a mess when I called you that day. I thought I'd been doing fine, then all of a sudden it just hit me," she said, lifting her short blond hair away from her neck and fastening it into her usual ponytail.

"I get it. I had a similar experience. But you're good? You're okay being here?" Meltdowns from stress were to be expected, but their safety and that of the team required them all to be mentally capable of the challenges they were going to face in the coming months.

She nodded. "I'm good, Mitch." She paused, staring at her hands, and his heart raced.

Oh shit. There was that look. The "we need to talk" look. Should he tell her about Jess? Should he say something first to save her any embarrassment when he said they couldn't be the way they were? Things had changed for him. He couldn't be with anyone else but Jess...

"So, I met someone," she said quickly. Her gaze, when it met his, was apologetic, nervous. She wrung her hands together in the way she always did when she had to tell someone bad news. "On the plane heading over here. He's a volunteer and we hit it off like wildfire..."

Mitch blinked. "He's here?"

She nodded quickly. "I'm sorry...I know we..."

Oh God, she was breaking it off with him. His shoulders relaxed. He wouldn't have to be the one to do it. He wouldn't have to potentially hurt her or cause an awkwardness between them at camp. Relief was the best feeling he'd had in days. But he also didn't want her to know he'd been about to do the same.

He cleared his throat and nodded. "Of course. I understand."

She smiled as she put her hands on his shoulders

and looked into his eyes. "You're a great guy, Mitch, but we both know this life is your one and only passion, and a girl just can't compete with that." She leaned forward and kissed his cheek, then left the tent.

Leaving him standing there feeling a gut shot, not at being dumped but at the harsh reality of her words.

CHAPTER TWENTY-FIVE

DECEMBER 30ᵀᴴ...NEW YEAR'S EVE EVE...

"I don't know how I'm supposed to choose a design—these are all so beautiful," Amber Parsons said, sitting at the bakery counter, flipping through the wedding cake binder.

Jess smiled at the young twentysomething. She was happy for the beaming bride-to-be, despite her own conflicted heart.

Since Mitch had left Blue Moon Bay, they'd Skyped once, as his schedule and workload were already busy and the time difference made it difficult to connect. He said there was essentially no cell phone service, which was disappointing, and the internet connection wasn't great, but Jessica had cherished the opportunity she got to see his face and hear his voice. Even for just a few minutes.

Things were different, though. He wasn't the relaxed man on vacation she'd gotten to know. He was working long hours and stressed about the conditions and situations he faced on a daily basis. He was slightly distant, and despite him telling her that he missed her, she'd felt a little worse at the end of the call.

She wasn't sure how much longer she could do it. She missed him so much, and unfortunately, "out of sight, out of mind" was not the case. Each day, the tightening in her chest grew more desperate whenever she thought about him. In her kitchen, she couldn't stop reminiscing on the day he'd worked alongside her, and her freezer was an absolute torturous reminder of their passionate sex. Her Friday morning deliveries were plagued with the memory of their fun together. And the volunteer sign-up sheet still sitting on top of the offer from Not Just Desserts in her drawer was taunting her.

She didn't regret her decision not to go with him. Whitney needed her. Sarah needed her. Blue Moon Bay was where she needed to be. For now. She just selfishly wished Mitch was here with her.

"This one! This is definitely the one," Amber said excitedly, pointing to a three-tier, pink fondant wrapped cake with doves as the centerpiece on top. Her green eyes sparkled with excitement as she stared at it.

"You sure, because you said that about three others," Jessica said with a laugh. It was the same with every bride—these decisions were important. "No rush, take all the time you need to be confident this is the one."

In no time at all, Jessica had been confident that Mitch was the one…

But Amber was nodding. "Nope. I've made the decision. This one is perfect."

"Okay. Great." Jessica reached for an order form and filled in the appropriate information. "What is the date of the wedding again?" Her grandfather had said it was sometime in February, but Jessica had been too caught up in her feelings of jealousy that day to take note of the actual date.

"February 14th. Valentine's Day. I'm not thrilled about a winter wedding, but I love the idea of getting married on the most romantic day of the year." The wistful note in the young woman's voice had Jessica longing for a special Valentine's Day, too. Would she even get a Skype date with Mitch that year?

"It will be beautiful and very romantic," Jessica said, adding the date to the form.

"Oh, and here's an invite. We'd love to have you there," Amber said, sliding a pale pink, embossed invitation across the counter as she stood.

Jessica picked it up and smiled politely. "Thank you." She wasn't sure she'd attend. Could her heart handle seeing any other blissfully wed couples right now? Or in the near future? Maybe weddings were ruined forever for her now. Not exactly wonderful when her business depended on her passion for wedding cakes.

"I have to run, I have a wedding dress fitting down the street…but thanks again, Jess," Amber said, before leaving the bakery.

Jessica sighed, tucking the invite and the cake order form into her upcoming order drawer, then she went into the kitchen as her oven timer chimed. She took a tray of oatmeal raisin cookies from the oven and placed them on a cooling rack, and checked the time on the clock on the wall. Four fifteen. Her laptop was sitting on the counter and she had fifteen minutes before her next Skype chat with Mitch.

Common sense was telling her what she needed to

say—that they shouldn't talk anymore, because it just made things harder for her. She needed to start distancing herself.

Maybe when and if he returned, they could see what happened then, but chats weren't enough for her, and it had painted a clear picture of what a relationship with Mitch would be like. Unfortunately, she wasn't strong enough to do it. The timing wasn't right for either of them.

Her cell chimed with a new text and her pulse raced, seeing it was from Mitch.

They never texted, since his cell service wasn't great. Was something wrong?

Mitch: *Sorry, I can't chat today. Something important came up.*

Something important. More important than her. Her gut instinct about where things were heading was right. Maybe he was realizing it, too. A lump rose in her throat as she fought for the right way to answer the text.

He was giving her an out. A great opportunity to say that maybe they shouldn't chat for a while. Take a break and see how they felt if he ever came home again.

She stared at her phone, unable to type the words. Maybe she was struggling now because it was new. Maybe in time she could get used to being second on Mitch's priority list. Being with him in any capacity was better than not being with him at all, right?

What the hell should she do?

The front door bell chimed, and she put the phone away. He was busy. He wouldn't be waiting with baited breath for a reply anyway.

Pushing through the swinging door, she saw Mr. Dorsey standing at the counter. Great. This was what she needed that day. More pressure from him. "Hi, Mr. Dorsey," she said tightly.

"Jessica! I trust you had a nice holiday?" he asked, leaning against the counter.

"It was nice. What brings you by?" she asked, despite knowing the obvious reason.

"Time is running out on the offer, and I wanted to personally let you know that the million dollars won't be on the table for long." He gave her a look that suggested she would be the dumbest person on the planet if she didn't accept it.

And maybe she would be…

But opening the drawer, she took out the volunteer application form for Doctors Without Borders and the offer from Not Just Desserts, and staring straight at Mr. Dorsey, she didn't even hesitate before ripping both of them in half right down the middle.

His hardened expression was cold as he straightened. "So that's your answer?"

"That's my answer." To both choices she'd been struggling to make. "You can see yourself out," she said, disappearing through the swinging door to the kitchen before he could see the impact that finally closing the door on a different path for her future had actually cost her.

• • •

Mitch was running.

Sweat pooled on his flesh and his heart was beating out of his chest. Every single decision he'd ever made seemed to be chasing after him as he dodged tree branches and stumbled over thick overgrowth, making his way through the forest. Away from the camp, away from the danger…

Hot, humid weather enveloped him, and it was difficult to breathe. The blood in his veins threatened to burst through, and his legs were like jelly beneath him as he forced them to keep moving. The weight of his full backpack grew too heavy, so he quickly grabbed only what he needed and ditched the rest.

His small Jeep had broken down on the trail and there was zero cell service where he was. Where that was, he couldn't even be certain in this unfamiliar area. He was alone with no way to reach anyone. His old-fashioned compass as his only guide. One mission. One goal driving him forward.

He kept running and running…until finally, salvation came into view.

CHAPTER TWENTY-SIX

December 31ˢᵀ…New Year's Eve…

Was there anything more depressing than spending New Year's Eve surrounded by couples in love?

If there was, Jessica never wanted to experience it.

Dressed in a black sequined mini-dress and red heels, a glass of champagne with cranberries floating on top in her hands, Jessica scanned the New Year's Eve party happening inside Dove's Nest. Sarah was hosting the event for the community, and it seemed like it was *the* hotspot to be the last day of the year.

The Christmas decorations had been replaced with black and silver garland and confetti. New Year's Eve logo'd banners and top hats sat on the dining room tables for guests to wear if they chose to. Noisemakers and streamers were everywhere she looked. Even battling morning sickness, Sarah had pulled off one hell of a party.

She spotted her friend now, in the foyer, dancing with Wes and Marissa. She was laughing so hard and looked so completely in love with her new growing family that Jessica's heart burst with happiness for her. Sarah had told Wes and Marissa about the pregnancy on Christmas Day as Jessica had suggested, and they were predictably over the moon about it. Marissa was already picking out names she liked.

In the dining room, she could see Whitney and Trent sitting at a table enjoying some of the desserts Jessica had brought. Whitney's casted leg was propped up on a chair, but she'd painted it a silver color to match the beautiful silky silver gown she wore. Trent, dressed in a suit with a matching silver tie, looked barely able to keep his hands off her. He hadn't left her side since the accident. She hoped it would help her friend realize what was important in life and maybe not work so much in the new year.

She walked slowly through the inn, taking in all the festive sights and sounds all around her. Laughter, happiness as one year came to an end and everyone looked forward to the next. All of her friends and family were inside. Mitch may not be there, but everyone else she cared about was, and this was where she needed to be that evening. Better than being alone again at home, missing him, thinking about him.

In Cambodia, it was already New Year's Day. Mitch was already moving forward with the new year ahead... leaving her, leaving them behind. She wasn't sure how to do that, but she hoped to gain clarity once the clock struck midnight in... She checked the big countdown clock Sarah had hung on the foyer wall... Eight minutes and four seconds.

She turned slowly in a circle and everything around her seemed to blur, fade slightly in the background of her own harsh reality. Surrounded by so many people and yet still so alone.

She had to get out of there. In eight minutes, the sound of Auld Lang Syne playing while couples kissed all around her would break her into a crumbling mess. She wouldn't tell anyone she was leaving; they'd just try to encourage her to stay. She set her champagne glass down on the nearest table and removed her top hat. Then she stealthily made a beeline for the front door.

Where she stopped and her mouth fell open.

"Hi. Sorry I had to cancel our Skype chat," Mitch said, slightly out of breath.

Mitch was here.

In person. Standing right in front of her.

At the inn. In Blue Moon Bay.

Jessica blinked.

He was still here. Dressed in a pair of wrinkled khakis and a dirty, ripped, tight black T-shirt, his hair a mess and a short beard covering his face, he was really here. Exhausted-looking, but vibrant, hopeful eyes staring at her with the most love she'd ever seen.

"What are you…? How did you…?" Confusion overtook all other emotions. She was frozen on the spot while he walked almost as if in slow motion toward her.

"I made a last-second decision," he said, still fighting to catch his breath. Had he run all the way from Cambodia? "I missed you."

He missed her. "Right…but you were overseas…" Shocked to see him here had her incoherent. Thoughts, words, feelings were all a jumbled mess, and she couldn't articulate any of them.

"I was," he said, taking her hips and pulling her

toward him. "But then I started to think about bowling and axe throwing…started *missing* those things."

She swallowed hard, shaking her curls around her shoulders. "You missed boring, small-town life activities? You hate those things."

His gaze burned into hers as he pulled her closer. He smelled like the outdoors and sweat and day-old aftershave, but she couldn't breathe it in fast enough. "I missed doing those things with you."

"Enough to come back here?" Her stomach was in knots. Hours ago, she'd been contemplating cooling things because she wanted to avoid a broken heart. Now he was standing there, holding her, telling her he'd missed her. The whirlwind of emotions spiraling through her had yet to decide on which one to land. She was surprised and happy to see him, desperate for clarity, afraid to let her guard down, and overwhelmed with a desire to kiss the face off him.

"Yes." He paused, gently touching her cheek. "But unfortunately, I can't stay."

There it was. The bomb drop. He'd flown all this way…but ultimately he was leaving again. They'd be right back where they were five minutes ago.

She eased out of his arms and folded hers across her chest, hoping to shield herself from the pain of having to tell him face-to-face what she'd barely been able to text. "Mitch, I miss you *so much*, but I'm not sure I can do this. After logging off our Skype chat, I felt hollow, empty inside. Knowing I can't reach you by phone and having you cancel because of important things taking priority hurts too much. I'm not strong enough to be with you in this way." Despite how much she loved him, she had to be honest with him and herself.

"Good," he said.

Her eyes widened. "Good?"

He nodded, stepping toward her again. He was so close she could feel his breath on her forehead, but he didn't touch her. "Yes, good. Because I'm not strong enough for that, either. That's why I'm here."

"Yes, but you're leaving again. And again. Who knows how many times? And I can't do that. Can't do us that way." The words killed her to say, but they needed to be said. Full transparency. She was looking for someone to share her life with and she'd always feel a void, living life with him between his time away. Knowing she'd always be the second passion in his life.

He reached out and touched her cheek. "What if I only left once in a while? What if I go back and finish what I started on this trip, then work locally with the organization here in California? I'd only have to go overseas for two months every year."

What was he saying? That he'd give up traveling with Doctors Without Borders full time? For her? Having him gone two months a year was certainly better than all the time, but did he really want that?

"You can't do that. You love your life. This is your passion and I'd never ask you to give that up."

"You're not asking, and I wouldn't be giving it up. The truth is, I can't see any other way. I used to pack up and leave everything behind and never feel a pull to come back to it. Nothing, nowhere ever had a hold on me. But that changed when I fell for you," he said, running his thumb along her jawline.

She couldn't breathe. She couldn't move. She was afraid that any second the magic of this moment would disappear.

"Jess, I want to see where this new path could take me. Take us."

"I do, too, but..."

"Shhhh...no buts. I've made my decision. It wasn't an easy one, but it's the right one. Now, I just need to know where you stand. What do you want and can you live with that compromise?"

She wrapped her arms around his neck and tears of happiness burned in the back of her eyes as she hugged him tight, savoring the feel of him in her arms, breathing in the familiar scent of him that she'd craved.

"I can definitely live with that." And she could always close the bakery two months a year and go with him. They didn't need to be apart. She didn't need to sacrifice everything and neither did he. "I'm so happy you're here."

He squeezed her tight, then pulled back slightly. "Me too." He kissed her forehead...her cheeks, her nose... then his lips found hers. She pressed her entire body to his as she separated his lips with her tongue and deepened the kiss. She had everything she ever wanted right here, right now.

Her chest filled with so much joy, she thought it might explode.

He held her tight as his passion for her poured out in his kiss and she knew everything he'd said was true.

Slightly breathless, she broke the connection with their mouths. "I'm in love with you, Mitch."

He smiled. "Turns out there might be some truth to that Good Luck Charm curse after all. I did fall in love after dating you," he said with a laugh.

Suddenly the curse didn't seem so bad. She kissed him again and stared up at the face of the man she loved more than anything else. "So, how long do we have?"

"About fourteen minutes."

Her mouth gaped. "You flew here for fourteen minutes?"

He nodded. "My flight back to Cambodia leaves again in three hours from LAX. But I needed to say this in person," he said.

She laughed. There was no time for any of the things she longed to do with him, but it could all wait. He was coming back. For her. Because he loved her. "Okay, well…when do you come home again?"

He held her tight. "I'm coming back on the early trip home. Feb thirteenth."

The day before Valentine's Day and Amber's wedding. The timing couldn't be more perfect. Mentally, she RSVP'd "yes" to the wedding. This time with a plus-one.

The music stopped playing, and all around them, everyone started to count. Jessica turned to look at the countdown clock. Nine seconds to midnight.

She turned back to Mitch, and they joined in the

countdown, but they'd barely made it to three before Mitch's mouth was crushing hers.

And as the familiar notes of Auld Lang Syne started to play, Jessica closed her eyes and sank into the love and affection all around her, knowing with the arrival of a new year, she was about to go on the best life adventure yet, and the best was yet to come.

EPILOGUE

THE FOLLOWING CHRISTMAS…

Mitch left his office and removed his lab coat as he approached the waiting room at his father's clinic. *His* clinic now, too. It was quiet that day, and he was slowly learning to appreciate the slower pace. They'd replaced the overhead awning on the clinic to read Dr. Jameson and Son, and Mitch didn't feel the pressure that he'd always thought he would, taking over his father's practice.

"Hey, Mrs. P.," he said. "I'm going to head out for an hour."

Dressed in an ugly Christmas sweater and elf hat on her graying hair, the older woman decorated the waiting room Christmas tree with homemade ornaments. The personalized snow couple baking ornament he'd given Jess the year before was already positioned in a place of honor in the front. Sarah had kept it for them and had given it to them the day before. Her friends had really accepted the two of them together as a couple, and he knew how much that meant to Jess. It had surprised him how much it actually meant to him, too. They were his friends now as well and he'd even started participating in the men's fantasy football league, even though he still had no idea what he was doing.

"Need to finish some holiday shopping," he said as he grabbed his coat.

"Going shopping for anything special?" The older woman's eyes twinkled with mischief.

"Maybe..." He winked, then left the clinic and headed along Main Street. The familiar festive sights and sounds felt almost as though he were seeing them for the first time. The storefront's decorated windows held more magic to him. Familiar holiday music playing on the radio had him humming along. Last Christmas he'd gone through a major transformation, a full change of heart and direction. This year, he was settled into the community that he once again called home and he appreciated the holiday traditions in a new light.

Life was headed in exactly the right path. He had no doubts about his future here in Blue Moon Bay with Jess. He didn't second-guess his decision to only go overseas two months every year and he had zero regrets.

Now it was time to prove that to Jess.

. . .

"That's the last of them," Jessica said from inside of the van where she stacked the last of the empty trays on the shelf. That holiday, she had more deliveries than ever before, and she was relieved that Not Just Desserts had been bluffing when they'd threatened to take over her bakery with or without her selling. Mr. Dorsey had called a few times in the new year and had even tried to get the mayor's office to put some pressure on, but

Jessica, Frankie, and Mrs. Barnett had held firm, united, and the big dessert chain had moved on.

Mitch climbed into the back and closed the door. Then he locked it.

The *click* had Jessica swinging around to face him. Her expression was first one of surprise…then intrigue. That past year together had been everything she could have hoped it would be. True to his word, he'd returned on February thirteenth and had escorted her to the first wedding where she hadn't been on the prowl, and her fears that he'd regret the decision of walking away from full-time postings eased with each passing day; he only seemed more in love and happy being in the small town with her.

He'd taken over his father's medical practice, and everyone in town loved him even more than ever before. And his father was thrilled to have the opportunity to still work two months every year when Mitch did his posting overseas. Ally had thanked Jessica a million times for convincing her wanderlust son to finally settle down, and even Lia was happy that the two of them were together.

He strode toward her and wrapped his arms around her waist. He kissed her gently. She pressed her body closer and deepened the kiss, but he reluctantly pulled back.

"We should get back to open the bakery."

She feigned a sigh. "If we must."

Five minutes later, they parked the van in the back and Jessica spotted Aunt Frankie waiting outside. "Hey, need a caffeine pick-me-up?" she asked, unlocking the door.

"Nope," her aunt said with a wide smile. "I'm here to officially put in an order for a wedding cake."

Jessica's eyes widened as she held the door open. "Really?" Her friend had finally chosen a design? Whitney hadn't said anything to Jessica. "Which cake?" she asked, sliding the binder toward her aunt.

Mitch joined them at the counter as Frankie flipped directly to the one she was looking for.

Jessica's stomach dropped, seeing the three-tier cascade cake. *Her* cake. She wouldn't show her disappointment. This was a big deal for her aunt. This was a special moment. If this was the cake Whitney wanted, this was the one she should have.

"This one is absolutely perfect," her aunt said, beaming.

Mitch nodded his agreement. "Definitely the best one."

What does he know about wedding cakes all of a sudden?

Jessica cleared her throat and reached for her order pad. "Great, well let's get this order in for the lucky couple." She started to write Whitney's name on the slip, but her aunt stopped her.

"Wrong bride, sweetheart," Frankie said, emotion evident in her voice. She nodded behind Jessica toward Mitch. "It's for *your* wedding."

Jessica swung around quickly to see Mitch down on one knee.

Oh my God.

Tears burned the backs of her eyes as he stared up at her. "I was going to wait until Christmas, but I can't wait any longer to know if you'll do me the honor of marrying me." He opened the box, and she gasped upon seeing the beautiful solitary diamond in the center of a white gold set. "Spend the rest of this life with me, Jess. Let's live it one adventure at a time together?"

She was nodding emphatically, not trusting her voice to speak.

He laughed. "That's a yes?"

"That's definitely a yes."

Her hand shook as he slid the ring on her finger and kissed her palm. She knelt next to him and wrapped her arms around him tight.

"I have no idea how you did it, but you've made this Christmas even more special than the last one," she whispered.

He kissed her gently and stared at her with all the love in his expression. "And I plan to year after year."

She frowned. "But wait, how did you know that was my favorite cake?"

"Lia might have told me," he said with a grin.

Jessica's heart swelled with even more happiness than she ever thought possible. With the love and support from their families, she and Mitch were about to start their lives together. She was finally going to get to make the most special cake for her special day.

ACKNOWLEDGMENTS

I loved writing this fun, heartwarming holiday story, and I'm so grateful for all the notes and feedback from my agent, Jill Marsal, and my editors, Liz Pelletier and Lydia Sharp, who always make each book stronger. Thanks so much to the Entangled art department for the lovely cover and everyone on the team for all the marketing and promotion! A big thank-you to my readers who continue to support me and my stories—I couldn't do this without you! And as always, a huge thank-you to my family. Reagan and Jacob, you two are my world. XO

What happens when a city girl crashes a small-town wedding and crashes right into her nemesis?

The WEDDING CRASHER *and the* COWBOY

ROBIN BIELMAN
USA TODAY BESTSELLING AUTHOR

Kennedy Martin is shocked when her ex calls days before his wedding, expressing serious second thoughts. Doesn't he see his fiancée's actually the glaze to his doughnut? Now Kennedy has no choice but to crash his wedding and convince the man he's with the right woman.

Instead, she crashes into the absolute last man she ever wanted to see: Maverick Owens, her old college nemesis. Maverick is still as awful, infuriating, and just The Worst as ever—even if he looks way too sexy in his cowboy hat. And of *course* he's convinced she's actually at the seaside ranch to ruin the wedding.

Now the only way to get some face time with the groom and save this marriage is to participate in all sorts of pre-wedding events…with Maverick. Stuck on a canoe, making small-talk at cocktail hour, and even a hoedown with her worst enemy? This just might be the longest week of her life…

NY Times bestselling author Ginny Baird is back with another sweet, heartfelt, and unique take on the wedding genre.

The
Matchmaker
Bride

Successful Boston matchmaker and television personality Meredith Galanes's reputation is on the line. During a guest appearance on a morning talk show, she's broadsided by questions about her own romantic attachments, just as she's trying to secure a syndication deal. Afraid to admit her love life is a total disaster, Meredith blurts out that she's seriously involved with a very special man—a boatbuilder in Maine. She never expects that small slip to get spun into a story about her supposed engagement.

Or that the paparazzi will track the guy down…

Derrick Albright is laid-back about many things. Being hounded by the press about some imaginary engagement to a woman he's only met once—and couldn't stand—isn't one of them. Then Meredith actually shows up at his cabin in Blue Hill, Maine, with an apology, a pot roast, and a proposal—play along until she secures her TV deal, and she'll help him win back his ex.

It's a simple plan, but if they have any chance of pulling it off, they'll have to survive each other first…

Want the spirit of Christmas to continue?

CHRISTMAS GRACE

MINDY STEELE

Grace Miller believed herself in love with the charming Englischer who eventually broke her heart. Now alone except for the secret life growing inside her, she arrives in the unfamiliar small village of Walnut Ridge, Kentucky, to hide and hopefully gain forgiveness.

She is pleasantly surprised, however, to find a tight-knit, welcoming group who help her heart grow right alongside her belly. And with the holidays around the corner, there's plenty of preparations to occupy her mind. Also occupying her mind? Her strong, protective neighbor, Cullen Graber, the town's blacksmith, who seems intent on not allowing her to ever suffer alone.

Cullen Graber gave up on love after too many losses early in life. He planned to live out his days focusing on his smithy business, yet the beautiful and mysterious Grace refuses to leave his thoughts. But can they open their hearts to God's grace and create a new family together before Grace must return home?

AMARA
an imprint of Entangled Publishing LLC